THE
LIONS
OF
LITTLE
ROCK

By the Author of

The Best Bad Luck I Ever Had

THE LIONS OF LITTLE ROCK

KRISTIN LEVINE

G. P. PUTNAM'S SONS

An Imprint of Penguin Group (USA) Inc.

G. P. PUTNAM'S SONS
A division of Penguin Young Readers Group.
Published by The Penguin Group.
Penguin Group (USA) Inc., 375 Hudson Street, New York, NY 10014, U.S.A.
Penguin Group (Canada), 90 Eglinton Avenue East, Suite 700, Toronto, Ontario M4P 2Y3,
Canada (a division of Pearson Penguin Canada Inc.).
Penguin Books Ltd, 80 Strand, London WC2R 0RL, England.
Penguin Ireland, 25 St. Stephen's Green, Dublin 2, Ireland (a division of Penguin Books Ltd.).
Penguin Group (Australia), 250 Camberwell Road, Camberwell, Victoria 3124, Australia
(a division of Pearson Australia Group Pty Ltd).
Penguin Books India Pvt Ltd, 11 Community Centre,
Panchsheel Park, New Delhi—110 017, India.
Penguin Group (NZ), 67 Apollo Drive, Rosedale, Auckland 0632,
New Zealand (a division of Pearson New Zealand Ltd).
Penguin Books (South Africa) (Pty) Ltd, 24 Sturdee Avenue,
Rosebank, Johannesburg 2196, South Africa.
Penguin Books Ltd, Registered Offices: 80 Strand, London WC2R 0RL, England.

PUBLISHER'S NOTE

This is a work of fiction. Names, characters, places, and incidents either are the product
of the author's imagination or are used fictitiously, and any resemblance to actual persons,
living or dead, businesses, companies, events, or locales is entirely coincidental.

Published simultaneously in Canada. Printed in the United States of America.

Design by Annie Ericsson. Text set in Columbus MT Std.
Library of Congress Cataloging-in-Publication Data is available upon request.

ISBN 978-0-399-25644-8
1   3   5   7   9   10   8   6   4   2

To my mother,

for telling me about the lions

1

THE HIGH DIVE

I talk a lot. Just not out loud where anyone can hear. At least I used to be that way. I'm no chatterbox now, but if you stop me on the street and ask me directions to the zoo, I'll answer you. Probably. If you're nice, I might even tell you a couple of different ways to get there. I guess I've learned it's not enough to just think things. You have to say them too. Because all the words in the world won't do much good if they're just rattling around in your head.

But I'm getting ahead of myself. To understand me, and how I've changed, I need to go back to 1958.

It was a beautiful day in September and I was standing on top of a diving board. The blue sky was reflected in the water below, the white board felt scratchy under my feet, and the smell of hot dogs wafted up from the snack stand. It was a perfect summer day—the kind you see in the movies—and I was positive I was going to throw up.

You see, it wasn't just any high dive. Oh, no. It was the super-huge, five-meter-high platform diving board, the tallest at Fair Park Swimming Pool, probably the highest in all of Little Rock. It might have even been the highest in all of Arkansas. Which wouldn't have been a problem if I hadn't been afraid of heights. But I was.

Sally McDaniels had told me she was going to jump off and asked if I wanted to come too. Everyone over the age of ten had already jumped off the board a dozen times that summer. Except for me, and I was practically thirteen. It was easier to nod than say no, so there I was.

Sally was waiting behind me on the ladder. Blond and blue-eyed, she wore a pink suit the exact color of her toenails. Sally wasn't really pretty, but no one ever noticed because she acted like she was. "Are you all right?" she asked.

No, of course I wasn't all right. I mean, I wasn't sick or anything, but I was standing perfectly still, frozen as a Popsicle, counting prime numbers in my head. A prime number is a number that can only be divided by itself and one. There are twenty-five of them under a hundred, and reciting them sure does help me when I'm nervous.

"Go ahead and jump," said Sally.

I didn't move. A plane flew across the clouds . . . 2, 3, 5, 7, 11 . . . I wished I were a stork and could fly away. Or a flamingo. Or a penguin. Except I didn't think they flew.

"Marlee," Sally said. "There's a bunch of people behind us."

I hated holding them up, so I took a step toward the edge of the platform . . . 13, 17, 19, 23 . . . but then I got dizzy and fell to my knees.

"Come on," cried the boy on the ladder behind Sally. "Hurry up and jump."

I shook my head and clutched the board . . . 29, 31, 37, 41. It didn't work. I wasn't ever letting go.

Sally laughed. "She said she was really going to do it this time."

I squeezed my eyes tighter and kept counting . . . 43, 47, 53 . . .

2

"Isn't that Judy Nisbett's little sister?" someone said.

It must have only have been a minute or two, but I got all the way to 97 before I felt Judy's hand on my shoulder. "Marlee," she said quietly, "come on down. I already bought a Coke and a PayDay. We can share them on the way home."

I nodded but didn't move.

"Open your eyes," Judy commanded.

I did. Not that I always do what my sister says, but—well, I guess I usually do. In any case, when I saw my sister's clear brown eyes looking at me, I felt much better. She was sixteen and going into the eleventh grade. I could talk to my sister. She was smart and calm and reasonable.

"Do you want me to hold your hand on the way down the ladder?" Judy asked.

I nodded again. It was embarrassing, but I didn't think I could do it on my own. Once I felt her palm on mine, it only took a minute for us to make our way down together.

"What a baby!" said the boy who had been behind me as he brushed past us to climb up again. Sally laughed, and I knew they were right. I was a baby.

"Come on," said Judy. She picked up her book and her bag from the lounge chair where she'd been reading.

"See you at school tomorrow," said her friend Margaret.

"See you," Judy replied, waving good-bye.

Judy hadn't even gotten her hair wet. She'd recently cut it into a short bob and wore it pulled back with a ribbon. My hair was the same brown color as my sister's, but it was long and wavy, and sometimes I still wore it in braids. Sally said I looked like Heidi, but I didn't care. I liked Heidi. She had that nice grandpa and her friend with all those goats.

Goats are okay, but what I really love are wild animals, like the ones you find at the zoo. The Little Rock Zoo was right across the street from the swimming pool. In the gate and down the hill, I knew the lions were pacing in their cages. At night, Judy and I listened to them roar, but during the day they were quiet like me. Judy and I sat on the wall by the zoo entrance as we shared a candy bar and a Coke.

"Sorry," I said. I'd ruined our last day at the pool before school started again.

Judy sighed. "Why are you even friends with Sally McDaniels?"

I shrugged. Sally and I have been friends ever since we were five and she pushed me off the slide at the park.

"She likes to boss you around," Judy said.

That was true. But she was also familiar. I like familiar.

"You need to find a friend you have something in common with," said Judy. "Someone who likes to do the same things you do. That's what . . ."

I stopped listening. I knew all her advice by heart. I needed to find someone who was honest and friendly and nice. I knew all the ways I was supposed to meet this imaginary friend too. *Just say hello. Ask someone a question. Give a compliment.* Maybe it would work, if I could ever figure out the right words.

I know it sounds odd, but I much prefer numbers to words. In math, you always get the same answer, no matter how you do the problem. But with words, *blue* can be a thousand different shades! *Two* is always *two*. I like that.

Judy finally finished lecturing, and I said, "It's easier to put up with Sally. Sometimes she's really nice."

"Yeah," Judy said. "Sometimes."

2

COFFEE, TEA OR SODA

That evening after dinner, we all sat down in the living room to watch TV. By "we" I mean my family: Mother, Daddy, Judy and me. I have an older brother too, David, but he'd just moved out the week before to start college. My sister and brother and Daddy are the only ones I feel really comfortable talking to, so I missed David something terrible. In fact, when Mother made a fresh batch of iced tea for dinner, I almost started crying.

You see, to me, people are like things you drink. Some are like a pot of black coffee, no cream, no sugar. They make me so nervous I start to tremble. Others calm me down enough that I can sort through the words in my head and find something to say.

My brother, David, is a glass of sweet iced tea on a hot summer day, when you've put your feet up in a hammock and haven't got a care in the world. Judy is an ice-cold Coca-Cola from the fridge. Sally is cough syrup; she tastes bad, but my mother insists she's good for me. Daddy's a glass of milk, usually cold and delicious, but every once in a while, he goes sour. If I have to ask one of my parents a question, I'll pick him, because Mother is hot black tea, so strong, she's almost coffee.

Mother and I don't exactly see eye to eye, or even elbow to elbow. She's always trying to get me to do stuff: *invite that girl over, volunteer at church, read to that poor blind lady down the street.* I know she loves me, but sometimes I think she wishes I were more like Judy. Mother and Judy like to read fashion magazines and go shopping. They get their hair done once a week and read long, romantic novels like *Gone With the Wind.* Despite our differences, Judy and I get along, but Mother expects me to be thrilled when she brings me home a new skirt or a sweater set, when what I'd really like is a new slide rule.

Ever since the Soviets sent up that Sputnik satellite last year, I've been studying really hard. Maybe someday I'll study mathematics at college and become a rocket scientist. Only thing is, when our teacher told us last year that our country needs more of us to study math, I think she meant more boys. I watched all those talks on TV about the satellite really closely, and I didn't see any experts who were women.

That evening we were watching our brand-new 1958 RCA 21-inch mahogany television console. It was so large, we had to move an armchair into the garage to make space for it in the living room. With rabbit ears on top, it got three whole channels.

Governor Faubus was on television, giving some sort of talk about Southern pride and communists and, okay, I tried to pay attention, but it didn't really make much sense. I was more worried about who my teachers would be this year. Teachers are definitely coffee. When they call on me in class, it makes me so nervous, I can't say a thing. Even when I know the answer. So there's always a rough patch at the beginning of the year when I'm breaking them in.

People sometimes think I'm stupid because I'm so quiet. But I'm not stupid, I'm scared. Scared my voice will get all squeaky and people will laugh. Worried I'll look dumb if I say the wrong thing. Concerned about being a show-off if I get the answer right. Convinced that if I start talking, people will notice me, and I won't like the attention.

"Turn off the TV, Marlee," Daddy said suddenly.

I jumped up to do as he asked. I could tell by his tone that something was wrong.

"I can't believe the governor would rather close the schools than have you go with a couple of Negroes," Daddy said to Judy.

"That's not what he said," Mother snapped. "It's about states' rights, preserving our way of life and respecting Southern traditions. Not to mention maintaining the peace."

"There you have it, girls." Daddy's voice was pleasant, but there was a bite to it.

Judy frowned. "But what will I do all day?"

"You can get a head start on the fall cleaning," said Mother. "Maybe wash the windows?"

Judy made a face.

"Or you can help Betty Jean with the laundry. It's up to you. I'll bring home a reading list and a math book to keep you busy after that."

Betty Jean was our new maid. We'd never had one before, but with Mother going back to work, we needed someone to do the laundry and the cooking. Daddy's been an English teacher at Forest Heights Junior High for a long time, but Mother's first day of teaching home economics at Hall High School was supposed to be tomorrow.

"Do you have to go to work?" Judy asked.

"Yes," said Mother. "Hall is closed to the students, but I signed a contract, so I have to go."

"What about Marlee? Does she have school?" Judy asked.

That was just what I wanted to know.

"Yes," said Daddy. "Only the high schools are closed. No one is trying to send Negroes to the junior highs."

"Not yet," said Mother.

Daddy ignored her.

We kissed our parents good night and went back to our room. "Lucky you," I said to Judy as I walked into the bathroom to brush my teeth. I was starting at West Side Junior High, and I wasn't too excited about it.

"Yeah," Judy whispered. "Lucky me."

As I brushed my teeth, I wondered how I'd feel if a colored girl were sent to my school. Sally said you'd get lice if you sat too close to one of them, but Sally also said if you lit a candle in a bathroom and turned around three times, you'd see a ghost in the mirror. I'd tried it once when I was seven, and there was no ghost, just a lot of melted wax on the countertop. I didn't believe much of what Sally said after that.

There had been a colored girl in one of Judy's classes last year at Central High School, the best high school in all of Arkansas. For the first time, nine Negroes had enrolled: Minnijean Brown, Elizabeth Eckford, Ernest Green, Thelma Mothershed, Melba Pattillo, Terrence Roberts, Gloria Ray, Jefferson Thomas and Carlotta Walls. That was a mouthful, so people just started calling them the Little Rock Nine.

The integration had gone so badly that President Eisenhower sent in soldiers to help keep the peace. I remembered Daddy talking about being polite to the Negroes and Mother biting her lip. I'd been so busy watching both of them, I'd never thought to ask Judy how she'd felt about it. All I knew for sure was that she hadn't gotten lice.

When Judy walked into the bathroom, I opened my mouth

to ask. But my mouth was full of toothpaste and by the time I'd rinsed and spit, her mouth was full of toothpaste. And then it was time to go to bed.

Judy fell asleep quickly, but I kept tossing and turning. Usually the lions' roaring lulled me to sleep, but they were silent tonight, as quiet as the halls of Central would be tomorrow. Finally I got up and went into the kitchen for a glass of milk. Mother and Daddy were talking in the living room.

"Almost sounds like you're an integrationist," I heard Mother say.

"I don't think it's such a big deal if Judy's at school with a few—"

"You want our girls associating with Negroes?" asked Mother.

"A few colored students wouldn't—"

"Race mixing. That's what it'll lead to," said Mother.

I stood in front of the open fridge in my nightgown, clutching the bottle of milk, and shivered. Race mixing was a scary thing—at least people always talked about it like it was polio or something. The thing was, the races didn't really mix in Little Rock, not in the bathrooms of department stores, nor in the water of the swimming pools. In fact, I don't think we'd ever had a colored person in our house until Betty Jean showed up ironing last week.

"There wouldn't have even been any trouble last year if the governor hadn't—"

"Richard, watch what you're saying!"

"I'm not saying anything I don't mean."

"Do you want people to call us communists?" Mother asked.

The milk bottle slipped from my hand and crashed to the floor. So much for eavesdropping. My parents ran into the kitchen.

"Oh, Marlee!" Mother grabbed a towel and began to mop things up. "Now there'll be no milk for breakfast."

"Sorry," I whispered.

Mother just kept wiping up the mess.

My father poured me a glass of water and walked me back to my room. "We weren't arguing," he said when we got to my door.

I nodded. But when he leaned over to kiss me good night, his eye twitched like it always did when he was lying.

3

QUEEN ELIZABETH

The next morning Judy woke up early to eat breakfast with me, even though she didn't have to. She's such a good sister. I made two bowls of oatmeal and put one down in front of her.

"Promise me something," Judy said.

"What?" I asked.

"Promise to say at least one complete sentence today."

"Yes, ma'am," I said. Sometimes Judy was as bad as Mother.

"I mean it," said Judy. "At least five words. Together. In a row. *Yes* and *no* don't count."

"I promise."

"That's only two," said Judy.

"To talk a lot," I added. "That makes six."

Judy laughed. I grinned and finished my oatmeal.

"Marlee!" My father poked his head into the kitchen. "You ready?"

Last year, Daddy had started driving me to school. The first time was the day after one of the colored girls from Central had been surrounded by a mob at the bus stop. In the picture in the paper, the white people were yelling at her, and yet she'd held her head up high. I couldn't understand why half of Little Rock was screaming over a few colored kids. Surely they weren't all stupid enough to believe Sally.

It happened again a few months later. Daddy had invited a colored pastor to come talk to his Bible study group at church. He said the meeting had gone well, but the next day, he'd found a note tucked in with the morning paper. He didn't let any of us read the note, not even Mother, but he drove me to school every day after that.

Daddy and I didn't talk in the car, but it was a comfortable silence. The closer we got to school, the more nervous I became, so I started counting prime numbers in my head again. I'd reached 67 by the time Daddy dropped me off at the front entrance to West Side Junior High. It was a large building, but of course I'd visited when Judy had been a student, so it only took me a minute to find my seventh-grade homeroom and sit down.

I knew pretty much everyone there. Sally was two rows over, talking with Nora. Unlike Sally's strong cough syrup, Nora was a weak fruit punch. She had horn-rimmed glasses and was convinced they made her ugly, even though she had a long neck and the straightest, smoothest hair I'd ever seen.

In the back was a new girl. She had short dark hair, just like Judy's, tied back with a ribbon. She had neatly trimmed fingernails (which reminded me to stop chewing on my pinkie) and a lovely tan too, like she'd been at the pool all summer, though I hadn't seen her there once.

Sally got up and walked over to her desk. Nora went too. "Hi, new girl," Sally said in her bright, clear voice. "What's your name?"

The new girl looked up and smiled. A wide, honest, open smile. I knew she thought Sally was being sincere, but I would've bet you all the money in my piggy bank that she wasn't.

"Elizabeth," said the new girl. "What's yours?"

"Sally," said Sally. "It's nice to meet you, Bethie."

"Oh, it's not Bethie," said the girl.

"Lizzie?" guessed Sally.

"No, Elizabeth," said the girl. "Like the Queen."

Sally looked at her blankly.

"The Queen of England."

"Did you hear that, Nora? Her name is Elizabeth, like the Queen of England." Sally burst out laughing.

I couldn't bring myself to look at the new girl. I was sure she felt awful. I started counting prime numbers again: 2, 3, 5, 7, 11 . . .

But the new girl started laughing too. "Yeah, like the Queen of England. But you can just call me 'Your Highness.'"

Nora tittered.

"Your Highness?" repeated Sally.

"That's right," said Elizabeth. "Unless you prefer 'O royal one.'"

Nora had to gulp down a giggle. I couldn't quite tell if she was amused or nervous. No one spoke this way to Sally.

The new girl suddenly grinned and slapped Sally on the shoulder. "I'm just kidding, of course. Liz is fine."

Sally gave a little smile. Before she could say anything else, Miss Taylor, our homeroom teacher, walked in, and Sally and Nora sat down.

Miss Taylor was one of those teachers you just can't imagine anywhere but school. She'd been teaching forever and always pulled her blond hair back into a bun. As she handed out our schedules, I noticed her sweater had a couple of dropped stitches on the back, as if she'd made it herself. I had Miss Taylor again for history in the afternoon. She frowned a lot as she talked, and I couldn't decide if she was plain old coffee or something worse, like the vinegar pooled at the bottom of a jar of pickles. Though I'm not sure why anyone would drink that.

After homeroom came English, then science, and right before lunch I had math. Since math is my favorite subject, sometimes I talk in class, but only if the answer's a number. Like 43. Or 3,458. Or 36.72. But if the answer is "eight apples," all you'll get out of me is "eight." You'll have to provide the apples yourself.

My math teacher this year was Mr. Harding. It was his first year at West Side, and he was young, almost as young as my older brother. Mr. Harding got to work right away, writing problems on the chalkboard. By the end of the period, chalk dust had turned his hair (and his suit) prematurely gray. He called on everyone in the class at least once, even the girls. Even me. (I answered. It was 345.) My old math teacher had asked the boys to answer three times as often as the girls. I knew because once, last year, I had gotten really bored, and I'd kept track of who she'd called on for a whole week. I decided Mr. Harding was a chocolate malt shake, and I liked him a lot.

Pretty soon it was lunchtime. Mother always packed me a lunch, because I didn't like to tell the lunch ladies what I wanted. I sat down at an empty table and wondered if Sally would sit with me like she had in elementary school. If she didn't, I'd just sit alone. There are worse things in life than sitting alone. Like leprosy. Or losing a limb. Or maybe getting your period in the middle of gym when you're wearing white shorts and the teacher is a man and you left all your sanitary napkins at home. Not that that's ever happened to me.

I was just biting into my pimento cheese sandwich when I

heard someone clear her throat. It was the new girl—Elizabeth or Liz or whatever she wanted to be called.

"It's Marlee, right?" she asked.

I nodded, wondering how she'd already figured out my name.

"Mind if I sit here?"

Truth was, I did mind. But if I shook my head, it would mean I didn't, and Liz would sit down. If I nodded, she might think that was a positive response and sit down anyway. I couldn't say no because that would be rude, and so I looked up at her, hoping she'd understand and go away. In that moment, with her hair pulled back and her clear brown eyes, she looked just like Judy.

"Please sit down."

Liz sat.

It took me a second to realize I had spoken. To a stranger. Mother would be thrilled. Judy would say this was real progress. Even if it had only been a reflex since she looked so much like my sister. I cursed myself for only using three words. Now I'd have to work another two in sometime this afternoon.

"Thanks so much." Liz smiled. "I hate eating lunch alone."

I hate eating lunch alone too, and I knew that was the polite thing to say. But I didn't say it.

"Don't worry," Liz continued, taking a bite of her sandwich. "You don't have to actually talk to me. Just sitting here is enough."

I snorted and looked up to see her grinning at me. A sense of humor was on Judy's list of what makes a good friend. But what was Liz's drink? Was she really as wholesome as whole milk? Or was she like a shot of whiskey given to you by your older cousin? I couldn't place her, and it made me nervous.

Sally and Nora finally arrived at the table. "That's my seat," Sally said, pointing at Liz's chair. Nora hovered behind her.

"Oh, is it?" said Liz mildly.

Sally stood there for a moment before she realized Liz wasn't going to move. "But you can sit in it," Sally said suddenly, like she was being really nice.

"Why, thank you," said Liz.

"Marlee doesn't talk," said Sally, pointing at me. "That's why I have to sit next to her. We've known each other a long time."

"She doesn't?" said Liz. "But she just invited me to sit down."

"She did?" Sally asked, and looked at me.

I was about to nod when I realized if I said something, I could bring my word count for the day up to five. So I kind of squinted at Liz until she went blurry and I could pretend she was Judy, and I took a deep breath and counted 13, 17, 19, 23 and said, "I did."

Liz nodded and smiled. Her teeth were straight and very white. Oral hygiene is very important. I never skip brushing my teeth myself.

"Why didn't we see you at the pool this summer?" asked Sally, tossing her blond hair. She always did that when she wanted someone to stop what they were doing and pay attention to her.

"You're Sally, right?" said Liz.

Sally looked pleased that Liz had already learned her name. "Well, my family just moved here . . ."

And with that, Queen Elizabeth started her reign.

4

FIVE LITTLE WORDS

I always walked home from school—guess Daddy figured I'd be safe enough with all the other kids around. Last year, I'd tagged along with Sally, but today she stayed late to watch the boys play football.

As soon as I opened our front door, I could tell Judy was in a bad mood. "School's not going to start until at least September fifteenth!" she yelled at me from the kitchen. "What am I going to do at home until then?"

I hung up my jacket and followed Judy's voice into the kitchen.

Judy was sitting at the table, watching Betty Jean pull a batch of cookies out of the oven. Betty Jean was tall and always wore a flowered apron over her clothes when she was at our house. To be honest, I'd been pretty upset about having a stranger hanging around, even if she was doing chores so I wouldn't have to. But Betty Jean didn't say much, and she never tried to get me to talk to her. Eventually, I thought of her as water. She took on the flavor of whoever else was around.

"There's a U.S. Supreme Court hearing on Friday, September twelfth," Judy explained. "To decide if the Little Rock schools have to follow the plan Superintendent Blossom came up with for integration."

"And after that?" I asked.

"Hopefully," said Judy, "the schools will open again, and they'll decide to give this whole integration thing a rest for a year or two."

It sounded like Judy was against integration. I knew Daddy supported it, and I'd always thought it was a good idea myself. Why have two sets of schools when one would do? But I didn't ask Judy about it, even though I knew she wanted me to. Judy does so much for me, I hate it when we disagree.

I watched Betty Jean use a spatula to put the cookies onto a piece of wax paper on the counter to cool.

"Mother agrees with me," said Judy, like she'd read my thoughts and was trying to convince me to come around to her side. "She said so this morning before she left." Judy picked up one of the cookies, then dropped it. It was too hot to eat.

Betty Jean poured me a glass of milk and handed me a plate of cookies. We nodded at each other. The cookies, oatmeal chocolate chip, were delicious. But even the warm cookies didn't erase the pit in my stomach. I wasn't sure I could trust Judy's opinion about integration, but I also wasn't sure I could trust my own.

And worst of all, Judy didn't even ask me about the five words.

I could have brought it up, maybe I would have, but it wasn't till Betty Jean had gone home and we were eating dinner that I got the opportunity. Mother told us all about her lesson plans and complimented Judy on the job she'd done washing the windows before she got around to asking me about the first day of school.

"Fine." I looked at my plate. "I said two sentences."

"What?" said Judy. "Marlee, why didn't you say something earlier!"

I shrugged.

"Oh, my goodness," said Mother, holding her hand to her heart, like women do in the movies when they are about to faint.

"Atta girl!" said Daddy.

"What'd you say?" asked Judy.

"'Please sit down' and 'I did.'" Then I grinned, embarrassed. "It's silly to get so excited about five stupid words."

"It's not silly," said Mother.

"What did Sally say?" asked Judy.

"I wasn't talking to Sally," I admitted.

Everyone stopped eating and turned to look at me. I didn't like it.

"It was a new girl," I explained quickly. "Her name is Liz, and she just moved here, and she has nice teeth." That was a stupid thing to say. No one cares about teeth. I should have mentioned her nails instead.

"Well," said Mother, and it sounded like she was just about ready to burst with pride. "I'm sure you made her feel quite welcome."

Mother was pleased with me! I didn't know what to say.

Daddy just grinned.

"Why don't you invite her over sometime?" Mother suggested. "Betty Jean could make lemonade and sandwiches and—"

Judy laughed. "Maybe tomorrow she could just say hello."

It was a really good dinner.

But that night in bed, instead of being happy, I felt kind of sad. Most of the time, I act like it doesn't bother me that I don't talk much. Usually I'm pretty convincing, even to myself. But some-times, at night, when I hear the lions roaring and they're really going at it, just growling and yowling, and roaring like a jet engine, sometimes I wish I could be like them, that I could just yell out whatever I was thinking or feeling and not care one whit who heard. Sometimes, in the middle of the night, I can almost convince myself that I'm going to do it. That I'll just start talking.

But by the time I wake up in the morning, the lions are always silent, and so am I.

5

JAMES-THOMAS

On the second day of school, James-Thomas Dalton ran in late.

JT, which was what everyone called him, was tall and blond and played football too. He had blue eyes and a dimple on his chin, and his nose was just slightly off-center; I thought it made him look even more handsome. Like half the girls in my class, I had a crush on him.

Not that anyone else knew. I hadn't even told Judy. It was embarrassing to like someone who still didn't know his times tables. But JT had flair. He had confidence. That and really long eyelashes.

"My brother's car had a flat," JT announced to everyone and no one in particular. "I had to help change it."

Miss Taylor nodded in sympathy. "I'll excuse you this time."

JT grinned at her, and his smile blinded us all to the fact that there wasn't a bit of grease or dirt on his clothes. The only open seat was next to me, so he strode over and threw his bag down. "Hi, Marlee," he said. Of course he knew my name. We'd been in school together since we were six, but it still gave me a thrill.

I smiled back and tried to move my bag out of his way, but I bumped it instead. Four or five new pencils rolled out across the floor. Sally giggled as I gathered them up. JT handed me one of the pencils and our fingers touched and I could almost hear the wedding bells.

Even though we were in homeroom, Miss Taylor couldn't help giving us a preview of what we were going to do in history that afternoon. She started going on and on about Arkansas and how we'd each pick a topic and give a presentation to the class. Pretty soon I stopped listening. Sally would ask me to be her partner, and I'd do all the work. That's how it always was. Besides, I was having too much fun imagining my life with JT.

By lunchtime I'd planned our honeymoon in Italy and was trying to decide if we should name our first son Orbit or Cosine, when someone slid into the chair beside me. I just about spit out my peanut butter and jelly sandwich when I realized it was JT.

"Hi, Marlee," he said.

I knew I should squeeze out a "hi" or maybe "hello," or maybe even "hello, JT," but of course he knew what his name was and my mouth was full of peanut butter. Still, I'd promised Judy I'd try to speak, so before I could talk myself out of it, I said, "Hi, JT."

I was pleased. I sounded so smooth and calm, at least until I reached for my milk to wash down the peanut butter and knocked over the carton instead.

JT, always the gentleman, mopped up the mess. "I was wondering if you'd be willing to help me with math this year," he said as he pushed a pile of soggy napkins around the table.

I was too surprised to move. There was still a big blob of peanut butter stuck to the roof of my mouth. If I said something, JT would be totally grossed out.

"Mr. Harding is a hard teacher," JT went on. "I'm sure to fail if I don't find a tutor, and I don't want to have to repeat the seventh grade like my brother did. I'm not so good at math, and you're great at it. So, what do you say? Do you want to help me?"

I swallowed. This was my chance. "I do."

He grinned, pulled out his math book and handed it to me. "The first assignment is on page twelve, numbers one through twenty-one."

I knew that. We were in the same class. Still, I didn't mind being the brains in the family.

"Let's meet up before school tomorrow, and you can explain it to me," he suggested. "Say at the picnic table by the football field?"

I nodded.

He patted me on the shoulder. "Thanks, Marlee," he said. "You're a real sweet girl." Then he walked off to join his friends at their regular table.

I was on cloud nine. I had a date—a real date—with JT. We'd had a whole conversation. He liked me. He—

"He just wants you to do the work for him," Sally said, sitting down at our table.

I shrugged. I was happy, and I wasn't going to let Sally take that away from me.

"Maybe," said Liz as she put down her tray. "But he sure is cute."

I didn't hear the rest of the conversation after that. I was too busy thinking about Cosine and his little sister, Isosceles.

The next morning I had Daddy drop me off at school extra early. I had pencils, paper, both our math books and my homework. JT could use it as an answer key if he got stuck. He wasn't at school when I arrived, so I sat down on top of the picnic table to wait.

I waited a long time. Cosine and Isosceles were in college by the time JT's brother, Red, finally pulled up to the curb. JT might be a cup of hot chocolate with whipped cream and sprinkles on the top, but his brother was castor oil. Red was seventeen, a year older than Judy. He had blond hair and blue eyes like his little brother, and his features were so regular, they looked like they had been laid out with a ruler. If you ask me, it's people's imperfections that give them character—a nose slightly off center or a dimple or one ear slightly higher than the other. There was something creepy about Red's perfectly symmetrical face.

Or maybe it wasn't about his face at all. Once, when we were all little kids playing in an old quarry near our house, Red had called me over to see a butterfly he'd caught. It was beautiful—black and orange—and fluttered like a tiny, pulsing heart in his hand. Then suddenly, he'd torn off its wings with his fingertips and laughed when I started to cry.

"You've got the mute girl tutoring you?" asked Red loudly as he pulled up to the curb. I knew he wanted me to hear.

JT shrugged. "She's pretty. And good at math. What else do I need?" He opened the door and got out.

Red sped off, almost hitting one of the colored women who worked in the cafeteria and was trying to cross the street. He leaned on the horn, and she hurried out of his way.

I wanted to say something to her as she walked toward the side door of the school. *Are you all right? Isn't he a jerk?* Or maybe even just *hello.* But before I could get up the nerve, she was inside the building and the moment was gone.

"Hi, Marlee." JT sat down next to me on the picnic bench.

24

I smiled at him.

"So," said JT.

So. I guessed I'd have to say something. In my excitement over planning the JT and Marlee love story, I'd forgotten that tutoring him would involve actual speaking.

"You ready?" he asked.

I opened my math book, and my homework fell out.

The first bell rang.

Great. We only had five minutes to get to class. There were twenty-one problems. We'd never finish in time!

But JT's grin was as wide as ever. "You're a sweetheart."

Before I could swoon over his words of endearment, JT picked up *my* homework and put it into *his* book. He winked and slammed the book shut. "Thanks, Marlee. See you same place tomorrow. Okay?" He strode off without waiting for an answer.

All yesterday, I'd imagined the scene. JT and I would have so much fun working together, he'd say he wanted to spend more time with me. We'd do fractions at the Double Scoop Ice Cream Parlor and long division at Krystal Burger. I wanted to believe the best of him. Maybe he'd had another flat tire. Maybe his alarm clock hadn't gone off. Even though the truth was staring me in the face, I couldn't help thinking that maybe tomorrow he'd be on time.

6

A NEW PARTNER

I spent all of homeroom frantically doing my math homework. Again.

When I was done, Liz leaned over and whispered, "What are you going to do for your history report?"

For a minute, I didn't know what she was talking about. Then I remembered the project Miss Taylor had told us about yesterday. The one that involved an oral presentation. No wonder I'd done my best to block it out.

Liz kept talking. "Because I had this really good idea, and I wanted to ask you to work with me."

I glanced at Sally.

Liz saw who I was looking at, and her face dropped. But she pasted a smile back on so fast, if I'd blinked I'd have missed her true reaction. "Oh, of course," she said brightly. "That makes sense. You and Sally being old friends and all."

I suddenly knew she'd imagined this scene, just like I had pictured the one with JT. And this wasn't the way hers had ended either. I felt bad, but not bad enough to actually work with her.

Liz turned away, but as she did, she knocked her math notebook to the floor. I bent over to pick it up.

On the back was a square with lots of little squares in it. In some of the squares were numbers. I knew what it was—it was a magic square.

Magic squares have been around for just about forever. According to David's old math book (he used to let me read it when he wasn't studying), the Chinese discovered them way back before Jesus was even born. The simplest was a three-by-three square, with the numbers 1 to 9 arranged so that every row, column and diagonal added up to 15. Liz had a four-by-four square on her notebook with some of the numbers missing.

I ran my fingers over the numbers. The top row added up to 34.

"It's a magic square," said Liz, sounding a little embarrassed. "It's a silly game my mother taught me."

"Thirteen," I said, pointing to a blank square.

"Oh," said Liz. "Thanks. I couldn't figure that one out."

I stared at the square again. Yep. Each row, column and diagonal added up to 34. It was beautiful. I handed back the notebook and counted 2, 3, 5, 7. "What was your idea?"

"Well, I have this book about the founding of Little Rock and the Indians who used to live here and . . ." Liz paused and looked at me. Then she shook her head. "It's okay, Marlee. You don't have to pretend to be interested."

"It's just . . ." I took a deep breath. "Why me?"

Liz shrugged. "You seem like a hard worker. At my old school, I was the one who always ended up doing all the work."

I knew what that was like. I'd worked with Sally on every project since third grade. Maybe it was time for a change.

"Okay," I said.

"Really?" she asked.

I nodded.

"Great," she said. "Meet you at the public library tomorrow after school?"

I nodded again.

The bell rang, and homeroom was over. Liz gave me a little wave and walked off. What was she? A root beer? An extra-thick milk shake with two straws? Carrot juice? I didn't know, and I didn't really care. I just wanted to know everything she knew about magic squares.

On Friday I arrived early and waited by the picnic table, and again JT arrived just before the bell rang. He winked at me as he took my homework. "Like your hair."

Judy and I had stayed up late the night before, putting my hair into curlers. I knew I should feel mad about the homework, but I couldn't help being just a little tickled he had noticed. And at least this time, I'd known to do the homework twice.

When I walked into the library that afternoon, there was Liz, her hair pulled back in a ponytail, reading glasses balanced on her nose. When she saw me, she pulled off the glasses and waved.

"Hi, Marlee," she said with a smile. "I wasn't sure you'd come."

I shrugged. Clearly she didn't understand how much I liked math.

When she realized I wasn't going to answer her, she handed me a book, and I sat down and started reading. We read for a long time. The book she had pulled for me on the Quapaw Indians was actually pretty interesting. The Quapaws were the

Indians who had lived in Little Rock when the first settlers came. The book talked all about their families and how they got married and what they did when they died. When I looked up, Liz had two pages of notes in a crisp, neat handwriting.

"Find anything interesting?" she asked.

I nodded.

"What?"

I passed her a book and pointed to a paragraph about what they did with orphaned children. She read it quickly. "Cool. Hey, we could do this for the class—put on sort of a pretend ceremony. Pick some kids to be the orphans and some others to be the fathers."

That would be interesting. And more fun than just reading a boring old paper aloud.

"Only one problem," she said.

I looked at her.

"You have to talk," she said. "I mean during the presentation."

I shook my head. I did not talk in front of the class. That was like asking me to walk down the street in my underwear.

"You have to at least say something."

I just looked at her.

"If I do all the talking, people will think I did all the work. And that's not fair."

She was right. It wasn't fair. And I didn't care. I did not give oral presentations.

"It's important to face your fears," said Liz. "It makes you a better person."

I thought I was pretty good just the way I was. We stared at each other for a long moment. If it was a staring contest she wanted, I knew I'd win.

Sure enough, she looked away first. "I tell you what," said

Liz. "My mother has a whole book about magic squares. You speak during our presentation, and I'll give it to you."

Just when I thought I'd gotten the best of her, she went and turned it all around. A book of magic squares? There was no way I could resist that. And from the smug look on her face, I was pretty sure she understood how much I liked math, after all.

"Fine," I said.

Liz smiled at me.

The front door of the library opened, and a couple of colored girls walked in. Liz stiffened. I knew Negroes were allowed to use this library now—that rule had passed a few years ago—but I didn't see them there much. It was like the bus—officially, anyone could sit anywhere they wanted now, but most of the time, the colored folks stayed to the back.

"I think we've done enough for one day," said Liz, closing her book. She glanced over at the colored girls again. They were waiting, trying unsuccessfully to get the librarian's attention.

I wondered if Liz was like some of the other kids at school, calling colored folks names I wasn't allowed to say. I wondered if I could do this project with her if she was.

"They aren't hurting anyone," I said quietly.

"I know," she said. "I'm just tired of studying."

But I didn't quite believe her.

7

A NEW ROOMMATE

Every Saturday we had to clean the house from top to bottom. It wasn't my favorite thing to do, but it wasn't so bad either, not since Judy and I got a record player last Christmas. Now every Saturday morning, we put on our latest album and sang along. This week it was *South Pacific*.

I like singing. The song gives you the words, so you don't have to think about what to say. Sometimes I dream about being in the church choir. But that involves getting up and standing in front of a group of people. Which is not something I like to do.

Every time I thought about how I had agreed to talk during our presentation, I felt sick. Even reciting prime numbers didn't calm me down. I hadn't even told Judy about it yet, since I'd already decided twenty times to tell Liz *no* on Monday. But then I'd think of that math book and change my mind again. Especially since last year, I'd spent a week building up my courage to ask the librarian for a book on magic squares, and when I did, she said they didn't carry books about witchcraft.

"Mother," Judy said, bringing me back to the world of scrubbing tubs and toilets, "is it okay if I move into David's room?"

What? David might be at college, but that didn't mean he wasn't ever coming back. Did it?

"I asked him before he left, and he said he didn't mind," said Judy.

I mind! But I didn't say it. I just scrubbed harder.

Mother stopped shining the mirror over the sink. "What about when he comes home for the holidays? Christmas and spring break."

"I'll just move back in with Marlee then. She can have the double bed; I'm happy with the twin."

"All right, then." Mother went back to work.

"No," I said. "I don't want you to go."

Judy laughed. "Marlee, I'm not going anywhere. Just down the hall."

"You'll love having some space to yourself," said Mother. "You'll see."

But I knew she was wrong.

As soon as we were finished with our chores, Judy moved into David's old room. We'd shared a room my entire life, and it only took her half an hour to disappear.

That night, it was as quiet as a graveyard in my room. Even the roaring of the lions couldn't break the silence. I missed the sound of Judy breathing, the squeak of the bed as she rolled over, even the ticking of her alarm clock. Finally I took my blanket and snuck down the hall into my brother's old room. The moon shone in the window, and I could just make out Judy asleep on the bed. I crept inside and curled up on the floor. It was hard and uncomfortable, but I fell asleep easily, listening to Judy's quiet snoring.

• • •

"Marlee!"

I woke up to Judy staring at me. The sun was shining in the window.

"Why are you sleeping on the floor?" she demanded.

I shrugged.

"Marlee, I changed rooms because I wanted to be alone! Tonight, make sure you stay in your own bed." Judy stepped over me and marched off to the bathroom.

I picked up my blanket and went back to my room. My sister, the one I could always talk to, didn't want me around anymore. I didn't know what I was going to do.

Sally wasn't pleased either. Not when Liz told her we were working together.

"But Marlee always works with me," she said.

I'm right here, I wanted to yell. I can hear what you are saying about me.

"Well, you are so nice," said Liz smoothly, "to make sure a new girl like me doesn't have to work alone."

Sally opened her mouth, then closed it again.

"I'll work with you, Sally," said Nora.

Sally shrugged, and Nora beamed.

What I wouldn't give to be like Liz, to be the one who could make Sally speechless.

That afternoon when I got home from school, Betty Jean was in the kitchen making sweet tea. Everyone has their own recipe, but Betty Jean makes it by boiling water in a saucepan on the stove. She adds in a pinch of baking soda, and then when the water's boiling, puts in the tea bags, all tied together. Once it's dark enough, she pours it into a pitcher and adds a cup of simple syrup. She stirs, adds enough water to fill the pitcher to the top, and stirs again.

Betty Jean was just getting ready to put it into the fridge when she realized I was watching her. "Oh, Marlee, I didn't see you," she said. "Would you like a glass of tea?"

What I really wanted was for my sister to come down and talk to me, but she was up in *her* new room, even though I knew she'd heard the front door open when I came in. But I didn't want to sit in my room alone, and I guess I was a little thirsty, so I nodded.

I sat down at the table while Betty Jean filled a tall glass with ice and poured in the tea. "Do you mind if I sit down for a minute?" she asked as she put the tea down in front of me. "The heat makes my ankles swell."

Of course I didn't mind. Betty Jean was a hard worker. All the clothes were folded and put away, dinner was cooking in the oven, and the living room floor was so clean, I'd be willing to eat off it. I was embarrassed she'd even asked me—like I was her boss or something—and gestured for her to go ahead.

Betty Jean pulled out a chair and sat down. It was hot, and she used the flowered apron to wipe the sweat from her face. I wondered why she didn't pour herself a glass of tea, then re-membered that there seemed to be an unspoken rule that she could cook our food but never taste it. Kind of like the one about girls and math and satellites.

It made me mad, thinking about that, and before I knew it, I had jumped up and poured another glass of tea. Betty Jean looked surprised when I held it out to her, but she took it. "Thank you, Marlee." She drank half the glass in one long gulp, then wiped her mouth daintily and said, "Did you have a nice day at school?"

"I'm doing a presentation in history," I said, then sat down, embarrassed. I'd never spoken to her before.

"Good for you," said Betty Jean.

I counted prime numbers in my head until I realized she wasn't going to ask me anything else. We sat like that for a long time. Silent. But not bad silent. Just quiet. When I was done with my tea, I snuck a look at Betty Jean.

She was about my mother's age, with big brown eyes and high cheekbones. Her skin was dark and smooth, and at her temples was just a bit of gray. She was staring off into the distance, thinking of something else. But when she felt my gaze on her face, she looked over at me and smiled.

I smiled back. Turns out, Betty Jean wasn't just plain water after all. She had a twist of lime that was all her own.

After dinner, I sat in bed, trying to figure out what to do about JT and his homework. Sure, he always thanked me or told me I was a nice girl, but I'd expected more. He never brought me candy or asked me to the movies or did any of the things a boyfriend was supposed to do. Then again, he wasn't really my boyfriend. I was pretty sure you had to talk to have one of those.

Also, I didn't suppose those Soviet scientists who had sent up Sputnik had gotten where they were by cheating. If I wanted to work on a top-secret space project someday, I couldn't have any blemishes on my record. Not to mention that I knew cheating was just plain wrong.

But every time I resolved to hand JT a blank piece of paper, I wondered if this would be the day he came to his senses and asked me out.

I had decided to give him just a little more time, when there was a knock at the door. Without waiting for me to answer, Judy poked her head into the room. "You got a minute?"

I nodded.

Judy held up a covered bird's cage. "I heard Daddy say he hasn't had much time for Pretty Boy lately." That was Daddy's pet parakeet. He usually kept him in the living room.

I kept my eyes on the parakeet. I was still too angry to look at Judy. Too worried that if I started talking, I might say something I couldn't take back.

"Do you want to keep him in here with you?" Judy asked. "Daddy said it was okay."

I shrugged.

Judy set him down on the dresser.

I didn't say anything.

"I'm sorry, Marlee," she said. "I've been so upset about not having school, not seeing my friends, and wondering how I'm going to get to college if I can't even start eleventh grade that I haven't really been thinking about you."

It was embarrassing. I was almost thirteen. I shouldn't need my older sister to fuss over me or tell me what to do. But I did. Without her, I was afraid I'd just get quieter and quieter, until even Mother and Daddy didn't remember I was there.

All of a sudden, Judy leaned over and gave me a hug. I tried not to melt into it, tried to stay stiff and cold, but my sister gives really good hugs.

"Pretty Boy!" the parakeet sang. "Pretty Boy!"

"Come back," I begged. "Please."

"I can't," said Judy. "It's not personal, Marlee. I just need some more space. You'll get used to it."

Maybe she was right. Maybe I would. But I didn't have to like it.

8

A NEW FRIEND

The next day at lunch, Liz showed up with a schedule. "I've got it all worked out," she said. "We have three weeks until our presentation. If we work Monday, Wednesday and Friday after school, and Saturday afternoons too, I think we'll be ready. Maybe. I hope."

"Why are you two working so hard?" asked Sally when she heard about our plans.

I was wondering the same thing myself. Judy had told me Miss Taylor was an easy grader. We could probably wait until the weekend before and still get an A.

"Marlee is going to talk," bragged Liz.

Oh, yeah. That was why we couldn't wait. I kept trying to forget that part. If the bribe had been anything but a magic square math book, it would have been so easy to refuse.

"Oh, really?" said Sally, as if that was about as likely as me jumping off the diving board. I suddenly wanted to do it, magic squares or no, just to prove her wrong.

Liz elbowed me in the ribs. "Tell her," she said.

"I am," I squeaked.

Sally rolled her eyes.

"Ignore her," ordered Liz. Sometimes she could be as bossy as Sally herself. "Now, we just need a place for you to practice speaking aloud. The library's out, of course. It needs to be somewhere you feel comfortable, but where we don't have anyone else like a maid or an older sibling hanging around. You don't have a tree house, do you?"

I shook my head.

Liz thought in silence for a moment. A few tables over, JT shoved a whole slice of orange into his mouth. His bangs fell into his eyes as he started jumping around like a monkey, but somehow, he still managed to look cute.

"The zoo?" I suggested.

"Perfect!" said Liz. "You can talk to the animals."

Great, I thought glumly. Just call me Dr. Dolittle.

We started the next afternoon in front of the gorillas. I watched the mother gorilla picking the bugs off her baby for a good five minutes before Liz cleared her throat.

"Okay," said Liz. "Now I've prepared a few questions to get you warmed up."

I gave her a look. This was sounding pretty stupid.

"Come on, Marlee. They're easy. Give it a shot."

"Fine." I crossed my arms and stared at her.

"What's your favorite color?"

"Blue."

"Who's your favorite singer?"

"Buddy Holly."

"I like him too. Did you see him sing 'Peggy Sue' on *Ed Sullivan*?"

I nodded. That had been pretty neat.

"What's your favorite subject?" Liz continued.

"Math."

"I knew that."

"And the point of all this is?"

"To get you talking," said Liz.

I hated to admit it, but her plan had worked. We'd just had a whole conversation.

The next day we met, we moved on to the elephants. Liz had me read part of the notes I had written up. Even though Ruth the elephant was the only one listening, my hands were still trembling.

"The Quapaw families had lots of traditions," I mumbled. "The Quapaw—"

Ruth stomped her foot.

"Go on," coaxed Liz.

"Fathers were really important to the Quapaw—"

Stomp. I paused again.

"Quapaw, Quapaw," said Liz.

Stomp, stomp.

"Why is the elephant . . . ?"

Liz shrugged.

"Quapaw, Quapaw, Quapaw, Quapaw," I said. Ruth stomped her feet so fast, it looked like she was dancing. Liz and I glanced at each other and burst out laughing.

It was fun after that. Singing to the seals and hollering to the herons. Liz always helped me "warm up" (like an opera singer) by asking me a few silly questions:

"Would you rather be a hippo or a rhino?"

"Rhino."

"If you could only eat one food for the rest of your life, what would it be?"

"Peanut butter."

"It's the night of the big dance. You're there with JT and—"

"I don't like JT," I said.

"You give him his homework every morning," Liz pointed out.

Okay, so I did.

"It's the night of the dance," Liz went on. "Would you rather have a pimple on your chin or your forehead?"

"Forehead, of course," I said. "I could wear my hair down and hide it."

"Great," said Liz. "Now it's your turn."

"My turn to what?" I asked.

"Ask me questions."

Actually, I wanted to. We'd been meeting for two weeks now, and she knew all sorts of random facts about me. I knew next to nothing about her, except that she was bossy and organized, and actually kind of fun. But when I tried to think up something witty or funny to ask, my mind went blank.

"What's your favorite color?" I said finally.

"Green," said Liz. "Like the grass."

"Who's your favorite singer?"

"Elvis Presley."

"What's your favorite subject?"

"English," said Liz. "But my mother wishes it were math."

Interesting. Part of me wanted to follow up there, but there was something else I was dying to know. "Why are you helping me?"

"Because I like to see Ruth dance when you say 'Quapaw.'"

This was hard for me. I'd always told her the truth—and she was turning it into a joke. "Seriously."

For the first time, Liz was silent. Behind her, the giraffes chewed their cud. "I thought it might be hard always being quiet," Liz said finally. "I thought you needed a friend."

She was right. I did.

"I needed a friend too," said Liz.

And I suddenly knew what Liz was—a cup of warm milk with a dash of cinnamon.

We stuck to the assignment for the rest of the afternoon, walking past the zebras and the flamingos, and finally ending up at my favorite place in front of the lions. There were two lions out that day. Both females, playing together, jumping over a log, batting an old pumpkin with their paws. I'd never seen them so active. We watched them a long time.

"Sometimes I feel sorry for them," Liz said suddenly.

"Why?" I asked. "They look like they're having a great time."

"Yeah," she said. "And I know they get their food and everything, and if they get sick, a vet gives them medicine. But don't you think they'd rather be chasing a zebra across the savanna?"

"Probably," I agreed.

"I like to listen to them," Liz said.

"What?"

"At night. I like to listen to the lions roar."

"Me too." I'd never thought anyone else did that. I wondered where she lived. I wondered if she'd ever invite me to her house. Should I invite her to mine? Wasn't that what friends did?

"When we first moved here, the roaring used to scare me. But now, I find it . . ." Liz paused.

"Comforting?" I suggested.

"Yeah," she agreed.

And for the first time, I understood what Judy was saying about finding someone who shared interests with you. Someone you can sit quietly with. For the first time, I thought I might understand what it was like to have a real friend.

9

THE FOOTBALL GAME

By mid-September the Supreme Court had decided that integration in Little Rock should proceed, but the schools still didn't open. For a while it seemed that with the high schools closed, there'd be no football too. But the public outcry was so great, the governor called the superintendent and told him to start up the football program again, school or no school. Daddy nearly turned purple when he heard this news. "They'll let their kids go without an education, but Little Rock won't stand for no football?"

Mother shrugged. She and Judy weren't fans, so they didn't care either way. It was certainly strange that football seemed more important than school, but I was glad they had decided to continue the football program. Friday night football games were something Daddy, David and I had always done together.

Even though he was upset, Daddy called David and asked if he wanted to go to the first game with us. David was actually just down the road at Little Rock University, but he was living in one of the dorms. Mother thought it was a waste of money when he could have stayed at home, but Daddy had had so much fun when he was in college, he wanted his son to have the same experience.

David was busy (having fun I guess), so I'd asked Liz to join us. She was going to meet us at the game, and I was so excited I couldn't help bouncing up and down on the front seat. Elvis's "Jailhouse Rock" came on the radio, and Daddy winked at me and turned it up louder. Mother was always telling us to turn the music down.

Liz was waiting for us by the gate. She yelled, "Marlee!" when she saw me and ran to give me a hug.

"Hi, Liz," I said, and grinned.

Daddy held out his hand for Liz to shake. "You must be the history partner," he said.

She took his hand and shook it hard. "You must be the English teacher."

Daddy laughed.

"Did Marlee tell you she's going to talk in front of the whole class?" Liz asked.

Daddy glanced at me. "No, she didn't."

"Liz!" I hissed.

"You have to tell people," she said. "That way you can't back out."

Daddy laughed again.

"When Marlee's ready to tell me, I'm sure she will," said Daddy. "Now, who wants something to eat?"

Daddy bought us popcorn and hot dogs for dinner. We gobbled them down and went to find seats in the bleachers. Every time one of the Central players made a good play, we screamed and waved homemade tissue-paper pompoms in the air. Daddy laughed and went off to talk to a colleague from work.

JT was sitting a few rows in front of us. He was wearing a Little Rock Tigers varsity jacket (probably Red's) and tufts of his blond hair were sticking up as if he'd forgotten to comb it. I had an overwhelming urge to go and slick it down.

"Staring at the back of his neck isn't going to make him turn around and say hello," Liz said finally.

"I don't know what you're talking about."

"Oh, come on," Liz said, laughing. "This is the perfect opportunity."

I gave her a look. "The perfect opportunity for what?"

"Well, you can't just talk to animals forever. We're giving the presentation to our class. Which is made up of people."

I didn't like where this was going.

"And JT is in our class."

Before I could protest, Liz pulled me up and practically pushed me down the bleachers. "Go talk to him."

I glanced back at her. She grinned and gave me a thumbs-up. Maybe I could do this. All I had to do was say hello. I took one step forward, then another. I was wearing my cream sweater and the pleated skirt, which was really cute and—

I kicked over someone's Coke bottle, leaned over to try to catch it before the glass broke, slipped, almost fell headfirst down the bleachers and only managed to save myself by grabbing onto JT's jacket, which I pulled halfway off his shoulders before I finally landed at his feet.

"Oh, hi, Marlee," JT said, like girls threw themselves at him every day of the week. (Who was I kidding? They probably did.) "Enjoying the game?"

I nodded and struggled to my feet.

"Sit down," JT said. A big burly guy with slicked-back hair moved over to make room for me. He was wearing a T-shirt and leather jacket, and I didn't know him from school. He was probably one of Red's friends, and he smelled funny, like a warm beer.

I sat down between them. I was so nervous, all I could think about was the smear of ketchup on my cream sweater. It must have happened when I fell. At least Red was playing in the game, so I didn't have to sit next to *him*.

"I'm really glad you stopped by," JT said. "I wanted to ask you something."

Finally! After all those math problems, he was going to ask me on a real date. "What?" I said, looking up at him expectantly. It was the first time I had ever spoken to him. I thought about batting my eyelashes, but he'd probably just think I had popcorn or something in my eye.

"It's about the homework," said JT.

The homework. Okay. Maybe he really wanted me to tutor him. I could live with that. Liz would say it was good speaking practice and—

"You're getting all the problems right."

Well, of course I am. I thought that was the point.

"You can't do that. See, if I get them all right on my homework, but I don't do well on the tests, Mr. Harding is going to get suspicious. I need you to throw in a couple of wrong answers here and there."

Get more wrong? He could just do the homework himself if he wanted to get more wrong.

"Do you like the movies, Marlee?" He looked at me with big, smoky blue eyes.

I nodded.

"I do too," JT said, "but Mother won't let me go unless I keep my grades up."

If I helped him, maybe someday he would ask me to come along.

"So what do you say?" JT cooed. "Will you help me out?"

I nodded again.

"Great," he said, and grinned. "See you on Monday?"

I smiled, stood up and practically ran back to my seat. At least I didn't trip on anything this time.

Liz patted me on the back when I returned. "There you go, you did it!" she cheered.

"Liz," I said, "all I said was 'what.'"

"That's something."

"And I nearly fell into his lap."

"Yes," she said. "But you did it *gracefully*."

We both started to laugh, harder and harder, until my stomach started to hurt, and Liz wiped tears from her eyes.

"You two sound like a pack of hyenas," said Sally. She was walking up the bleachers with her mother behind her.

"Who are your friends?" Mrs. McDaniels asked.

"You know Marlee," said Sally.

"Yes, of course."

"And this is Liz, she's new at school. Liz, this is my mom." Sally waved her hand in introduction.

"Hi," said Liz.

Sally's mother gazed at Liz intently for a moment. "I've heard a lot about you, Elizabeth."

Liz blushed. "Sally's been real welcoming to me."

"Glad to hear it."

A woman in a large white hat, sitting a few rows behind us, waved in our direction. "Well, it was nice to meet you," said Mrs. McDaniels. She headed up the bleachers, but Sally sat down with us.

"What did you tell your mother about me?" asked Liz. I knew her well enough now to hear the annoyance in her voice.

"Nothing but the truth," said Sally. She flipped her hair, then smoothed it down. "Does my hair look okay? In a minute I'm going to talk to JT."

"Oh," said Liz casually, "Marlee already did that."

Sally turned as red as the ketchup on my sweater, and I had to force myself not to start laughing again.

It was dark when we drove home. "You know," Daddy said quietly, "I like that Liz girl."

"Me too."

"Are you"—he paused—"are you really going to speak during that presentation?"

"I think so," I said.

Daddy patted me on the shoulder, and when I glanced at him, I could see the pride in his eyes.

10

BEHIND THE GRIN

Mother and Daddy started arguing again on Sunday. Mother was frying hamburgers on the stove when she said to Daddy, "States do have rights, you know. Those politicians in Washington can't be telling us how to run our schools."

Daddy bit his lip. He was grating carrots so briskly, I was afraid we would find fingers in the salad. "The schools have already been closed almost two weeks. The students are the ones who are suffering."

"If the governor gives in, what's next?" Mother asked. "Negroes at the swimming pool?"

Daddy shrugged. "They're already sitting at the front of the bus. And you still manage to find a seat."

"Richard!"

"It's not right to keep the schools closed, Maurine, and you know it."

At that moment, the back door flew open and David burst in. I squealed and dropped the bowl of potatoes I was mashing. "You came home!"

"Hi, Marlee," said David, and he gave me such a big hug, he picked me up off the ground. David always wore a dazzling smile, which transformed him from a nice-looking guy into a movie star.

"Classes going well?" asked Daddy.

"Never better," said David. But his eye twitched just like Daddy's did when he was lying. He popped a tomato from the salad into his mouth. "Where's Judy?"

"Hi, David," said Judy, coming into the room.

"Hey, sis!" David grinned. "Wanted to tell you the university's going to offer correspondence classes to all the kids without school." He took a spoon and swiped a bit of mashed potato. "Needs more salt," he told me. Then to Judy, "Thought you might be interested."

"Correspondence classes?" asked Judy.

"Yeah," said David. "They give you a list of assignments, and you send your work in. The professor grades them and sends you the test and you send it back and—"

"And who's going to help me if I don't understand something?" asked Judy.

"I can help you, sweetie," said Mother.

"Yeah, if it's English or history," said Judy. "But what if it's chemistry?"

"If it's chemistry, I'm sure one of my colleagues in the science department would be glad to help you. In fact, maybe we could organize study groups for you and Margaret, at least until—"

"And Marlee could help you with the math!" David teased.

"Wonderful," said Judy as she carried the plates into the dining room. "I get to be tutored by my mother and my little sister."

Daddy laughed.

It was a great dinner, even if the burgers were dry and the potatoes were salty and the salad didn't have any tomatoes because David had swiped them all. The whole family was together, and for an hour, that was enough.

After dinner, I pulled David into my room. "So how's it really going?" I asked.

"What?"

"Your classes."

"Oh, great." David picked at a piece of lint on his sweater.

"Come on, David."

"What?"

"I can tell you're lying."

He looked around, though there was no one else in the room with us. Then he sighed and sat down on the bed. "Promise you won't tell Mother and Daddy?"

"Course not!"

"It's awful. All those math classes I signed up for . . . well, I don't have the foggiest idea what's going on. The professor's talking in the lecture hall, and it's like he's speaking another language."

That sounded awful. I mean, David has never been as naturally good at math as me (I'm not bragging, it's just a fact), but we'd had so much fun talking about all the things we were going to invent together. He was the one who'd explained what an engineer was and how they built things—like spaceships and satellites.

David shook his head. "If you were there, I bet you'd understand."

"Me?" I asked. "No way."

"Yeah, Marlee. I think you would."

Then we heard Daddy calling, and David stood up. "Bye, sis," he said. "It's up to you now to beat those Soviets." He pasted his usual grin back on. "Now, remember, not a word to Mother."

I nodded.

• • •

That night I lay in bed wondering how many other times David had grinned and fooled me too, even though he'd felt awful inside. The idea that my big brother sometimes felt not good enough was strange, and a bit scary. But the idea that he thought I'd be able to do those math classes, maybe work on a spaceship someday, well, that made me feel awful good.

11

THE TALISMAN

Pretty soon, it was the last weekend in September, the last weekend before our presentation. There was an election going on that Saturday, and both Mother and Daddy were in a bad mood. I think the grown-ups were trying to decide if they should keep the high schools closed or open them again. But of course they didn't say it that way. No, it was more like, *Do you think it's a good idea for whites and Negroes to go to school together?*

That was kind of tricky, if you ask me. There aren't too many people in Little Rock who'd say yes to that kind of question. Mother and Daddy voted first thing in the morning, even before we cleaned the house. They didn't say how they voted, and I didn't ask.

But I thought about it. I tried to imagine what it would be like going to school with Betty Jean, since she was the only colored person I'd ever really talked to (if you call drinking a glass of tea a conversation). I tried to picture Betty Jean as a twelve-year-old girl, but I kept imagining a smaller version of her in a big flowered apron. It made me giggle as I vacuumed my room.

Soon as I was done cleaning, I ran out of the house to meet Liz at the zoo. We were going to go over our presentation one more time. I'd done my part at least twice for every animal in the zoo. I'd said my lines in front of the mirror at home, trying to maintain eye contact with myself. I'd even said my part for Judy, late at night, when Mother and Daddy were asleep. I'd done everything I could to prepare. I knew my lines perfectly. And I was still terrified.

Liz was late. I watched the lions, but they were just lying there, sleeping. I got more nervous every second I stood there alone, so I thought about all the ways Liz had taught me to relax.

One: take a deep breath.

Two: imagine all the people at school in their underwear. This didn't work too well. Just thinking about JT in his underwear made my heart beat way too fast.

Three: my good old friends the prime numbers. I'd actually told Liz about them, and she hadn't laughed. I'd reached 83 by the time Liz finally appeared. She was clutching a paper bag.

"Sorry I'm late," she said. "I've got a surprise for you."

"What?"

She reached in the bag and pulled out two small green turtles. Their claws scrabbled gently on her hand. "I got them at the variety store," she said. "Let's have a race."

"Liz," I said, "we have to practice."

Liz waved a hand in the air. "Marlee, there's one more rule of giving a presentation I haven't taught you yet."

"What?" I should have brought a pencil to write this down.

"You have to know when you're done."

"But I'm not done," I said.

"You know your part cold," said Liz. "Heck, I bet you even know mine too."

I shook my head. "Let's go over it a few more times."

"Marlee, at some point you just have to believe that you can do it."

"Well, I don't."

Liz sighed.

She was getting frustrated. This wasn't going to work. Any minute now, she'd give up and say she'd do all the talking after all, and I'd be incredibly relieved and incredibly disappointed. That's what Sally would have done.

But Liz wasn't Sally. Instead of giving up, she started looking around like she'd lost something on the ground.

"What are you doing?" I asked.

"Looking for a talisman."

"A what?"

"A talisman. A good luck charm."

Like she was going to find a gold amulet or a magic ring lying around on the ground amidst popcorn and peanut shells.

But after a few moments she said, "Aha!" and picked up a single black crow's feather. "You've seen *Dumbo,* right?" asked Liz.

I nodded. I'd seen the movie a bunch of times when I was little. I could relate to the little elephant with the big ears. He didn't talk either.

"Well, this is a magic feather. Put it in your pocket, and if you get nervous during the presentation, just touch it, and you'll be fine."

"A magic feather?"

"Yeah," said Liz.

"That's kind of silly."

"Just try it."

"Fine." I held out my hand.

Liz placed the feather carefully on my palm.

It weighed nothing, just a wisp of air. The feather tickled

my hand, but as for making me less nervous, nope, it didn't do a thing.

"Better?" Liz asked.

I nodded. I didn't have the heart to tell her no.

"Good." Liz pulled out a small bottle from her pocket. "Because I brought nail polish so we can paint our names on the back of the turtles. That way, you'll know for sure that it was mine when it wins."

So instead of working, we painted our names on the backs of the tiny turtles and let them run up and down our arms as we waited for the polish to dry. Then we raced the turtles across one of the large stones that made up the lion's den. My turtle won.

"Least we know for sure it was mine," I said, and Liz laughed.

It was getting late, so we walked down to the ducks and let the turtles go. They slid silently into the murky green water and paddled away.

"That was really fun," I said. At least it had taken my mind off the presentation for a little while.

"You'll be fine," said Liz. "I'll bring the magic square book with me to school on Monday."

"I'm still not sure I can do it," I admitted.

"I believe in you," said Liz.

"Thanks," I whispered.

She put her arm in mine, and we turned to go home.

12

BLOOD LIKE A JEWEL

All Saturday evening and through half of Sunday, I got more and more nervous. I started pacing through the house, clutching my note cards. The third time through the living room, Judy caught my arm. "Your presentation's tomorrow, isn't it?"

I could only nod. I'd lost my voice. How was I going to find it again? I'd—

"Come on," said Judy. "Let's go to the rock crusher."

Though we lived in the city, our house was in one of the newer neighborhoods. There were still patches of undeveloped land only a few blocks from our house. The rock crusher was an old abandoned quarry. The open mine sometimes filled with rainwater, making a small pond, but mostly it was just hills and trees and lots of rocks.

David and Judy and I used to take picnics to the rock crusher, but I hadn't been there in ages. The pond was too shallow for swimming, so mainly it was a place for little kids to run around and collect rocks during the day. At night, sometimes teenagers would park there on dates or sneak off to drink beer. Mostly, though, there was no one around and the woods were calm and peaceful.

"Okay," I said. I could practice there as well as at home. I started to gather up my note cards.

"Margaret said the old man who lives next to the rock crusher just got a horse," said Judy. She plucked the cards out of my hands and handed me two apples instead.

The day was hot, so we walked slowly. Judy chattered on about the classes they had started broadcasting on TV for all the high school students. Eleventh grade was on channel eleven. Seven A.M., history; seven thirty A.M., algebra; eight A.M., English; and so on. I knew she was going on and on to try to distract me from worrying, and even though I could see right through her, it kind of worked.

"When the classes first started, they were scary," said Judy. "I kept thinking I was going to miss something and wouldn't be able to ask the teacher to repeat herself. Turns out, they keep it really basic, and it's pretty easy to follow along. I actually like the classes now. It seems familiar, a way to get to go to school after all."

"Like the lions," I said softly.

"What?" asked Judy.

"Like how the lions roar at night," I said. "You'd think it'd be scary, but I've heard them for so long, it actually makes me feel safe."

"You're right," Judy said finally. "It's like the lions."

We walked in silence for a moment. I felt for the black feather. Even though it didn't work, I still had it in my skirt pocket. It was a gift from Liz. JT had only ever given me his math book—and I already had one of those.

"Judy," I asked, "you ever have a crush on anyone at school? I mean, last year when you got to go."

"Yes," she answered slowly.

"Who?"

She shook her head. "I'm not going to tell you."

"I'll tell you who I like if you tell me," I said.

"Fine," said Judy. "Who do you like?"

"JT," I admitted. I tried not to blush, but I think I did, just a little.

"Red's little brother?" Judy asked.

I nodded.

Judy laughed, but it was good-natured.

I pouted. "What?"

"Heard he's not the brightest."

I shrugged. "Awful cute, though." I waited for her to tell me who she liked, but before she could, a group of teenagers in cars pulled up in front of us at a red light. They were all honking their horns and yelling, and one boy even waved at my sister.

"Who's that?" I asked.

"Some stupid kids from school," said Judy. "They've got nothing better to do."

Most of the cars had signs in their windows: HIGH SCHOOL STUDENTS AGAINST INTEGRATION; SUPPORT FAUBUS; CHRISTIANITY, NOT COMMUNISM. One girl leaned out of the window and yelled at us, "Two, four, six, eight. We don't want to integrate!" Then the light turned green, and they drove off.

"Do all the students at Central feel that way?" I asked.

Judy shook her head. "Only the loud ones."

She didn't say anything else. Pretty soon, we came to an open lot with a barbed wire fence. In the middle of the field was a gray horse. We crawled carefully under the wire and fed the horse the apples. I scratched her nose, and she looked at me with wide eyes as brown as Judy's and Liz's.

I stuck my hand in my pocket again, and this time when I

touched the feather, I felt my fingers tingle. A surge of bravery swept over me, but I didn't trust it. I had to do something scary to test the feather, to see if it really was magic.

"I'm going to ride the horse," I said.

Judy shook her head.

"Come on," I said. "Just give me a lift."

Judy held out her hands, and I stepped onto them. She lifted me onto the horse's back. The mare was very tame and stood still as I tried to arrange myself. I'd ridden a horse once or twice before at Girl Scout camp, but of course I'd had a saddle then. I sat straight up and grabbed her mane just like they did in the movies. The horse turned her head back to look at me, then continued to chew the last apple core.

I gave her a little kick, but I guess it was harder than I planned, because the horse took off so fast, I had to wrap my arms around her neck just to stay on. I could feel the horse's muscles moving under her skin. It was scary at first, but thrilling too, and pretty soon I was imagining I was a cowgirl, riding off into the sunset. No, an Indian. I could take the feather from my pocket and put it into my hair and ride forever.

The horse stopped when she came to the far end of the pasture. I slid off and rubbed her nose as I waited for Judy to make her way over to us.

"It was great," I said. "You have to ride her too."

Before Judy could answer, a man yelled out, "What are you kids doing with my horse?"

We looked up. In the next field, there was an old man in worn coveralls, clutching a shotgun. "Get out of there," he yelled. "Now!"

We turned and ran, scrambling under the fence. Judy and I

headed into the old quarry. After a moment, I realized I had cut my thumb on the barbed wire and stopped, shocked. It hurt, a lot, and I started to cry.

Judy stopped too and made me sit down on a large boulder. She took one look at my hand, then pulled out a handkerchief and wrapped it around and around, holding it tight. I kept sobbing.

"His name's Robert Laurence," Judy said quietly. "He's really smart, and not that cute, but I like him anyway."

I stopped crying, and we sat there in silence. My sister pressed her handkerchief into my thumb. I would have a scar, but I didn't care. One final drop of blood oozed out and sat on my fingertip like a jewel, a secret given to me by my sister.

13

NOT THE STOMACH FLU

The next day was Monday. The big day. The day of our presentation. I thought I'd be nervous, but I wasn't. I was excited. No more waiting. I was actually going to do it. I was going to talk in class.

JT was waiting for me by the picnic table when Daddy dropped me off. "Big day," he said.

"Yep," I agreed as I handed him his homework, which had four problems wrong, nicely scattered throughout the assignment.

"Last week Liz told everyone you were going to talk," JT said. "That true?"

"Yep." My voice didn't even wobble. I felt for the feather in my pocket. The magic was still there. I was ready. I could talk in front of a thousand people! Well, maybe not a thousand. But thirty in my history class definitely seemed doable.

Liz wasn't at school when the bell rang. The bus was sometimes late, so I didn't worry, not until homeroom was almost over and Miss Taylor cleared her throat and said, "Marlee, would you step into the hall with me for a moment?"

The class froze. I stood and slowly made my way toward the door, everyone watching me. A month ago, I would've fainted dead away. But now I felt eerily calm. The feather was still in my pocket. Liz would be here any minute. What could go wrong?

Miss Taylor didn't say another word until we were in the hallway. "Marlee, I'm afraid I have to tell you that Elizabeth will not be returning to West Side Junior High."

I stared at her. I mean, I heard the words, and I knew what they meant, but they didn't make any sense. Why would Liz leave West Side?

"Liz is very ill, and she . . ." Miss Taylor paused. "I'm sorry. I will give you a few days to write down your report and turn it in."

She turned and walked back to the classroom, leaving me in the hall. The bell rang, and students swarmed around me, but I didn't move. I was a balloon that had been blown into a cactus. One *pop,* and all my confidence was gone.

I couldn't concentrate in math. Mr. Harding called on me twice, and I didn't even answer. At lunch, JT and Sally and Nora sat down at my table. "So what did Miss Taylor say to you?" JT asked.

I shook my head.

"She said Liz isn't coming back to West Side," reported Nora, peering over the top of her glasses. "I was standing by the door and heard her. She said Liz is real sick. But I don't think that's true, because Liz was in school last Friday and she was fine."

JT thought for a moment. "My cousin got the stomach flu last week. That can come on real sudden."

"Yes, but that only lasts a few days," said Nora.

"Liz isn't coming back because she's a Negro," said Sally.

We all turned to look at her.

Sally flipped her hair to make sure we were all paying

attention. "That's what my mother told the principal. They were talking outside the teachers' lounge."

That's ridiculous, I said, but not out loud.

"What?" JT sounded confused.

"My mother and I saw Liz last night." Sally leaned forward and lowered her voice. "Way down by Ninth Street."

That was the colored part of town.

"What were you doing there?" asked Nora.

"Our maid, Sue Ann, was sick. We had just dropped her off at her house when I saw Liz come out of the Baptist church on South Chester. She was holding hands with a colored boy."

"You're kidding," breathed Nora.

Sally shook her head. "I was so surprised, I called out her name, and I think she heard me because she looked right at me. Then my mother saw her and recognized her from the football game. Mother was so surprised, she almost ran into a lamppost. She wouldn't say one word about it all the way home, but first thing this morning, she came in to talk to Principal Watkins.

"But then," Sally continued, "when we got here this morning, the principal said Liz had already withdrawn from school. She didn't even come by to pick up her records. When he heard our story, he said it all made sense. She must have been colored."

JT shook his head.

"Last week I even loaned her my hairbrush," whispered Sally.

"Ewww," squealed Nora.

"I know," Sally said. "Of course I already threw it away."

"Can you believe it?" JT said. "A nigger at our school?"

I stood up, suddenly furious, but I wasn't sure at whom. JT, Miss Taylor, Sally, Liz, myself?

"Where are you going?" asked JT.

My thumb was throbbing. "I . . ." I shook my head and ran out of the room.

In the bathroom, I thought I was going to cry, but I didn't. Just stood in front of the sink and took the bandage off my thumb. I was careful not to glance in the mirror and see my brown hair and brown eyes that looked so much like Liz's.

Could it be true? Can a girl be white one day and colored the next? It seemed much more likely that she was sick. Or maybe she was moving. But if she were moving, why wouldn't she have told me? She said she believed in me. But how could she believe in me if she wasn't there?

The bell rang, and I splashed water on my face. I glanced in the mirror. My skin was the same beige color it had been before. Liz was the first person outside of my family I could really talk to. I couldn't lose her. It must be some big misunderstanding. When it was resolved, when she came back, I wanted the magic square book. I wanted to have earned it.

History was right after lunch. Miss Taylor looked surprised when I raised my hand. "Yes, Marlee?"

"I want to do the presentation." My voice shook, but the words were clear.

Miss Taylor was speechless. She just nodded and gestured for me to go to the front of the room.

Everyone was silent. Every eye was on me. It took forever. Finally, I reached the front of the room. I pulled the black feather from my pocket and stuck it in one of my braids, like an Indian headdress. I took a deep breath.

Nothing came out.

I counted 29, 31, 37, 41.

Still no voice.

Finally, in desperation, I imagined them all in their underwear.

It made things worse. In a moment, I was going to faint dead away. JT was grinning at me like a monkey.

A monkey.

Sally was stroking her hair, preening like a peacock.

Nora's long neck turned her into a giraffe.

A boy in the back row had his head down, sleeping like a lion.

They were all animals. It was a zoo.

I started to talk.

"The Quapaw Indians were one of the tribes that lived near the river when the first French explorers came to Little Rock. The Quapaw had respect for all living things. After hunting, they would thank the animal they'd killed for giving them food."

I stood up in front of the class and told them how the Quapaw smoked the peace pipe with the Europeans. I explained how unmarried women wore their hair braided and pinned up, while married women wore their hair down.

"Who did you marry, Sally?" JT called out, and everyone laughed. Sally turned bright red and stopped fiddling with her hair.

Miss Taylor shushed them, and I went on, explaining what crops the Quapaw planted (corn, beans and squash) and where they slept (on woven mats). Finally, I got to the last part of our presentation—the Peach Seed Ceremony.

"Fathers were real important to the Quapaw, so if yours died, you had to get another one. Instead of letting the grown-ups decide, they let the kids choose."

I held up the peach pit I had been clutching in my hand. It left a mark on my palm.

"If your father died, they gave you a peach pit and put you in a circle of all the men. The man you gave the pit to would be your new daddy."

I held up the pit and all the boys starting oohing and ahhing.

"Pick me!" yelled JT.

That had been my plan. It was going to be fun. Flirty. But he'd called Liz that name, and now I was determined to pick someone else. Anyone else. I scanned the room.

Little Jimmy was quiet and shy and bad at football and, well, little. I'm not sure he'd ever spoken to me before. I know I'd never spoken to him. But when I placed the pit in his hands, he looked up at me with shining eyes, as if I'd given him a diamond.

14

FACING FACTS

After history I went to the bathroom and threw up. I'd done it. I'd spoken aloud in a class at school. But I didn't feel powerful. I didn't feel triumphant. I felt like I was getting the flu.

I got halfway to the nurse's office before I turned and walked out of the building. I tried to make myself feel bad about skipping school, but it didn't work. I just kept hearing Sally saying she threw away her hairbrush. Imagining Mother complaining about states' rights. Remembering racing turtles with Liz in the sunlight.

I walked home slowly. I needed to talk to Judy. She would know what to do. She would know what to say. But as soon as I went into the kitchen, I remembered Judy was at Margaret's for a tutoring session.

Betty Jean glanced over at me. "You're home early."

I didn't answer.

"You've got something in your hair," she said.

I put my hand to my head. It was the black feather.

Betty Jean poured me a glass of sweet tea. "Drink it," she said. "And then you can tell me what's wrong."

I had no intention of telling *her*, but I was thirsty, and after I drank the tea, I felt a little better. Betty Jean had her back to me and was stuffing a chicken for dinner. I was going to tell her I wasn't feeling well (which was true) and go to my room to wait for Judy. But when I opened my mouth, what came out was, "Have you ever heard of a light-skinned Negro pretending to be white?"

Betty Jean stopped what she was doing, her hands full of chicken guts, and gave me a funny look. "Why are you asking that, Marlee?"

The kids at school said . . . this girl I know . . . I was just wondering . . . I couldn't get any words to come. Finally, I just stood there, helpless, praying Betty Jean would understand.

I guess she did, because she finally pushed the basting pan aside and went to the sink to wash her hands. She cut two pieces of blueberry pie, then sat down at the table. I sat down too, and she pushed the pie across the table to me.

"It's called passing," she said. "Some Negroes who are really light skinned and have straight hair try it."

"Why?" I asked.

"Better schooling. More opportunities." She shrugged. "Maybe they're just tired of being seen as second best."

I didn't say anything. It suddenly seemed like there was more gray around her temples than had been there just a moment before.

"It's a hard life," Betty Jean went on. "You have to give up seeing family and friends. Stop going the places you used to go. And you have to lie—every day—to everyone you meet."

Like Liz had done to me.

"Lying like that, well, it's exhausting. I hope you never have a secret like that, Marlee. A secret so big, your whole life depends on it."

I swallowed. "What happens if someone finds out?"

"I'm not sure your mother would like me talking to you about this, Marlee."

"Please," I said. "Please, Betty Jean. There's no one else I can ask."

She took a few more bites of blueberry pie. When she spoke, she kept her eyes on her plate, mashing a bit of crust with her fork. "If you're really lucky, you lose your job or you're kicked out of school. If you're a little less lucky, you get beat up, but after a few weeks your injuries heal and you're left alone. If you're not lucky, a lynch mob comes and firebombs your house, killing you and everyone you love."

And that's when I knew it was true. I didn't know her phone number or where she lived. I'd never even asked if she had a sister. No wonder she had picked me as a friend. No one else was stupid enough not to ask any questions.

"Marlee," said Betty Jean quietly, "are you all right?"

I nodded as I stood up and went to my room. I lay on my bed, numb. Even my mind was empty. After talking in school in front of everyone, I guess my words were all used up.

It was late afternoon by the time Judy poked her head into my room. I must have fallen asleep, because I jerked awake when I heard her ask, "How'd it go?"

It took me a minute to realize she was asking about the presentation. If I told her the truth, she'd make a big deal about it and tell Mother and Daddy. I'd have to act happy and proud or explain what had actually happened. On the other hand, if I said I hadn't done the presentation, that I'd chickened out, she'd console me and tell me it was okay, and I could not handle that now either, because everything was definitely *not* okay. But I had to say something.

"Liz is colored."

"What?" asked Judy, a puzzled look on her face.

That's when I started to cry.

By the time I'd calmed down enough to tell Judy the whole story, it was getting late. Judy pursed her lips tighter and tighter as I talked, until finally they were just one straight line across her face. "Oh, Marlee," she said. "I'm so sorry. I don't know what to say."

I didn't either. Part of me was angry at Liz for lying, part of me wanted her to come back, and the other part just wanted the magic square book.

"You think it's okay if whites and Negroes go to school together," I asked Judy, "don't you?"

Judy said nothing.

"Don't you?"

"I guess so," said Judy slowly. "But I hated it when those soldiers came to Central. They stared at me each time I had to walk by them in my gym shorts."

"It doesn't have to be that way."

"Doesn't it?" asked Judy.

Before I could answer, Mother called us for dinner. I splashed some water on my face, but my eyes were still red. The chicken Betty Jean had made was moist and delicious, but it stuck in my throat.

"Marlee," Mother said softly, "we need to talk about it."

I ignored her.

"Mrs. McDaniels called today and told me about your friend Liz. The one who turned out to be"—she looked around and lowered her voice—"a Negro."

70

Did she think there were radical segregationists lurking under our sideboard?

"We just wanted to say we're sorry," Daddy jumped in. "Because I know you don't find it easy to make friends, and she seemed like a nice girl and—"

"A nice girl?" Mother interrupted. "She lied to Marlee and everyone else at school. That's not what I call the behavior of a nice girl. Marlee's probably feeling betrayed and—"

"Marlee's missing her friend," Daddy countered.

Great. Arguing again.

"I'm not hungry," I said, even though I was.

No one answered.

I pushed in my chair and went to my room. I crawled into bed without brushing my teeth, expecting to toss and turn all night. But the lions roared once, and I was asleep.

15

TALKING TO DADDY

I woke up the next morning in a good mood. The presentation was over, and I'd done my part. Everything was as it should be. Except my teeth felt fuzzy, like I hadn't brushed them before bed. But I *always* brushed them before bed, even when . . . then I remembered.

I went into the kitchen and made myself a bowl of oatmeal. Daddy was reading the paper. There was an article about the election the weekend before on the front page:

Little Rock votes against integration 19,470 to 7,561. Schools to be closed indefinitely.

Daddy slammed down the paper, making me jump. "Sorry," he said. But he scowled as he said it, and I realized then, certain as could be, that when asked if Negroes and whites should go to school together, he had voted yes. "Are you ready to go, Marlee?"

I nodded, even though I'd only had two spoonfuls of my oatmeal.

It was quiet in the car. Daddy gripped the steering wheel like he was driving in a snowstorm. Not that it snowed much in Little Rock, but I'd seen a movie where there was one once, and the actor clutched the steering wheel so tight, his knuckles turned white.

"Daddy?" I asked.

"What?"

"Can you find her for me? Maybe get her phone number?"

Daddy shook his head. "Marlee, you need to leave that girl alone."

"But she's my best friend."

"She was your friend. Now she's someone else."

No, she wasn't. Liz was funny and outspoken and clever, and I didn't see how all that had changed, just because people were now calling her colored. But Daddy and I usually got along so well. I trusted him. "I don't know," I said finally. "I want to hear her side of the story first."

"Marlee, you can't still be friends with Liz."

"Why not?"

"Segregationists don't take kindly to Negroes who try to pass as white. Liz and her family are in real danger. The farther away you stay from them, the better."

"You're worried about me?" I asked.

"Yes, I am," said Daddy. "Why do you think I drive you to school every day?"

I shrugged.

Daddy ran a hand through his hair. "Do you remember when I invited that colored minister, Pastor George, to come speak at our church?"

I nodded.

"The next day there was a note tucked in with our paper. It said, *You let your youngest walk to school tomorrow, she won't make it.* And it was signed, *KKK*."

"The Ku Klux Klan is in Little Rock?"

Daddy nodded.

"Who's in it?"

"Hard to tell, since it's a secret organization. However, the Capital Citizens' Council, or CCC, is not a secret club. Their avowed purpose is to support segregation in Little Rock. It seems reasonable to assume that some of their members are Klan sympathizers, at the very least."

"Do we know any CCC members?" I asked.

"Mr. Haroldson, from next door."

He was a nice old man who sometimes gave me penny candy. At least, I'd always thought he was nice.

"And Mrs. McDaniels, Sally's mother, is a member of the Mothers' League."

"What's that?" I asked.

"A women's group, associated with the CCC, that formed last year to oppose integration at Central."

This was a lot to take in. "Isn't everyone allowed to have their own opinion?"

"Of course," said Daddy. "But the reason there were police all over David's graduation last May was not because people have different opinions. The FBI was there to protect Ernest Green because they were worried that someone was going to try to kill him."

I had never really thought about why we'd gotten so few tickets to David's graduation that Granny hadn't even been able to go. Apparently, there was a lot I hadn't thought about.

"But you still support integration, right?"

"I do," said Daddy. "And I still talk to Pastor George. He's Betty Jean's husband, you know."

I hadn't known. How could I? "Why haven't you ever told me any of this?"

"These are issues for grown-ups to deal with, not children."

"The Little Rock Nine weren't much older than me."

Daddy sighed, but he didn't answer.

"I thought things settled down at Central once they called the soldiers in."

"Somewhat," said Daddy. "At least that was the official story. But things were not ever pleasant for them there. Minnijean Brown got expelled."

She was the colored girl who'd dumped a bowl of soup on the boys who were picking on her. That was something Liz would do.

"If they were still being harassed, why didn't they complain?"

Daddy shrugged. "Maybe they did and nothing was done. Maybe they thought if they showed any weakness, it would only get worse. In any case, last year the pictures from Central told the whole world Little Rock is filled with hate. And now the town's gone and voted against opening the schools. We are not *just* a town of racists, but those of us who believe in integration . . ." He shook his head. "We can't seem to find our voice."

Daddy was so upset, for a minute I thought he was going to cry. That scared me as bad as anything he'd said. I knew what it was like to have trouble finding your voice, so I reached over and patted his arm. He didn't look at me.

"I mean it, Marlee. I don't want to scare you too much—I'll keep you safe—but I do want you to be careful. Which means you stay away from Liz."

I nodded to show him I understood what he was saying.

But I didn't promise that I would.

16

SENT AWAY

That day at school passed in a blur. JT was surprised when I didn't have his homework. His mouth made a big round O, and I could tell he was talking, but I couldn't concentrate on what he was saying. For the first time, I noticed his ears were too small, his teeth were crooked, and his eyebrows looked like fat, blond caterpillars wriggling on his face when he spoke.

I couldn't stand the thought of Sally talking about what had happened with Liz, so when it was time for lunch, I didn't leave Mr. Harding's classroom. Just sat in my seat and pulled out my math book to make up the homework I had missed. The first homework I had *ever* missed in math. Mr. Harding finished grading a few papers, then came over to my desk.

"Marlee," he said, "it's time for lunch."

I didn't move.

Finally, he left me alone, doing long division in the empty classroom.

When I got home from school, Mother and Daddy were already there. Daddy still had on his work clothes, but he'd taken off his jacket and loosened his tie, like he was going to dig a ditch in his suit. Mother'd taken the opposite approach. She'd put on pearls, a fresh coat of lipstick and a new pair of white gloves. One look at them, and I knew it was bad news.

My dread only grew when Mother announced that we were all going to a cafeteria for dinner. That was another bad sign. My parents believed in telling a person bad news in public so they couldn't make a scene. Maybe occasionally we'd go by the cafeteria after church on Sunday. But out to dinner on a Tuesday night could only mean something was wrong.

They waited until we all had our food. Then Daddy cleared his throat and said, "Girls, we have something to tell you."

I kept my eyes on my plate. They already knew about Liz. Had they found out about JT and the homework too?

"Since it appears that the schools are going to remain closed indefinitely," Daddy continued, "and she's already missed a month of school, Judy is going to go to live with Granny in Pine Bluff. She'll go to school there."

Judy and I stared at Daddy in confusion.

"What?" Judy asked finally. I glanced over at Mother, but she was stirring circles in her mashed potatoes.

Daddy sighed. "You're going to live in Pine Bluff with—"

"I heard you," Judy interrupted. "But I don't want to go. My friends are here and Marlee and—"

"I'm afraid you don't have a choice," said Daddy. "You've missed so much school already."

"I'm doing the TV classes."

Daddy shook his head. "Watching a teacher on TV is no substitute for real instruction. You can't ask questions. I know you've been working hard on your assignments, but we don't even know how long the TV classes will continue."

"There are study groups," Judy insisted. "Parents help out and—"

"Why can't she just order those correspondence classes David talked about?" I asked.

"This doesn't concern you, Marlee," said Daddy.

My face stung like Daddy had slapped me. Of course it concerned me—my only sister was being sent away!

"Why can't I just go to T. J. Raney with Margaret?" asked Judy.

"What's that?" I asked.

"It's a private school that's just starting up," Judy explained. "It's free."

Daddy put his fork down, a little too hard. "It's not free. They're using public money, money that should be going to the public schools. It's Governor Faubus's way of trying to get around the integration order. I will not allow my child to be a part of that."

"But—"

"I know this isn't ideal, Judy," said Daddy. "But Mother and I have talked it over."

I glanced at Mother, but she wouldn't meet my eye. It didn't seem like she was too excited about this plan. But she wasn't speaking out against it either.

"You can't send me away. You can't!" Judy was yelling now. Other people at the cafeteria started looking over at us. So much for not making a scene.

"I'm afraid we can, Judy. I know you're upset, but we're your parents. We know what's best for you." Daddy spoke quietly, but firmly.

"No you don't," Judy hissed. She jumped up out of her seat and stormed off, knocking over Mother's cup in the process. The coffee dripped off the saucer onto the tablecloth.

Mother and Daddy looked at each other. It was like they

had forgotten I was there. "It's the right thing to do, Maurine," said Daddy. But he didn't sound too sure about it himself.

First my best friend, and now my sister. Who was left? There'd be no one for me to talk to. Daddy might as well lock me in a tower like Rapunzel. At least *she* had the prince come by occasionally for a visit. But my hair wasn't long enough to climb up, and of course that was just a fairy tale, anyway, and now that I knew what it was like to have a friend, I didn't think I could stand being so awfully lonely again.

"Marlee?" Daddy repeated sternly. I looked up, wondering how long he'd been calling my name.

"What?" I tried to keep my voice icy, tried to tell them with one word how angry I was. But I think I just sounded kind of scared.

"Go into the bathroom and tell your sister we're leaving. If we go right now, we can swing by Margaret's house and she can tell her good-bye. Tell her . . ." His voice broke, "Tell her she's leaving tomorrow."

"Tomorrow?"

But Daddy wouldn't look at me again. He fiddled with his wallet, pulling out a few dollar bills. "Just go get your sister."

I pushed my way into the bathroom. Judy was sitting in one of the stalls, crying. I didn't know how to handle this. I wasn't old enough. I wanted to cry myself. "Judy?"

"Go away." She sniffed.

"They want to leave now."

"I don't care what they want."

I didn't either. "I'll come with you."

"What?"

"We can run away."

"And go where?"

I thought for a minute. "Granny's house." I looked around the bathroom. "We can climb out that window and walk to the bus station and—"

"That's a stupid idea. That's where they're sending me."

That was true.

"And we don't have any money."

Another good point. But I felt a little better that she had stopped crying.

"Come on, then," I said. "Daddy said we can go by Margaret's house on the way home."

Judy went to the sink and splashed water on her face. I didn't tell her it didn't help. Her face was still red and blotchy.

I sat in the car with my parents while Judy went inside Margaret's house. I kept waiting for someone to say "I'm sorry, Marlee," or "we know this is hard on you too," but they didn't. Daddy just drummed his fingers on the steering wheel, over and over again, tapping out some melody I couldn't hear. Mother laid her head against the window and closed her eyes. A vein pulsed in her head the way it did when she had a headache.

Finally, Judy appeared on the porch. I watched Margaret's mom give her a hug, and then she climbed into the backseat of the car.

"Thank you for ruining my life," Judy snapped.

No one said a word as we drove home.

17

THE NEGRO CHURCH

In the middle of the night, I woke up and went into David's room. Judy was curled up on the bed. Her suitcase was packed on the floor beside her. In the morning she'd be leaving, just like David had done, just like Liz. After a moment, she rolled over and looked at me. "You can't sleep either?"

I shook my head.

Without a word, she picked up her blanket and came back into our room, the one we had shared ever since I'd been born. She lay down on her old side of the bed.

Soon I heard her quiet, even breathing, but I still couldn't sleep, not until the sky began to lighten and I heard Pretty Boy stir under his cover.

My stomach hurt something awful the next morning. I wanted to stay home from school, but I didn't have a fever, so I knew Mother wouldn't let me. Daddy made a special breakfast, pancakes and bacon, but no one ate much. Judy's green suitcase sat by the door like a wart.

"We'll drop you off at the bus station on the way to school," said Daddy. "I spoke to Granny last night. She'll be waiting for you in Pine Bluff."

I stared at my plate, a half-eaten pancake wallowing in a pool of maple syrup.

"Come on, girls," Daddy said quietly. "It's time to go."

Mother gave Judy a hug and kissed her cheek. Daddy put Judy's suitcase in the trunk while Judy and I got into the car.

All the way to the bus station, I rehearsed heartfelt good-bye scenes in my head. I would say something like "good-bye, dearest sister of mine," and Judy would burst into tears, and Daddy would be so touched, he'd relent and take us all home. But what actually happened when we reached the bus station was that Judy gave me a hug, I whispered "bye" and then she was gone.

I gave JT his homework as soon as I got to school. He didn't even notice that they were all wrong. After math class, I stayed in Mr. Harding's classroom again for lunch. In history, Sally was still retelling the story, though everyone at school must have heard it about a hundred times by now. It was good gossip, sure (at least I might have thought so if it hadn't been about my friend), but Sally was acting like she was a hero who'd personally saved us from a Soviet invasion. It was ridiculous. All she'd done was go by the church and . . .

Gone by the church. The Baptist church on South Chester. If Sally could go there, so could I. Maybe I could find Liz. Talk to her. Maybe learning how or why or *something* would help me feel not quite so confused and alone.

I pulled a piece of paper from my math notebook and thought for a moment. It would have to be a short note, no names, but somehow she'd have to know who it was from. I had an idea and scribbled furiously.

"What are you writing?" Sally said.

I shook my head.

Nora snatched the note away before I could finish. I reached for it, but she jumped up and read it aloud. "You owe me a magic book."

"What does that mean?" asked Sally. "Marlee, are you studying to become a magician?"

"Maybe she has an imaginary friend," suggested Nora.

They both laughed.

The bell rang, and Miss Taylor rapped on her desk. I didn't even bother trying to get the note back from them. It was short. I could just write it again.

That afternoon, I rode my bike over to the Baptist church. I was worried about finding it, since I'd never been there before, but I'm good at reading maps, and I didn't have any trouble. It wasn't until I got there that I remembered what my father had said about staying away from Liz. I glanced around the parking lot. Was someone going to jump out and call me a race mixer, steal my bike, beat me up? But the parking lot was empty.

Finally, I left my bike in the bushes and went inside. The Baptist church looked a lot like the Methodist one we went to, pews, altar, a couple of stained glass windows. A colored man in a dark suit and tie came up to me. He had short hair, was clean-shaven and had that serious yet helpful expression on his face, just like the reverend at our church. I wondered if they practiced it in the mirror between services.

"Hello," he said. "I'm Pastor George. What can I do for you?"

I couldn't believe my luck. Pastor George was Betty Jean's husband and Daddy's friend. If anyone could help me, it would be him. I handed over the note. I'd folded it into quarters and written "To Liz (Elizabeth)" on the front.

His smile faded when he read the name. "She doesn't go here," he said, and handed the note back to me.

That's when I realized he knew exactly who I was looking for. Elizabeth is a real common name, and he didn't even ask me what her last name was. Not that I knew it. I mean, she was listed on the rolls at school as Elizabeth Templeton, but I was pretty sure that wasn't her last name. I wasn't even sure if Liz was her real first name. Maybe it was really Wanda or Darlene or Phyllis.

"I'm sorry I can't help you," Pastor George said politely, though his tone made it clear that what he really wanted was for me to go home.

I unfolded the note and handed it back to him. He took it like it was the tail of a dead mouse. "You owe me a magic book. Friday after school, the usual spot."

"She'll know what it means," I whispered.

Pastor George gave me a funny look. "Are you Richard Nisbett's daughter?"

I nodded. Sure hoped he wouldn't tell my father what I was doing.

Pastor George still didn't smile, but his face softened a little. "Youth group is tonight. I'll ask around."

"Thank you." And I went home to wait.

18

WHEN PRETTY BOY DIED

The next evening at dinner was quiet, not the good quiet where you're all thinking your own thoughts and smiling at each other, but the bad quiet where you're walking on eggshells even though the mean words are still in your head. I was mad at Daddy for sending Judy away and mad at Mother for not standing up to him.

For their part, my parents seemed to have almost forgotten I was there. No one spoke, except to say "pass the salt" or "where's the butter?" I wondered if this was what dinner was going to be like, now that Judy was gone. If so, I thought I'd run away to live at Granny's too.

Halfway through dinner, I dropped my glass and spilled water all over my blouse. "Excuse me," I said, and it sounded way too loud as I stood up and went into the kitchen.

I was just reaching for the dish towel when I heard Mother say, "There's something I need to tell you, Richard."

"What?" asked Daddy. They were whispering, but I was only in the kitchen so I could hear every word.

"You know that private school, T. J. Raney?" Mother asked. "The one Judy wanted to go to."

"Yes."

"It's opening next week," said Mother. "I've been asked to teach there."

"Just tell them you're not interested."

"No," said Mother. "I signed the contract this afternoon."

Daddy started coughing.

"It'd mainly be the same students I would have been teaching at Hall High."

"No."

"And if I could help get the school started, then maybe Judy could come home," explained Mother.

I crept over to the doorway. I didn't want to hear them argue, but like a moth near a candle, I couldn't pull myself away, either. Daddy shook his head. "Governor Faubus is just trying to find a way to get around the integration order. It's going back on all the progress those nine students made last year."

Mother said nothing.

"You knew I wouldn't approve," said Daddy.

"That's why I didn't ask you first," snapped Mother. "Sometimes I think you care about those Negroes more than your own family."

Daddy slammed his fist down on the table. "That's not fair. Of course I'll miss Judy, but we have to do what's best for her education and—"

Mother stood up and walked out of the room. Daddy threw down his napkin like he was going to follow her, then changed his mind and sat with his head in his hands.

I wanted to sneak off and hide under my covers, but I couldn't reach my room without going through the dining room. I considered going out the back door and climbing in my bedroom window like a burglar, but it seemed simpler to wait and see if Daddy would leave too.

Finally, he looked up and saw me standing in the doorway. "Marlee," Daddy said automatically, "we weren't . . ."

But I guess he realized there was no point in lying, because he sighed and said, "Sit down and finish your dinner."

I didn't want to, but I didn't want to storm off like Mother either. I decided, to keep the peace, I would take the high road and go sit down. Even if I couldn't eat a bite.

"We're all feeling stressed and . . ." Daddy rubbed his eyes. "You're probably pretty angry with me."

I didn't answer. The answer to that question was yes.

Daddy took a deep breath. "Do you remember when we thought Pretty Boy had died?"

I wasn't in the mood for a bedtime story. Pretty Boy was singing away in my room right now, so I was pretty sure he had lived through whatever misfortune had befallen him. But Daddy wasn't deterred by my lack of interest.

"You were little, maybe four or five," he went on. "David let Pretty Boy out of his cage to fly around, but then, after a while, he couldn't find him. He searched everywhere. Finally he went up into the attic. There was Pretty Boy, lying on the rafters in front of the attic fan.

"Pretty Boy was lying awful still, not moving. David picked him up and gently stroked his feathers. Nothing. There wasn't any injury he could see, but Pretty Boy didn't move. David brought him back downstairs and put him in his cage. When I came home from work, that was where I found you all, gathered around Pretty Boy's cage, crying."

I vaguely remembered that. Not that I was interested in Daddy's story, but . . .

"You were already planning his funeral, but I wasn't sure he was dead. I'd seen birds like that before, stunned, but if you left them alone long enough, they'd shake it off and be as good as new. So we put the cover on his cage and went to bed. And in the morning, when we took off the cover, there was Pretty Boy sitting on his perch, singing. Singing just as pretty as he ever had.

"What I'm trying to say is . . . our family is like Pretty Boy. Things might seem awful bad right now, with your new friend gone and your sister at Granny's and Mother so angry with me, but we'll get through this. You'll see." He patted my hand.

It was a nice story. But I wasn't totally sure he believed it himself.

There was a knock at the front door, and Mother went to answer it. We could hear a man's voice, low and gruff, but we couldn't make out the words.

"Who is it?" Daddy called out.

"A policeman," said Mother, and she sounded afraid.

All sorts of horrible ideas went through my head as Daddy and I ran for the front door. Maybe David had been in a car accident. Maybe Judy had run away. Or maybe the policeman was here to arrest me for trying to contact Liz. Daddy had warned me to leave her alone, and I hadn't listened.

"Actually," said the man, "I'm a federal marshal."

Sure enough, he had an armband that read U.S. MARSHAL and held up a badge with an eagle on it for all of us to see.

"Does Mrs. Lillian Maurine Nisbett live here?"

"Yes," said Mother. "That's me."

He handed her an envelope with a golden seal. "This is a restraining order forbidding you from working at T. J. Raney High School."

"I don't understand," stammered Mother.

"There is a current contract on file placing you at Hall High School. You need to honor that contract."

Mother took the envelope, but didn't move to open it. "Oh."

"Do you understand, ma'am?" the man asked. "You are not to teach at T. J. Raney. This is an order from the federal government, which supersedes any state laws. You need to remain at your old school. Even if there aren't any students."

"I understand." But Mother didn't look at him.

The marshal tipped his hat. "Good night, then. Sorry to bother you." He turned and left our front porch.

Mother stood perfectly still in the hallway. Daddy opened his mouth, then closed it again. I went back to the dining room.

The silence was horrible, and I found myself wishing for the yelling. Thoughts were bouncing around my head like the balls in a pinball machine, and I didn't want to hear any of them. *Was Mother going to get arrested? Were my parents going to keep fighting? When was Judy going to come home? Would Liz show up tomorrow afternoon?* I scraped all the leftovers into the trash and focused on doing the dishes, scrubbing each plate in clockwise circles. The area of each plate was pi times the radius squared. If I thought about that hard enough, I wouldn't have to worry about anything else.

In the middle of the night, I woke up hungry. I decided to go into the kitchen and make myself a bowl of cereal and milk. But when I got halfway down the hall, I heard crying. I peeked into the kitchen.

It was Mother sitting at the table, holding a cup of tea.

Parents were not supposed to cry. They weren't supposed to fight, either. And sisters weren't supposed to be sent away.

And if your friend was white, she should stay white, and not suddenly turn out to be a Negro.

I wanted to comfort Mother, but I didn't know what to say. For a long while, I just stood in the hall and listened to her crying and thought, what if Pretty Boy hadn't woken up? What if flying into the fan had killed him? Daddy had said sometimes birds shook off a collision and sometimes they didn't. Which one would it be for us?

I crept back to my room and picked up the drape over the birdcage. Pretty Boy was sitting on his perch, his tiny chest moving up and down. I whispered, "Please don't die." Then I let down the drape and went back to bed.

19

COLORED

Friday afternoon finally came. I wasn't sure what I should do. On the one hand, the federal marshal showing up the night before had spooked me. And Daddy had told me to stay away from Liz. On the other, I really wanted that math book. I'd earned it. There could be no harm in meeting her, getting the book and leaving. At least that's what I told myself. But the truth was I just wanted to see Liz.

I meant for her to meet me by the lions, but she wasn't there when I arrived. After a few minutes, I decided to walk around the zoo to see if she was waiting somewhere else. The monkeys were chattering at each other and ignored me. The flamingos slept on one leg, their heads under their wings. Even Ruth wouldn't take the peanuts I offered.

I was in a foul mood. How dare Liz not show up? She probably wouldn't even bring the magic square book if she did. She'd lied to me. She'd used me. Picked the dumb white girl for a friend, because even if I did find out her secret, I wouldn't tell anyone. Part of me knew that didn't make sense—if she'd wanted me only to stay quiet, why had she worked so hard at getting me to talk?—but as I walked around the zoo, my disappointment grew, and I nursed my anger like a jawbreaker that grew hotter and hotter as I rolled it around on my tongue.

I went back to the lion's cage. There was a strange girl on the bench, with a bandanna tied around her head and big sunglasses and a patched coat. She was looking off in the other direction. I had just decided to give Liz five more minutes before I left when I noticed there was a book on the bench next to the girl. A big book. A math book.

"Liz?" I ventured.

The girl turned to face me. "You came," Liz said.

"Of course I came," I said. "I invited you."

"You weren't here when I got here."

"I was," I insisted. "*You* weren't here, so I went to look around. Visited Ruth and her friends."

We stared at each other for a minute, not exactly scowling, but not smiling either. Maybe Daddy was right—maybe now she was a completely different person after all.

Liz looked down at the ground. "Why don't you just say it," she said.

"Say what?" I asked.

"Ask me. Isn't that why you wanted to meet me here?"

Questions swirled in my head: *Why did you lie? Why didn't you tell me? Did you like me at all, or was our friendship a story too?* But what I said was the obvious question. "Are you really colored?"

Liz nodded.

I sat down next to her. "You don't look colored."

"It doesn't matter what you look like," said Liz. For the first time since I'd known her, Liz dropped her friendly mask. "I am colored. Do you have a problem with that?"

I wasn't sure. If you'd asked me last summer if I wanted a Negro for a friend, I'd have said no thank you. I'm sure they are very nice, but I'll stick to my own kind. Birds of a feather flock together, right? But this wasn't some random hypothetical Negro—this was Liz. "I'm not sure," I said finally. "Why did you—"

"I don't know," said Liz miserably. "My parents told me to go to West Side Junior High, so I went. Do you ever talk back to your parents?"

I thought about the conversation with my father in the car. Meeting Liz probably qualified as talking back. "Sometimes," I admitted.

"Well, I don't," said Liz. "They're my parents. They have their reasons. I have to trust them."

I waited. There was more she had to say. And if there's anything a quiet girl knows, it's how to listen.

Sure enough, after a moment Liz began to speak again. "My mother is real smart. She's like you in math, it comes natural to her without even thinking. But she had to quit school when she was fifteen and get a job working as a housekeeper in a rich white lady's house. When she should have been a scientist, designing one of those satellites."

I gave Liz a surprised look.

"What?" she said. "You think white people are the only ones who dream about going to the moon?"

For the first time I realized, not only were there no women among those scientists on TV, there weren't any Negroes either.

"We moved to Little Rock this past summer. My grandmother's getting old, and she has a nice little house but no one to help her take care of it. So we moved in with her. And when Mama told me to go register myself at West Side Junior High, I did, and I didn't ask any questions.

"I haven't gone anywhere with my family in months, just school and home and the zoo with you. My grandmother and I even said our prayers at home. Then last Sunday, my little brother was getting confirmed at church, and we figured this one time, it would be okay for me to go." She shrugged. "You know the rest."

No, I didn't. I mean, I knew about Sally and her mother, but what about Liz and me? What was going to happen to us? "Where are you at school now?" I asked.

"Dunbar Junior High," said Liz. "The colored school. The official story is that I've been real sick and my grandmother's been teaching me at home. But the truth is, everyone knows." Liz was crying now, small silent tears that dripped out from behind those ridiculous glasses. "No one will talk to me. If I ask a question, they don't respond. If I sit down at a table at lunch, the others get up and leave. Everyone ignores me as if I weren't even there."

I handed her my handkerchief, and she wiped her eyes. This wasn't the Liz I'd known at all. The Liz I'd met at school was strong and confident, and this one reminded me a lot of myself.

Liz blew her nose and nudged the math book closer to me. "Here's the book."

"You don't have to—"

"In your note you said to bring the book. I thought that meant you did the presentation."

I nodded. "I did. The whole thing. Your part too." I couldn't keep the pride out of my voice.

"Good for you, Marlee," Liz said, but she didn't smile. "You earned it."

This wasn't how I imagined things. I wanted Liz to be proud and happy. "Won't your mother miss her book?"

Liz shook her head. "She was so excited when I asked to borrow it. I didn't have the heart to tell her it wasn't for me."

I picked up the book and clutched it to my chest. It was warm from sitting in the sun. The last of my anger melted away, and suddenly I knew, despite everything, that I still wanted to be Liz's friend.

"Meet you here again next Friday?" I asked.

Liz shook her head. "Marlee, I can't meet you here anymore. It's dangerous. If the wrong person found out . . ."

She didn't finish and I thought about what Daddy had said. *You let your youngest walk to school tomorrow, she won't make it.* I guess that was why Liz had on the glasses and the bandanna. Though if she was trying not to be noticed, she probably should have picked something less conspicuous.

"Daddy's already talking about moving again," Liz went on, "but Mother has a housekeeping job she likes for once, and Grandmother has been here forever, so she won't leave no matter what happens. Besides, Mama's not the type to run. Even if it is dangerous."

"Are you scared?" I asked.

"Yes," said Liz. "I am."

I was too. At least, I tried to be. It was hard to believe that someone would really try to hurt us, when the sun was shining and we were at the zoo, and everything seemed so normal.

"Well," I said, "you can always take a deep breath."

Liz snorted. "Imagine them in their underwear."

"Two, three, five, seven, eleven."

We both giggled.

Liz leaned over and put her head on my shoulder. "Aw, Marlee, you are a good friend. I'm sorry I can't—"

"Please," I said. "Daddy sent Judy away to live with Granny in Pine Bluff."

"What?" said Liz, sitting up straight.

"She's going to go to school there," I explained.

"But who is there left for you to talk to?"

"Exactly," I said.

Liz was silent for a long time. "I don't have anyone to talk to, either."

I held my breath.

"Give me the book for a minute."

I handed the book back to her. Liz pulled a pen out of her coat pocket and began to write on the front leaf of the book. When she was done, she handed it back to me.

1	9	5
2	9	3
7	5	8

"The first two and the last two digits are the year," said Liz. I looked: 1958.

"The other five are my phone number."

"Five, two, nine, three, seven," I repeated.

Liz nodded.

"It's not a magic square," I said. "The rows don't add up."

"Oh, Marlee." Liz laughed. "Only you would notice that. Ask for Elizabeth Fullerton when you call. Not Liz. Use my full name. Mother is worried about prank calls and won't let me answer the phone."

I nodded.

"Don't bother calling until next weekend," said Liz. "I'm going to be grounded for sneaking out today."

I nodded again.

"And we need new names. My parents know I have a friend named Marlee at West Side."

"Mary?" I suggested.

"Nice to meet you, Mary," said Liz. "When I call you, I'll be Lisa."

"Lisa," I repeated.

"I don't know if this is going to work," Liz admitted.

"Me neither," I said. "But isn't it worth a try?"

Liz smiled, and for the first time, she looked like herself again. "I have to go. See you, Marlee." And she ran off.

When she was gone, I opened the math book and looked at the square Liz had drawn. And I decided it was a magic square after all, because it was going to bring my friend and me back together.

20

THE WEC

We went to church as usual Sunday morning at Winfield Methodist Church, but I had a hard time keeping myself from yawning during the sermon. I'd stayed up late the night before reading *Magic Squares and Cubes,* and it was even better than I'd expected. Before, I'd only seen magic squares with three or four rows and columns, but this book had squares with five, six, and even seven. It had a picture of an engraving by Albrecht Dürer that had a magic square in it too. And it even talked about how magic squares were used as talismans to protect you from harm.

I closed my eyes to rest for a moment and thought about the book and Liz and talking. For a long time, I'd thought of myself as only speaking to four people: Judy, David, Daddy and Mother (if she asked me a direct question). Then Liz came along, and things started to change. I answered math questions in Mr. Harding's class most days, and squeezed out a few words to JT. I'd told Miss Taylor I was going to give the presentation, had given it and had a whole conversation with Betty Jean afterward. I'd even spoken to Pastor George. What was going on?

Mother elbowed me in the ribs. I opened my eyes, and she passed me the collection basket. I was supposed to put my one-dollar donation inside, but I was so distracted by magic squares and talking and presentations, I forgot and just passed the basket onto the next person. Drat. At least Mother hadn't noticed. I'd put in two dollars next week to make up for it.

After the service came Sunday school. My teacher, Miss Winthrop, was young, a college girl, I think. She'd only been at our church for a year or two and was sort of annoying and amusing at the same time. She was a little on the plump side and had dimples when she smiled, which was pretty much all the time.

Miss Winthrop was a glass of seltzer that had been pumped full of too many bubbles. Even if you skinned your knee or something, she'd say, "Oh, darling, there's no need to cry!" with a huge grin on her face, as if she enjoyed seeing you bleed. "I've got a Band-Aid right here in my purse. Isn't that fabulous luck!"

Uh, no. I didn't think I was lucky to have tripped on a rock. And she had the Band-Aids in her purse because it was her job to bring along the first-aid kit on the youth group hike.

That week in Sunday school, Miss Winthrop was talking about the apostle Peter and how he thought you should be good, kind and loving to everyone, even if it was hard. I was thinking, okay, it's just the Golden Rule. Then she read a quote from 1 Peter 3:14 that caught my attention: *But even if you do suffer for righteousness' sake, you will be blessed. Have no fear of them, nor be troubled.*

That got me thinking about what Daddy had said to me in the car. And for the first time, I didn't feel guilty. I was pretty sure Peter would say being friends with Liz was right; Daddy was the one who was wrong to be afraid.

Before I could decide how I felt about that, I noticed Little Jimmy was sitting across the circle, staring at me. I hadn't spoken to him since I gave him the peach pit, and well, actually, I hadn't spoken to him then, either. I had a vague recollection of seeing him at Sunday school once or twice before, but he wasn't a regular like me. He was short, of course, and I'd always thought he was as bland as a glass of apple juice. His eyes seemed too big for his face, like a child's, and his cheeks were chubby, though the rest of him was skinny as a pole. I noticed he had a notebook clutched in one hand. Little Jimmy gave a small wave and smiled at me.

I blushed. Did he like me?

When class was over, I let the others file out first so I wouldn't run into Little Jimmy. By the time he was gone, my mother was at the door.

"Mrs. Nisbett," Miss Winthrop said, "it's so good to see you!"

"Hello, Miss Winthrop," said Mother. "I do hope Marlee was well behaved in class."

"Oh, she's a doll, as always." Miss Winthrop was the only person who ever described me as a doll. And I didn't talk in class—how much trouble did Mother think I could get into?

"I've been hoping to run into you," said Miss Winthrop.

"Oh, really?" asked Mother. "Why?"

"Some women and I have started a little group. A committee, actually, and we were wondering if we could convince you to join."

Mother's smile brightened. "I'm always happy to do some volunteer work. And with things at school the way they are, well, let's just say I have plenty of time on my hands."

"Funny you mention the schools," said Miss Winthrop. "That's what our group's about. We're calling it the Women's

Emergency Committee to Open Our Schools, the WEC for short. Now, I know you are a teacher, so I was hoping you would join. Only costs one dollar, we'll put your name on our mailing list and you'll be informed of all our events. So what do you say?" Miss Winthrop finished breathlessly. "Will you join?"

Mother was red as she struggled to find the words. "Miss Winthrop, I'm honored, but . . . Of course, I want the schools to reopen, however . . . I'm not really sure Negroes should be going to our schools."

"No need to worry about that," Miss Winthrop continued smoothly. "The WEC isn't for integration or segregation, but for education."

"Still," said Mother, looking at the ground, "I'm afraid the answer is no."

"Oh." All the fizz went out of Miss Winthrop.

I hated Mother in that moment. She knew how important it was for me to have Judy come home. I thought it was important to her too. More important than who went to school where.

After a moment, Miss Winthrop's enthusiasm bubbled back. "Well, if you ever change your mind, please let me know."

Mother glanced over at me. I pretended to be studying a Bible. No reason to let her know I'd been listening. Just hoped she didn't notice it was upside down. "I'll meet you on the front steps, Marlee," she said, and walked out.

As soon as Mother was gone, I felt for the dollar in my pocket. Might as well add another name to my talking list. I looked over at Miss Winthrop and counted 2, 3, 5, 7 and said, "I want to join."

It wasn't as hard as I'd expected. Miss Winthrop looked

delighted, at least until she remembered my mother had just refused. "Are you sure your mother won't mind?"

"But even if you do suffer for righteousness' sake," I said, *"you will be blessed."*

"Thank you, Marlee," said Miss Winthrop as she took my money. "You really are a doll."

21

THREE GOOD THINGS

On Thursday, I was sitting in Mr. Harding's classroom, munching on my pimento cheese sandwich, when he came over and threw a thick book down on my desk. "Look at the cover," he said.

I flipped the book over. ALGEBRA I was written across the front in large letters.

"Here's the deal," said Mr. Harding. His face was serious, but his eyes were shining. "You get to eat lunch in my classroom. In exchange, you have to spend fifteen minutes every day doing math with me."

Algebra was a high school math course. I was only in seventh grade.

He read my mind. "Come on, Marlee. You know seventh-grade math is way too easy for you."

That was true. And even though Judy talked about algebra like it was a horrible torture device, David was convinced I'd love it.

"Do you need to hear the speech I prepared about how we need girls like you to save us from the Soviets?"

That's what my brother had said.

"All those American satellites aren't going to invent themselves." Mr. Harding grinned at me, just like David did.

Maybe I could talk. Mr. Harding was already on my list. Just fifteen minutes a day. And it was only about math.

"Okay," I said.

"Really?" asked Mr. Harding.

I nodded.

Mr. Harding winked at me and opened the book.

On Friday, I got some mail. Two pieces, actually. The first was a postcard from Judy. It said *Pine Bluff Welcomes You* on one side, and on the other was written a short note:

> Dear Little Sis,
>   I hate it here. Granny burned the pot roast, the toast and the scrambled eggs. The kids at school are mean. Please send a new pair of hose without holes. Lots of love.
>
> Judy

Mother also got a letter from Judy. Daddy kept trying to peek over her shoulder, but she kept turning away.

"What does yours say?" Daddy asked me. "I didn't get one."

I guess Judy was still mad at him for sending her to Pine Bluff. "Granny's a bad cook," I said, "and she needs some new underwear."

Daddy laughed.

I wasn't much of a letter writer, but I'd have to send her a note in return.

The other piece of mail was a flyer from the Women's Emergency Committee to Open Our Schools. "What's this?" asked Daddy.

"Miss Winthrop is a member," I explained. "She invited me to join."

The flyer said *Brotherhood Week* at the top, and there were four little buildings drawn with the names of the four closed high schools on them: Central, Horace Mann, Hall and Tech. There was a quote beneath it that read, "The world is now too *dangerous* for anything but the truth, too small for anything but *brotherhood.*" The post office box of the WEC was listed at the bottom.

"Nice," said Daddy, and patted me on the back.

Finally, it was Saturday, and I could call Liz. I waited until Mother and Daddy were busy in the backyard and then snuck into the kitchen to use the phone.

I don't like using the phone. In real life, I can usually tell if I say the wrong thing. Someone might roll their eyes or look away. But on the phone, I don't have those clues. To make things even worse, we have a party line. That means we share one phone line with two of our neighbors. We each have our own ring (ours is one short and one long) but if someone wants to be nosy, they can just pick up the receiver and listen right in. And it seemed like every time I tried to place a call, Mr. Haroldson chose that exact moment to call his mother.

So to deal with all those variables, I'd written out everything I was going to say on note cards. I laid them all out in front of me in short rows, took a deep breath, pictured the lions at the zoo and dialed Liz's number.

A woman answered on the fourth ring. "Hello."

"Hello," I read. "May I please speak to Elizabeth Fullerton?"

"Who's calling?" She sounded suspicious.

I had to look down at my notes to remember the name we'd picked out for me. "Mary," I said. "A friend from school."

The woman grumbled something under her breath, then I heard her yell, "Elizabeth! You have a telephone call."

A moment later, I heard Liz pick up the phone. "Hello," she said.

"Hi," I read. "It's me. Can you meet me at the zoo in twenty minutes?"

"No."

"No?" She was supposed to say *yes*.

"I'm taking my little brother to the movies," Liz continued.

I frantically searched through my cards for a response.

"Hello? Are you still there?" Liz asked.

"I thought we were going to do something today," I mumbled finally.

"I said I'd try. My mother needs me to watch my brother and told me to take him to *The Wizard of Oz*," she said. "I'd invite you to come too, but we're going to the Gem," she said.

The Negro movie theater. I looked at the only card I had left. *Great, see you there,* didn't seem quite appropriate.

"I need to help my mother clean the bathroom anyway."

"Maybe another time," she said brightly.

"Yes," I said, and hung up the phone, disappointed.

As I scrubbed the toilet, I started thinking. Why hadn't I said *Great, see you there*? I knew the Gem was over on West Ninth Street. If I could go to a Negro church, why not a Negro movie theater? I turned the idea over and over in my mind, like a lemon drop on my tongue. I imagined being the only white girl in a room full of Negroes and shivered. It was a little scary. But Liz had been the only colored girl in a whole school full of white kids. Negroes might not be welcome at the white theater, but I didn't think there was a rule against whites going to the Negro theater. If she could do it, so could I.

22

THE GEM

It was surprising to learn how easy it was to lie to Daddy. I'd just asked him if I could go to the movies, and when he said sure and offered to drive me, I'd said I'd ride my bike instead. He'd even given me money for popcorn.

I peddled faster, trying to drive out the knowledge that I was disobeying my father. I had the black feather in my pocket, but I wanted to get there before Liz went in or I was afraid I wouldn't have the nerve. I thought about Miss Winthrop: *Have no fear of them, nor be troubled.*

Liz was standing on the curb when I arrived. "Marlee." She frowned. "What are you doing here?"

I shrugged. "Going to the movies."

Liz gave me a look.

"You said you were going to the Gem. You didn't say I couldn't come."

She had to work real hard to keep the frown on her face.

A Negro boy walked up to Liz. He was dark enough that there was no way he could ever pass. "Who's this?" he asked, pointing at me.

"My friend Marlee," said Liz. "Marlee, this is my little brother, Tommy."

Her brother was only eight or nine. He had curly hair and

a cute, round face. I could probably talk to him. Kids weren't as intimidating as grown-ups. I decided he was Ovaltine, sweet and wholesome.

Tommy looked me over. "You look like a white girl."

"I am a white girl," I said.

"Then why do you want to come here?" Tommy asked. "My friend's cousin works at the Center Theater on Main Street, and he says they have a new popcorn machine and velvet seats."

I didn't know how to answer. Maybe he wasn't so sweet after all.

"You're going to get me in big trouble," said Liz. "I'm not supposed to see anyone from the old school. I'll be grounded again."

People were looking at me. "Sorry," I muttered. I hadn't thought this through. "I'll go."

"No," said Liz. "A bunch of people have already seen you. The damage is done. You might as well stay and enjoy the movie."

Enjoying the movie proved to be harder than I expected. I'd never been in a place with so many Negroes before. Heck, I'd never been in a room with more than one or two. People were staring at me as I bought my popcorn. I wanted to disappear. I felt my courage shrinking, like the Wicked Witch when Dorothy threw water on her.

I tried to tell myself I didn't know everyone when I went to the white movie theater, either. And the popcorn smelled exactly the same. But it didn't really work.

We walked down the narrow aisle single file, carrying the popcorn and looking for a seat, Tommy first, then Liz, then me.

"Now, hello there, Miss Elizabeth!" bellowed a voice from a fat woman in a large hat.

"Hello, Mrs. Johnson," said Liz quietly.

I tried to hide behind Liz, hoping she wouldn't notice me.

"Elizabeth, I can't tell you how nice it is to see you out having some fun."

"That's me," she said brightly. "Fun, fun, fun." She waved like she was trying to move on.

Mrs. Johnson took in a deep breath and started coughing like she'd swallowed a fly. When she caught her breath, she said, "Elizabeth, may I have a word with you?"

I knew what was wrong. She was upset that I was white. My face burned red with shame. It reminded me of Miss Taylor pulling me into the hall to tell me Liz was colored. Now Mrs. Johnson was doing the same with Liz about me.

Mrs. Johnson took Liz's hand and pulled her a step or two away, causing her to spill half of her popcorn on the floor. She shouldn't have bothered. I could still hear every word she said. "What are you doing here with a white girl?"

"She's a friend," Liz said miserably.

"From the white school! What were you thinking bringing her here?"

"I didn't invite her," protested Liz. "She just showed up."

"Didn't she realize it could be dangerous for you? Didn't she think about the repercussions?"

I hadn't. I'd thought the brave thing to do was to go meet Liz at the Gem. I'd thought it was the right thing to do. Now it seemed like I should have just stayed at home.

"She's my friend," Liz protested.

"How can you be sure?" Mrs. Johnson went on.

Everyone was staring at us now. I prayed for the lights to go down and the newsreel to start.

"Elizabeth, people have been killed over less. After taking

such an enormous, and I might say foolhardy risk, you might at least—"

"Mrs. Johnson," a familiar voice said sharply, "what's going on here?"

We all turned and looked. There was Betty Jean, wearing a blue skirt and a white blouse. It was the first time I'd seen her without an apron. She looked real pretty.

"This white girl has snuck into this theater and—"

"I didn't sneak in," I told Betty Jean. "I paid for my ticket."

"She could be a member of the Mother's League. A spy who—"

Betty Jean laughed. "She's not a spy. She's the daughter of the family I work for. She's a good girl."

I was so grateful.

Mrs. Johnson harrumphed. "Are you saying you'll vouch for her?"

"Yes," said Betty Jean. "I'll vouch for her."

"Well, you're the pastor's wife," said Mrs. Johnson, but she still sounded annoyed.

"Thank you," I said to Betty Jean.

She nodded. "Enjoy the movie, Marlee."

But I didn't. My heart was beating so fast, it took me ages to calm down. Even though I was next to Liz, and Betty Jean was just a few rows back, I kept worrying Mrs. Johnson was going to come back and hit me with her hat. How had Liz ever concentrated at school? How had she done math problems and written essays when she was surrounded by people who might hurt her if they found out who she really was?

On screen, the Cowardly Lion was being given courage. That's what I needed—a wizard to pin a medal to my chest. For now, the old black feather would have to do.

• • •

After the movie, we went out for a soda at a little store on the corner. The owner was colored, but he didn't look at me like I had three heads, just took my money and went on to helping someone else. Tommy was friends with the owner's son and went to play with him in the back while Liz and I sat down to drink our sodas.

"It'll be Halloween before I'm allowed out again," said Liz.

"Sorry," I said. "I don't know what I was thinking."

"You were thinking like a friend," said Liz.

Yeah, I guess I was. "Is this good-bye?"

"Good-bye?" asked Liz. "Please, Marlee. For a girl who can solve a magic square, I'd think you'd be a little more inventive."

"But—"

"All we need is a time and place to meet. Mama's got me scheduled up to the gills, but Tuesday afternoons might work. I have to take Tommy to baseball, but I could probably sneak away for an hour or two."

"At the zoo?" I asked.

"No, too public. Anyone could see us there."

I tried to think like her for a moment, imagine that there was danger lurking around every corner. But it was hard when everything seemed normal, the movie and the soda in my hands. The cut on my thumb was almost healed. "How about the rock crusher?" I asked.

"What?" asked Liz.

"The old quarry on the edge of town," I said. "It's quiet."

"You mean the old forest with the rocks?" she asked.

I nodded.

"Sounds just about perfect."

23

THE ROCK CRUSHER

Betty Jean was waiting for me in the kitchen when I got home from school on Monday afternoon. "Marlee, we need to talk." Her arms were folded over the big red flower in the middle of her apron, and she was frowning.

I sat down at the table with a gulp. I knew what this was about. My time with a certain girl from Kansas.

"Have you told your parents you went to the Gem this past weekend?"

I shook my head. Of course not. I didn't want to get in trouble.

Betty Jean sighed. "Then I'm afraid I'll have to mention it to them."

"No!"

She looked up, startled to hear me talking so loud. Truthfully, I was kind of surprised too.

"Betty Jean, please. If you tell, I'll be in big trouble."

"Marlee, I know your father has some liberal views—and I applaud him for that—but you can't be friends with that girl."

"I know," I said.

Betty Jean sighed. "I wish it was different, Marlee, I really do. That girl's having a hard time of it and could use a friend like you."

"I made a mistake," I said. "Please don't tell."

"It can't happen again," Betty Jean said.

I nodded. I felt like Pinocchio, knowing I was going to meet Liz at the rock crusher on Tuesday. I told myself, "It's not a lie if you don't say anything," but even as I thought it, I knew it wasn't true.

Guess I did fool Betty Jean, though, because she went over and cut me a piece of apple pie. "Lucky for you," she said, "I sometimes have a very bad memory."

She handed me the pie.

"Thank you," I said.

She nodded. "Now, don't make me regret it."

On Tuesday afternoon I had Daddy and Betty Jean in my head telling me what a naughty girl I was for being friendly. Still, I managed to ignore them both and wait in the little clearing in the woods, sitting on the very rock where Judy had bandaged my hand. Liz was late. I started to worry that she wasn't going to come at all, so I did what I always did when I started to worry. I started to count.

It was prime numbers at first. But somehow, it changed into counting all the new people on my talking list. I'd added Miss Winthrop. And Mr. Harding. Now that we were doing math together, sometimes I said more than just numbers. Maybe, *I don't understand.* Or more often, *Oh, I get it!* I'd spoken to Liz's mother on the phone, even if I was reading from cue cards, and chatting with Tommy hadn't even made me sweat. For so long I'd been the quiet girl. If I wasn't her anymore, who was I?

"Finally!" said Liz, stepping into the clearing. "I've been wandering around for twenty minutes trying to find you." She looked, taking in the large stone I was sitting on, the ring of trees, the path leading out into the woods. The grass was tall and turning brown, but a few wildflowers still poked their heads up above the meadow.

"Sorry," I said.

"No, it's good," said Liz. "It means other people won't be able to find us."

She sat down on the rock next to me. "So," Liz said.

"So," I said.

We sat there in silence for a moment. "How are things at school?" Liz asked.

"The same," I said.

"JT ask you out yet?"

"No." I remembered what he'd called Liz. Even if he did ask me out now, I wasn't sure I would go. "How are things at your school?"

"Fine," said Liz.

But there was a catch in her voice, and her smile seemed just a little too tight.

"Really?" I asked.

"No." Liz's face fell like a house of cards. "Things are terrible! Everyone is still ignoring me. This morning in English, the teacher asked Janet to hand out books and she skipped me. I thought it was an accident, so I said, 'I didn't get one.' She looked right in my face, so I know she heard me, but she just kept on going down the row."

"That's awful!"

"And when I walk down the hall, people move away to let me pass so I won't accidentally bump into them. Like I'm a leper or something! They talk about me like I'm not there too. At least Shirley does. She's like Sally, only a hundred times worse. She's always saying stuff like, '*Some people think they're so fancy, they need to go to school with white folks.*'"

"I'm so sorry."

Liz shook her head. "I know I make it worse. The words build up and build up until I explode and start screaming. *I asked you a question! Why won't you respond! Don't you have any manners?* When I'm done, the other just laugh and go back to ignoring me. It's embarrassing."

"What does your mother say?" I asked.

"My mother is so angry at me, she nearly made me go live with my aunt. She yelled at me for an hour when she heard about the Gem, until I convinced her I really didn't know you were coming. Besides, I know what I need to do. I need to learn to ignore them."

"How are you going to do that?"

Liz looked at me and grinned. "You're going to teach me."

"Me?"

"Of course! You're the best at being quiet."

I'd always thought of being quiet as a negative, something that was wrong with me. Was it possible that Liz saw it as a strength?

"I know it won't solve everything," said Liz. "They probably still won't talk to me. But if I stop yelling, at least I won't feel like such a fool. What do you say, Marlee? Will you help me learn to keep my mouth shut?"

I nodded.

"Good," said Liz. "I knew I could count on you."

Now I just had to figure out how to teach her something that came so naturally to me.

24

HALLOWEEN

All October, we didn't get around to the silent lessons. It poured one week, so Tommy didn't have baseball, and the next, he got sick on the way to practice. I waited for an hour alone, worrying about how I was going to teach Liz to be quiet, until I realized she wasn't coming. And then it was Halloween.

Being almost thirteen, I was too old to go trick-or-treating, but being almost thirteen, I also really loved candy, so I volunteered to take the little girl from down the street. Jill was five years old and so shy, she never said a word. She was like a sip of water from a bathroom cup, and we got along great.

On the thirty-first, I threw on a cowboy hat and picked Jill up around seven P.M. By eight thirty, she was so tired, I practically had to carry her home. I'd just dropped her off at her house and was on the way back to mine when I heard a whistle.

"Howdy, cowpoke!"

I turned and saw a cowgirl with a leather skirt, chaps, a fringed jacket, hat and bandanna over her face. Beside her stood a little kid dressed as a horse, with a full mask over his head.

"Wow," I said. I recognized Liz's voice, even if I couldn't see her face. "You look great!"

"Granny can sew," she said. "Too bad every day isn't Halloween. We could go anywhere we wanted."

"You're not supposed to talk to your white friend," said Tommy.

"Shh," said Liz. "Horses don't talk. Besides, I told you I'd give you half my candy."

"Oh, yeah," said Tommy.

"Walk with us a bit?" Liz asked me.

A block or two would be okay. Mother and Daddy didn't expect me home quite yet. "What are you doing here?" I asked.

"We heard about the man who owns the Coca-Cola factory," said Liz. "He gave out hot dogs and Cokes."

"They were good," said Tommy.

"And the lady on Taylor gives out the best candy apples," said Liz.

"I wouldn't know," said Tommy. "You ate mine."

Liz pulled his mane, and they started squabbling, and I missed Judy and David so much, I could almost imagine they were there, taking me trick-or-treating, like they'd done when I was little.

We turned a corner, already to the edge of the white neighborhood. I'd never really thought about how close we lived to the colored part of town.

"Go on home," said Liz to Tommy. "I'll be there in a minute." Tommy ran off.

"I'd better be going too," I said.

"Want to try meeting again next Tuesday?" Liz asked.

Before I could answer, we heard a *splat*. We looked up.

A tall boy with blond hair was throwing eggs at a small white house on the corner.

"Mrs. Jefferson lives there," I said.

"The old white lady with the little dog?" Liz asked.

I nodded.

Splat. Splat. Eggs oozed down the front window. Inside, the little dog began to bark.

"Stop it," Liz yelled, walking toward him.

He took one glance at us and kept on throwing. When the first carton was empty, he reached into a bag to get another one. When he stood up with the new carton, I could see his perfectly straight nose in the streetlight. It was Red.

"Liz!" I hissed. I grabbed her arm and tried to pull her away, but she shook me off.

"She's an old lady," Liz yelled. "She can't get up on a ladder and wash those eggs off. What a stupid, mean—"

A second boy stepped out from behind a tree and into the light. It was JT.

Liz stopped talking.

JT was holding a whole bag full of eggs. "Marlee, what are you doing here?"

I didn't answer.

"Is that . . . Liz with you?"

Liz was standing still, frozen. At least her bandanna was still in place.

"No," I squeaked.

"It is," said JT. "I recognize her voice. You're still hanging out with that—"

I gave Liz a shove, and she finally turned and ran.

"JT," Red called out, "you got those extra eggs?"

JT watched Liz run off, then gave me a funny look.

"Who is that?" Red loomed over both JT and me in the darkness between the streetlights.

"It's Marlee," said JT. "My math tutor."

Tutor? Yeah, right.

"The mute girl?" asked Red.

"And she was with that colored girl who used to go to our school."

I shook my head furiously.

"It was Liz!" insisted JT. "I recognized her voice."

"Where's she now?" asked Red.

"Ran off," said JT, and gestured into the darkness.

"Aw, Marlee," said Red. "You shouldn't be hanging around with niggers." He plucked the cowboy hat off my head and crushed it between his palms. Then Red took an egg from the carton JT was holding and placed it in my hands.

I was shaking so much, I could barely hold it.

"Throw it," commanded Red.

I shook my head.

"Throw it!" Red barked.

I tried to throw, but it landed about a foot in front of us. A little yolk leaked out onto Red's shoe. JT stared at it, but Red didn't seem to notice. He took another egg and shoved it into my hands.

"Hit the house!"

I shook my head. Even if I had wanted to, I didn't have a good arm.

Red took me by the shoulders and shoved me up the front walk, until I was only about a yard from the front door.

"Throw!"

I threw, but the egg still landed in the bushes.

"Idiot!" Red roared, and pressed another egg into my hands, so hard this time that it broke. I had egg all over my fingers.

"Red," JT asked, "what are you doing?"

"Gotta make sure she doesn't tell on us. Now if she does, we can say that she threw them too."

The yolk was sticky on my hand. I wanted to wipe it off, but I didn't dare move.

JT glanced at me again, then looked back at his older brother. "She's not going to tell."

"How do you know?" asked Red.

"She does my math homework for me," said JT. "I know she doesn't want anyone to find out about that. Besides, she doesn't talk."

I could feel Red's electric blue eyes boring into me. "You know where that colored girl lives?" he asked.

I shook my head.

Red picked up my flattened hat and shoved it back on my head. "You make sure you stay quiet," he said. "'Cause if you don't, I'll be coming after you and your little friend too."

I nodded to show I understood.

"Come on, JT," he said. "Let's go somewhere else." They started walking away. After a moment, Red turned back. "And keep on doing my brother's homework!"

I could hear them laughing as they wandered off.

When they finally turned the corner and were out of sight, it was like a spell was broken. I ran and ran, and it wasn't until I reached our front porch that I realized I was crying.

"Marlee, that you?" Mother called out.

"Yes, Mother!" I frantically wiped my eyes. I was going to be stuck doing math homework for JT forever. And if I confessed and told my parents, they'd find out about Liz. I pulled myself together and opened the front door. I was splashing some water on my face when the phone rang. "Hello?" My voice was shaking.

"It's me," said Liz. "You got home okay?"

I nodded.

"I can't hear you nod over the phone," said Liz.

"Yes," I said, but I didn't even smile.

"I had to give Tommy all my candy, but don't worry. My little brother knows how to keep a secret."

I listened to my heart beating . . . 2, 3, 5, 7, 11.

"I really need those quiet lessons," said Liz, and she sounded scared too. "Next Tuesday?"

"Okay." I hung up just as Mother walked into the kitchen.

"Marlee, you're white as a sheet," said Mother. "What's wrong?"

I wanted to tell her then. I wanted to go back to the days when I sat on her lap and she read me stories and I told her everything. But they were gone.

"I ate too much candy," I said finally.

Mother nodded. "Go to bed. You'll feel better in the morning."

I crawled into bed and pulled the covers over my head. I missed Judy something awful. If she'd been there, I could have told her what had happened. She'd have known what to do. I listened to the lions. But it still took me a long, long time to fall asleep.

25

BETTY JEAN'S SON

On Monday, I gave JT his homework. I didn't look at him. I didn't like him anymore. But after what had happened on Halloween, I was too scared not to do it.

As soon as I stepped inside the house after school, I knew something was wrong. There was unfolded laundry in the living room, and the breakfast dishes were still in the sink. In the kitchen, Betty Jean had her head down on the table.

"Betty Jean?"

She sat up when I called her name. Her face was gray.

"What's wrong?" I asked.

"It's nothing." She jumped up and straightened her apron. "I'm sorry I haven't . . . I wasn't feeling . . ."

When she couldn't even finish her sentence, I realized something was really wrong. So I did what she'd done for me. I found some cookies in the cupboard, put them on a plate and poured us both a cold glass of tea.

"It's Curtis," she said, sitting back down.

I sat down with her. "Who's Curtis?"

"My son. He's fourteen. He's in ninth grade at Dunbar Junior High."

Betty Jean had never mentioned a son before. That was

another one of those unspoken rules: maids didn't talk about themselves.

"He's been arrested." Betty Jean looked like she was going to cry.

"Arrested? For what?"

"Egging Mrs. Jefferson's house on Halloween." She sobbed once, then took a sip of tea. "He didn't do it. I was making deviled eggs for a ladies luncheon at church, and I asked him to go out and buy some groceries and—" She choked down a sob again.

Egging Mrs. Jefferson's house. I knew who *had* done that. And if having to do JT's homework wasn't bad enough, now someone else had gotten into trouble too.

"But if you explain to the police that—"

Betty Jean shook her head. "A white woman gets her house egged and the police find a colored boy nearby, that's all they need to know."

It wasn't fair. Betty Jean had helped me at the movie theater. And afterwards too. There had to be something I could do for her.

Betty Jean drained the iced tea and wiped her face with a corner of her apron. "I'm sorry. Time got away from me. I'll hurry now to get my work done." She went into the living room.

I saw the list of emergency phone numbers posted on the fridge—Mother's school, Daddy's school, police, fire and so on. If this wasn't an emergency, I didn't know what was. My note cards were upstairs, so I scribbled a few sentences down on a napkin and picked up the phone.

"Forest Heights Junior High," said a woman's voice.

I froze and gulped down air. It was just a stupid phone call. Why was I so nervous? And then I was mad at myself for being nervous, which made things worse and—

"Hello?" said the woman again. "This is Forest Heights Junior High."

I looked down at the napkin. "May I speak to Richard Nisbett, please?"

"I'm sorry, he's in class now. May I take a message?"

They got out later than we did. But luckily I had thought of that. I read, "It's his daughter. It's an emergency."

I hoped that was all I would have to say, because I was already sweating, and I didn't have anything else written down. The woman said something else, and then there was a long pause, and then Daddy was on the phone.

"Marlee," Daddy asked, breathing hard, like he'd run all the way to the phone. Which he probably had. "What's wrong?"

"It's Betty Jean," I said. "Her son was arrested."

"What?"

I tried to explain, but Daddy made me put Betty Jean on the phone, but then she started crying, so I had to get back on the phone and tell him what had happened.

"I see," said Daddy when I was finally done. I couldn't quite tell if he was annoyed or just worried. "Tell Betty Jean I'll go to the police station right now and see what I can do."

After I hung up, I helped Betty Jean fold the laundry and do the dishes. Her hands were shaking so badly, she couldn't hold the iron. Finally, I told her to sit down, and I'd press Daddy's shirts. An hour later, we were done with all the jobs, and Daddy still wasn't there. Mother played bridge on Mondays and wouldn't be home until late. We sat at the kitchen table and stared at the clock, until I went and got a deck of cards.

"You play hearts?" I asked Betty Jean.

She nodded.

I won the first two rounds. I was counting cards in my head, which was probably cheating, but it kept me from worrying too much. With all those numbers and suits in my mind, there wasn't room for anything else. I was just dealing the third hand when the front door flew open and my father came inside. "Don't worry," he said to Betty Jean. "I got him."

A tall colored boy stepped into the house. His clothes were crumpled, as if he'd slept in them all night.

"Oh, thank God," exclaimed Betty Jean, and ran to hug him. He was taller than she was, and she had to pull him over to kiss him. He looked embarrassed. Finally she let him go and said to my father, "I'm so sorry. My husband is out of town, and when they arrested Curtis last night, I didn't know what to do."

"It's all right," Daddy said kindly. "I'm glad Marlee thought to call me. I paid the fine, and they dropped the charges."

"Thank you so much!" She turned to me. "Thank you, Miss Marlee. I—"

"But I didn't do anything!" Curtis interrupted. "And the fine was fifty dollars!"

"Curtis," my father muttered, "I thought we agreed to keep that to ourselves."

Fifty dollars. That was a lot of money.

Betty Jean shook her head. "You'll have to take it out of my salary."

"Betty Jean, right now you don't have to—"

"Yes, Mr. Nisbett. Yes, I do." Betty Jean took a moment to think, then said, "Would a dollar a week be okay? I know it'll take almost a year for us to repay you, but . . ."

Daddy nodded. "A dollar a week will be fine."

Betty Jean reached over and gave me a hug. "You got a good daughter here," she said.

"That," said Daddy, "I already know."

Daddy sent Betty Jean and her son home early, and we made cold pork sandwiches for dinner. "Daddy," I asked as I sliced some bread, "why did you help Betty Jean's son?"

He thought for a long moment. "I've been a member of the Arkansas Council on Human Relations for a few years now," he said finally. "I met Pastor George there."

That wasn't really an answer. "But why did you join that group?"

Daddy looked at me, then sighed. "I suppose you're old enough now. Have you ever heard of Emmett Till?"

Emmett Till. I had heard of him. A few years ago, in whispered conversations that stopped as soon as I walked into the room. "Something bad happened to him?"

Daddy nodded. "He was a young Negro boy who went down to visit some relatives in Mississippi. One day someone saw him talking, some say flirting, with a white woman." Daddy stopped, like he didn't want to tell me what happened next.

"Did he get hurt?" I asked, thinking of JT and Red and the egg cartons.

"He was murdered."

"For talking to a white woman?"

Daddy nodded again. "He was only fourteen years old. About the same age as David was then."

"That doesn't make any sense."

"I know," said Daddy. "That's when I realized I had to do something. So I joined the Council on Human Relations. It's an integrated group and in 1955, when Emmett Till was killed, the council was active in providing legal advice to school board members in Hoxie, Arkansas. Their schools were integrated that year, and the group helped get injunctions filed against protestors who were trying to disrupt the process. Overall, things went fairly smoothly in Hoxie. When problems started here in 1957, we were hopeful that the council could help again. But the Little Rock officials refused to talk to the committee."

The kitchen was warm, but I felt cold. I guess I'd heard about things like what Daddy was telling me, but when you read it in a newspaper, it was different. "Curtis is fourteen too," I said.

"Yes, he is."

Liz had done worse than talking to a white boy. She'd fooled a whole school of white people. I wanted to confess and tell Daddy everything, but I couldn't. Liz needed me. I had to teach her how to keep her mouth shut when got mad so she wouldn't feel embarrassed. So she wouldn't anger people like Red. So she wouldn't get hurt.

Mother came home then, and we didn't talk about it anymore. But that night, after I was supposed to be asleep, I heard Mother and Daddy arguing again.

"Fifty dollars!" Mother exclaimed.

"We had the money saved," Daddy said quietly.

"It was for Judy's college fund," said Mother.

"Betty Jean will repay us."

"Why didn't you ask me first?" snapped Mother.

"Maurine, the boy was in jail and scared. Now, I got in trouble once or twice as a boy. Curtis is a good kid. He just needed someone to help him out."

"Why did it have to be you?"

"Who else should it have been?" Daddy asked.

Mother didn't have an answer.

I lay awake a long time, waiting for them to go to sleep. The lions started to roar, and I had a new thought. Maybe Mother wasn't selfish or uncaring. Maybe she was scared. Maybe she masked it like David did, not with a grin, but with a frown.

When my parents had finally gone to bed, I got up and copied the quote from Peter onto a pretty piece of pink stationery. Then I snuck into the kitchen and placed it inside Mother's purse, where she'd be sure to see it the next morning.

26

BEING QUIET

When I walked into Mr. Harding's room on Tuesday, I still didn't know how I was going to teach Liz to be quiet. But once lunch started and Mr. Harding and I spent fifteen minutes on x and y and solving for the unknown, I felt like a new person. A better person. One who could do things I didn't normally do. If numbers could do all that for me, maybe they could help Liz too.

Liz was waiting when I got to the rock crusher that afternoon.

"I have an idea," I said as I walked into the clearing.

"What?"

"You asked me how I managed to be so quiet. It's numbers. I count prime numbers in my head and—"

"That's when you *want* to talk," said Liz.

"It's when I'm trying to do something I'm not good at," I said. "And what you're not good at is being quiet when you're angry."

Liz thought for a moment, then shook her head. "I don't even know the prime numbers. And if you tell me to count to ten before I speak like my mother always does, I will scream."

Okay. So counting was out. "How about times tables?" I asked.

"What about them?"

"Well, which ones do you like?"

"I don't like any times tables!" exclaimed Liz.

Every once in a while, I just couldn't relate to her at all. Who didn't like the times tables? Such beauty! Such patterns! Such organization! Okay, so I knew it wasn't normal, but it was how I saw them. "We'll do the nines then," I said, rummaging in my purse for a pen. "Hold up your hands in front of you with your thumbs together."

With the pen, I labeled each of her fingers with a number from one to ten, left to right, starting with her left pinkie (one) and ending with her right pinkie (ten).

"Now put down your pinkie on your left hand," I said. "The one with the number one on it."

"How is this going to help me be quiet?" asked Liz.

"Just do it."

Liz sighed and put down her pinkie.

"How many fingers do you have left?"

"Nine."

"Exactly. One times nine is nine."

"I knew that," said Liz.

"Now put down your ring finger on your left hand. The one with the two."

Liz did so.

"How many fingers do you have to the left of the one that is down?"

"One."

"And to the right?"

"Eight."

"Two times nine is eighteen."

Liz gave me a look. "Does it work for all of them?"

"Try it."

She put down her middle finger, labeled three. Two fingers to the left; seven to the right. Three times nine is twenty-seven.

"Okay, so that is pretty cool," said Liz.

"So every time you feel words starting to creep out when you don't want them to, look down at your hands and recite the nines times tables. By the time you're done, you won't even remember whatever it was you wanted to say."

Liz wasn't listening. She had her thumb on her right hand tucked in and was counting. "Six times nine is fifty-four. I could never remember that one!"

"That's the point." I laughed. "You don't have to remember a thing." I wiggled my fingers at her. "All you have to do is count."

Liz liked the trick I had taught her, but I wasn't sure it was enough. When I got home, I found Mother in the kitchen, going through the mail. "Did you put this in my purse?" asked Mother, holding up the pink piece of stationery.

"Yes," I said.

"Oh," said Mother.

I waited for her to ask why, so I could explain what Miss Winthrop had said about Peter and tell her why I had joined the WEC. But she didn't. She just passed me my mail.

I was disappointed. I'd imagined us sitting down and having a long chat, talking and laughing like we'd done when I was little. Still, if she wasn't going to say anything, I wouldn't either.

I had two pieces of mail. The first was another postcard from Judy:

Dear Little Sis,

I hate it here. I didn't make pep squad, and I'm failing math. (Not really. But I have a C!) Please send two PayDays and a deck of cards. I'm playing a lot of solitaire. Lots of love.

Judy

The second was another flyer from the WEC. It read "People who care about their teachers, their children's education, their city's future, want open public schools."

I cared. Helping Liz and leaving notes for Mother and sending candy bars to Judy was nice, but it wasn't enough. Not when there might be more that I could do.

27

AT THE MEETING

That weekend, I hung around in the Sunday school classroom after the others filed out. When it was just Miss Winthrop and me, I cleared my throat. "Are you going to the WEC meeting this Friday?" I asked.

"Yes," she said.

"Do you mind if I come too?" It was a whisper, but it was quiet in the classroom. I was pretty sure she'd heard me.

"Oh, Marlee!" Miss Winthrop exclaimed. "That would be wonderful!"

I guess she had.

Daddy said it was fine when I asked his permission, so Miss Winthrop and I arranged to meet at the church Friday afternoon and walk to the meeting together.

The meeting was at Mrs. Terry's house. She was one of the founders of the WEC. From the outside, her house was large and fancy, much bigger than ours, and I was sure it was furnished with many breakable objects. I would have to be careful not to trip. Mrs. Terry herself opened the door. She was in her seventies but seemed as energetic as a glass of fresh squeezed orange juice. "Welcome, Marlee," she said when Miss Winthrop introduced me. She led us into the living room.

Mrs. Brewer was standing in front of a group of women sitting in folding chairs placed in neat rows. Miss Winthrop whispered that she was the chair of the WEC. Mrs. Brewer was about my mother's age, maybe a bit older, and wore a tailored blouse with pearls. She reminded me of white wine in a fancy goblet. The meeting was already in progress as Miss Winthrop and I slipped into our seats. "Remember, the Women's Emergency Committee to Open Our Schools stands neither for segregation nor integration, but for education," Mrs. Brewer said. "Our sole aim is to get the four high schools reopened and our students back in their classes."

The women nodded their approval.

"Now, on to new business," said Mrs. Brewer. "As you know, two days ago, the school board resigned in frustration over the school situation. A new election is scheduled for December sixth; however, new candidates must file their intention to run by Saturday, November fifteenth. Which leaves us"—she looked at her watch—"just over twenty-four hours to find six candidates who believe in public education."

"We have Ted Lamb," said Mrs. Terry.

"Well, that's one."

I let my eyes wander as Mrs. Brewer continued talking. I wasn't sure how I was going to help. I didn't know anyone who wanted to run for office. Miss Winthrop was taking notes, like it was the most fascinating discussion she'd heard in a long time. Of course, she always looked like that, even when a five-year-old at church wanted to tell her every single kind of animal that Noah took with him on the ark.

A woman sitting hunched over in a back corner caught my eye. I knew I knew her, but I couldn't place her. She saw me looking at her, and I expected her to smile, but she didn't, just cowered back in her seat and raised her flyer in front of her face.

It was Mrs. Dalton, JT's mother.

I'd seen her once or twice before, at a football game maybe. She always reminded me of a glass of iced tea so weak, you had to add a whole cup of sugar to make it taste like anything at all. The Daltons had more money than we did and lived in a big house with a maid and a butler and weren't really friends with my parents. But I remembered her because she had a scar over her left eyebrow, and she was shy like me. JT had said once she'd got the scar when she tripped on the stairs doing a load of laundry. But that didn't make sense, because I was pretty sure a lady like her never even turned on the washing machine. They had a maid to do that, probably a colored woman who . . .

I looked around the room. There wasn't a colored person there, except for the maid in the kitchen who was putting sandwiches on a table.

The meeting adjourned a few minutes later and Mrs. Terry invited everyone to have some refreshments before they left. "Grab me a cucumber sandwich, Marlee?" Miss Winthrop asked. I was hungry, so I grabbed two, and when I came back, Miss Winthrop was deep in conversation with an older woman I thought I recognized from church.

"All I'm saying," said Miss Winthrop, "is that it still seems odd to me that we haven't invited any colored women to join the WEC."

"Oh my," said the lady from church. "I'm not sure my Terrance would feel comfortable about me being here if he knew I was associating with Negroes."

"But the Negroes want their schools reopened too."

"I'm sure they do."

"So wouldn't it make more sense to work *with* the Negroes?" Miss Winthrop asked.

Before the church lady could answer, Mrs. Brewer came up and put a hand on Miss Winthrop's shoulder. "Would you help me in the kitchen for a moment?"

"Of course."

I tagged along, but I should have known she didn't really need any help, because as soon as we reached the kitchen, Mrs. Brewer said, "Miss Winthrop, I appreciate your idealism, but admitting Negro women to our group would be the end of the WEC."

"Don't you believe that the schools should be integrated?" asked Miss Winthrop.

"Of course I do," Mrs. Brewer whispered. "But if anyone calls me an integrationist, half the women here will run out. And it's in everyone's best interest to get the schools reopened. I've talked to the Negro leaders and explained what we are trying to do. They understand."

"Well," said Miss Winthrop, "I believe they've told you they understand."

"We're all doing the best we can," said Mrs. Brewer.

"I know." All the fizz was suddenly gone from Miss Winthrop. "Call me about the petitions?"

Mrs. Brewer nodded.

"Come on, Marlee," Miss Winthrop said. "Let's go home."

On our way to the door, we ran into Mrs. Terry, who was talking to a lady in a fancy hat with flowers on it.

"I'd love to help," said the woman. "You know I've been to every meeting since the first one in September. But Stephen works downtown, and if I agreed to lead a committee, my name might end up the paper. There could be problems with his job."

"I understand," said Mrs. Terry, though her teeth were clenched. It was obvious to me she didn't understand. Surely that lady's husband wouldn't really lose his job.

My sleeve caught on something, and I stopped, expecting I had snagged myself on a vase or a statue or a fancy carving. But JT's mother was clutching my sleeve. Her hand was thin and bony, like a skeleton's.

"It's Marlee, isn't it?" she said. "You go to school with James-Thomas."

I nodded.

"Would you . . ." She spoke so quietly, I had to lean forward to hear her. "Would you please not mention to anyone that you saw me here? I believe in public schools, but if my husband found out I was attending these meetings, he"—the scar on her eyebrow suddenly flushed red—"he wouldn't like it."

I nodded again and tore myself away, like a cricket escaping from a spiderweb. I looked back at her, and she looked so sad, I gave her a little smile. She did not smile in return.

Miss Winthrop and I waited at the bus stop together. It was raining. We were sharing her umbrella, but my toes were still getting wet. "Miss Winthrop," I asked, "is Mrs. Brewer right? If she invited Negroes to join the WEC, would the group really fall apart?"

"I don't know," said Miss Winthrop. "Probably. But that doesn't make it right."

I thought about that. Doing the right thing was harder than I'd expected it to be. And more confusing too.

"I know it's frustrating," said Miss Winthrop. "But sometimes change is slow."

"Will they find people to run for the school board?" I asked.

Miss Winthrop nodded. "Mrs. Terry is going to work the phones tonight. I said I'd go around tomorrow and help get the petitions signed. They only need twenty-five names for each one. That's not that many."

"Can I come too?" I asked.

"Sure." Miss Winthrop smiled as the bus pulled up. "I'd love the company."

The WEC found five people to run: Ted Lamb, Billy Rector, Everett Tucker, Russell Matson and Margaret Stephens. Miss Winthrop stopped by to pick me up around nine. My father was the third to sign the petition. Mother was busy with the wash and did not come to the door. We walked around the neighborhood and by noon we had the names we needed. It seemed simple. A few people had refused to sign, but everyone had been polite.

That afternoon, as I was scrubbing the toilet and doing my other chores, the phone rang. I thought it might be Liz, so I ran to answer it. It was a man's voice. "Is this Richard Nisbett's daughter?"

"Yes," I said politely.

"Little nigger lover," he snapped. "You'd better watch your-self because—"

I slammed down the phone.

Daddy walked into the room a moment later. "Who was that?"

I shook my head, too upset to say anything.

"Are you all right, Marlee?"

I realized I was trembling. "I don't feel well."

"Go to bed," Daddy said.

I did. I closed the curtains and pulled the blankets up to my chin, but it took me a long time to stop shaking. I wanted to tell my father about the phone call, but I couldn't. Because if I did, he might not let me go back to the WEC.

28

THANKSGIVING

The Tuesday before Thanksgiving, Liz and I met again at the rock crusher. I thought about telling her about the phone call, but I was too embarrassed to repeat the man's words.

"I did what you said," said Liz, when we were settled on our usual rock.

"And?"

"It didn't work," said Liz. "Shirley started talking to Janet about how other folks were going to pay for me being so uppity. I didn't say a word, just started reciting the nines times tables, counting on my fingers like you taught me. I got all the way to seven times nine is sixty-three before Shirley turned to me and said, 'What are you doing?' She said it in a nasty voice, but it was the first time anyone had spoken to me in weeks, so I decided to answer her. 'I'm reciting the nines times tables,' I said, and I showed her how to do it. I only got to three times nine is twenty-seven before she and Janet started laughing and I started yelling again. The rest of the day, whenever I walked by, everyone wiggled their fingers at me and snickered."

"I'm so sorry."

Liz shrugged, but I felt horrible. My plan had failed. It had made things worse for her. She'd helped me learn to talk, and I couldn't even teach her how to be quiet. I couldn't figure it out. When I was upset, calculating the area of a triangle, or adding up columns of numbers, or reciting pi always helped me.

Then I realized that was it. Liz simply wasn't a numbers person. She liked words. If she was going to be quiet, we had to go about it a different way.

"What if, when you felt the words building up, instead of saying them out loud, you wrote them down?"

"Wrote them down?" asked Liz.

"Yeah," I said. "You could carry around a notebook. Like Little Jimmy does."

"I guess that might work," Liz said slowly.

"You could say whatever you wanted. As long as no one reads it."

"Well." Liz smiled. "It's worth a try."

Thanksgiving morning was cold and gray. Central was playing its last football game of the season. Daddy and David were going, and I tagged along with them, leaving Mother at home to cook the turkey. Judy and Granny were coming in the afternoon, just in time for dinner. The game started at ten thirty A.M., and I shivered as I sat on the bleachers, wishing I'd put on a warmer coat.

In the first quarter, Red intercepted a pass. Everyone cheered. Everyone except for me.

David glanced over. "How you doing, sis?"

"Cold," I said.

David laughed, took off his own jacket and draped it over my shoulders. The jacket was warm and old, and it smelled like it hadn't been washed in a really long time.

"Mr. Harding is teaching me algebra," I said during a time-out.

"Algebra?" David didn't say anything about it being a high school class, and I loved him for it. "How's it going?"

"Fine," I said. Then 'cause it was my brother and I figured I could brag a little, "Actually, really well. I like it. And he says I'm good at it."

"Phew," said David, wiping his brow. "Marlee, you are making me feel so much better."

"Me?" I protested. "How?"

He glanced over at Daddy, but he was engaged in a conversation with a neighbor and wasn't listening to us. "I dropped out of all those math classes. I'm studying English now, like Daddy did." He wiped his brow again. "Sure is a relief to know someone else'll be taking care of beating those Soviets."

I grinned. "Mr. Harding says he sleeps better at night knowing there are girls like me to invent those satellites."

"That Mr. Harding," said David as he tousled my hair, "sounds like a real smart man."

Judy was waiting for us on the front porch when we got home from the game. I screamed and ran to give her a hug. She smelled different, like she'd been trying a new shampoo. After we'd said our hellos to everyone, Judy and I ran off to our old room.

As soon as the door was closed, I turned to Judy.

"Guess what!" we both said at the exact same time. We laughed. It was so good to be with my sister again.

"You first," I said.

"I have a boyfriend," squealed Judy. She pulled a picture out of her purse and shoved it into my hands. It was a snapshot of her and a skinny boy with thick brown hair sticking up in all directions. They were at a roller-skating rink, holding hands.

They were both grinning so big, a raccoon could have crawled up in their mouths and settled down inside.

"It's Robert Laurence!" she said.

"Who?" I asked.

"The boy I told you about when you cut your thumb." Judy didn't even take a breath before she continued, "His parents sent him to live with his uncle in Pine Bluff. I didn't even know, because we'd never really said much to each other at Central, but in Pine Bluff of course we started spending time together because we were both from Little Rock. And then he asked me out to the movies and then we started going steady."

I was beginning to think the new shampoo wasn't the only change. "Why didn't you tell me?"

"Mother reads all our mail," said Judy.

That was true.

"Besides, if Mother knew I had a boyfriend, she'd make Daddy bring me home."

"Don't you want to come home?" I asked.

"Of course I do," said Judy. "When the schools reopen and Robert Laurence can come too."

I'd spent the past two months thinking she was miserable, and it turned out that wasn't the case at all. She'd fooled me along with Mother, and I didn't like it.

Judy sat down on the bed and started unpacking her clothes. "What was your news?"

I'd been planning to tell her all about Liz and JT and the nasty phone call and everything. But now? It wasn't like anything had really changed. She just had a boyfriend. But I still felt like I'd been betrayed.

"I joined the Women's Emergency Committee," I said finally. "We're trying to get the schools reopened."

"That's great," said Judy. "Let me know if there is anything I can do to help."

Last I'd heard, she wasn't even sure she was in favor of integrating the schools. Now she wanted to help? More likely she just wanted to make sure she and Robert Laurence came home together. And even though Judy had always been the one I'd told everything, I kept the rest of my news locked up tight inside of me.

I'd always thought Judy was an ice-cold Coca-Cola. Now it seemed like she'd gone flat.

We went to bed early, but in the middle of the night I woke up. The phone was ringing, one short ring and one long. For a minute, I thought I was dreaming, then I heard my parents' door open and Daddy stumble into the hall.

I scrambled out of bed. Daddy was just slamming down the phone when I reached the kitchen. "Who was it?" I asked.

"Wrong number," said Daddy. "Go back to bed."

Before I got back to my room, the phone rang again. This time Daddy left it off the hook. Judy slept on.

29

GOOD ENOUGH

As soon as I saw Liz that next Tuesday, all my words about my sister just came tumbling out.

"Wow," said Liz when I was finished. "All I had to report was that we ate a lot of pumpkin pie."

We were folding a bunch of WEC flyers on the big stone. The flyers were asking people to come out and vote in the December 6 election. Miss Winthrop had dropped them off the night before. "I just don't understand how you get so much done," she marveled. I didn't tell her Liz was helping me too.

Each time the wind picked up, it blew a few of the flyers across the meadow, and either Liz or I had to run after them. As we folded and stamped all the flyers, I kept talking, telling Liz all about the Christmas float our church was doing.

Every year the Saturday before Christmas, all the churches in town (well, all the white churches) built a float and sent it down Main Street. The mayor voted on the winner, and that church got bragging rights for a whole year. Usually, everyone wanted to ride on the float and only one or two people were picked, but this year we had a theme from Matthew 19:14: *Let the children come to me, and do not hinder them; for to such belongs the kingdom of heaven.* Reverend Mitchell was going to be Jesus, sitting on a throne, and all the kids from Sunday school were going to be the children. Everyone who wanted to could ride on the float, and I was super excited.

"You'll come, right?" I asked Liz.

"Marlee, I can't."

"Why not?"

"Someone might recognize me."

"Can't you wear a disguise and—"

Liz shook her head.

I knew she was right, but it didn't make it any easier. For the hundredth time, I wished we could do all the normal things friends do. Go places for fun. Have the same circle of friends. Eat lunch together at school. "How's school going?" I asked. I'd been talking so much, I was embarrassed to realize I hadn't even asked about her.

Liz grinned. "It worked! I got a notebook over Thanksgiving break. I've already written five pages, and that was just yesterday. Today Shirley asked me why I was scribbling away, but I just wrote my answer down—making sure she couldn't see it, of course—and after a minute of my not responding, she left to talk to Janet. Maybe they started gossiping about me and maybe they didn't, but I was so busy writing about them, I didn't hear a word."

"That's great," I said.

"Tommy will be at the parade," Liz said. "I'll tell him to wave to you. I know it's not the same as being there myself, but . . ."

"Don't worry about it," I said. "It's good enough."

After Tuesday afternoons with Liz, I started spending Friday afternoons with Betty Jean. It started when she baked me an extra-special triple-layer chocolate cake to say thank you for

146

helping with Curtis. Then I did the ironing for her one week to say thank you for the cake, and she baked me a strawberry rhubarb pie to thank me for the ironing. After that, I said why don't we just help each other out each Friday, and she thought that was a great idea.

Betty Jean taught me a lot, starting with the NAACP. That stands for the National Association for the Advancement of Colored People. They filed lawsuits and stuff to help Negroes get more rights. They'd even been part of the *Brown v. Board of Education* lawsuit that had started this whole integration issue. I told her about the WEC and what we were doing with the election and how there weren't any Negroes in the group.

Betty Jean nodded. "Heard about that from Mrs. Daisy Bates."

Mrs. Bates was what Betty Jean called an activist. Her husband owned a newspaper, and she'd spent a lot of time helping the Little Rock Nine last year.

"I can't say we're thrilled about the 'No Negroes' policy, but Mrs. Bates says Mrs. Terry is a good woman."

What I learned most from talking to Betty Jean was that things were complicated. Take starting a private high school for the Negroes, for example. The whites had done it with T. J. Raney. At first it sounded like a good idea to me, but Betty Jean said the NAACP had asked the colored community in Little Rock not to do so.

"Why not?"

"It would be doing what the segregationists wanted—setting up separate schools. Not to mention that it would be betraying the nine Negro students at Central who suffered through last year."

"What happened to them?" I asked. "I mean, I know Ernest

Green graduated and Minnijean Brown was expelled, but what about the rest of them?"

"Minnijean is still in New York," said Betty Jean, "at the school she was invited to attend when she was expelled from Central last year. Carlotta, Melba, Thelma, Elizabeth and Jefferson are taking correspondence courses. Terrence moved to Los Angeles to live with relatives and go to school there, and Gloria went to Kansas City to do the same.

"You keep working with that WEC, Marlee," Betty Jean said. "We want to move forward so that Curtis and your friend Liz will have the same opportunities you do. Without having to leave town."

Yeah, I thought. That sounded pretty good to me.

30

THE CHRISTMAS PARADE

December 6 came and went. Three moderate candidates were elected (Lamb, Tucker and Matson) and three segregationists, so the school board was deadlocked again. Still, Miss Winthrop managed to put a positive spin on it when I saw her as I climbed onto the Christmas float. "Three is better than none. We'll get there yet, Marlee!"

I nodded.

"Besides, I've been getting a lot more threatening phone calls," said Miss Winthrop. "I think that's a good sign we're making a difference."

We hadn't gotten any more calls, thank goodness. Daddy hadn't said a word about it to me, but I'd seen him talking to Mr. Haroldson. I remembered Daddy saying our neighbor was a member of the segregationist Capital Citizens Council. He was also on our party line and probably didn't appreciate being woken up in the middle of the night. Maybe he'd put a stop to our calls.

In any case, I didn't want to think about that. Today was the Christmas parade and our float was impressive. There was a little hill built on a low platform, and the whole thing was being pulled by a tractor. The hill was covered with fake grass and flowers, and at the top was a throne. Reverend Mitchell sat in the chair and wore a fake beard and a long white robe, but every time he laughed, he kind of went "ho ho ho," and he ended up reminding me more of Santa Claus than Jesus.

I settled into a spot between a fake bush and a stuffed rabbit. Not sure why there was a rabbit—maybe it was left over from Easter? Practically everyone from our Sunday school class was there, so it was crowded. There was one space left right next to me.

"Wonderful! Wonderful!" exclaimed Miss Winthrop, clapping her hands. "You really do look like the poor masses."

At the last minute, Little Jimmy ran up and sat down next to me. His hair was sticking up in all directions, as if he hadn't combed it. "I overslept," he said. "Thanks for saving me a seat."

I hadn't, but it seemed rude to say that, so I just nodded.

There was a lurch, and we started off.

The crowd got larger and larger as we drove through town. Mother and Daddy were right near the start of the parade, smiling. Mrs. McDaniels and Sally stood next to them. Sally hadn't been selected to ride on her church's float. She'd complained about it for three days straight at school. Still, I waved to her, and she waved back.

A little further down the route, I saw Curtis and Betty Jean and Pastor George waving so hard, I was afraid their hands would fall off. Next to them was Tommy, and a man and a woman who I guessed must be Liz's parents. I waved at them too.

Little Jimmy was watching me wave at them.

Then the truck turned the corner and they were gone.

Little Jimmy leaned over and whispered, "JT is saying you're still friends with Liz."

I stared at him.

"Are you?" asked Little Jimmy.

I shook my head no.

"Oh," said Little Jimmy, "I was hoping it was true. I liked Liz." He pulled his notebook out and found a stub of pencil and started to write.

I wanted to tell him it was true, but when I counted 2, 3, 5, 7, what came out instead was, "What do you write in there?"

"Words."

"About what?"

"Things that are too hard to say aloud," said Little Jimmy.

Maybe I was the one who needed a notebook, not Liz. "What are you writing now?"

Little Jimmy gave me a funny look. I was sure he wasn't going to answer me, when he said, "How I think you're lying. And that I wish you'd tell her hi for me."

My mouth made a little round O. "If I run into her, I will," I stammered finally.

"Thanks," said Little Jimmy. And he went back to his writing.

I wasn't sure what to think. Now I'd added Little Jimmy to my talking list. He'd accused me of lying, but somehow, I still got the feeling that he wanted to be my friend. After all, he'd warned me about JT.

I thought doing JT's homework meant he would keep his mouth shut. I couldn't think of any other way to get him to be quiet, except to be utterly silent on the topic myself. That way, it'd only seem like mean-spirited gossip. At least, that was what I hoped.

The rest of the parade was ruined by worrying about JT, and when it finally ended and I climbed off, guess who was waiting for me? Yep, that's right. JT himself.

"Congrats, Marlee," JT said. "The mayor just announced your float won first place."

I glared at him.

"What?" he said. "What did I do?"

I turned my back to him. Red was across the street, watching a colored man who was cleaning up after the parade, sweeping trash into a pile. When the man was done, he turned to get his dustpan, and while he wasn't looking, Red walked through the pile, kicking his feet until bits of paper and bottle caps were strewn across the street again. He was humming "White Christmas."

"You missed a spot," said Red.

The man glared at Red once, then slowly started sweeping up the mess.

When he was done, Red stepped into the pile again. "Like jumping in leaves," he said. "Try it, JT. It's fun!"

JT walked into the street and halfheartedly kicked a bottle.

Their father, Mr. Dalton, appeared then. He was a large, beefy man who looked like his younger son, if you blew JT up with a bicycle pump to twice his size. "Come on, boys," he said. "Let's go." His voice was overpowering, like the smell of the schnapps my father sometimes drank after a big meal.

Mrs. Dalton hovered behind him, gray and silent. Red started singing as they walked off, but he changed the words: *"I'm dreaming of a white Central."*

Mr. Dalton laughed.

The colored man gripped his broom tighter and started sweeping yet again, but I could see the rage in his eyes.

31

AN UNWELCOME
CHRISTMAS GIFT

We spent every Christmas with Granny in Pine Bluff. She was short like me, and wore faded dresses that she'd bought way before I was born. Her hair was the color of buttermilk, and that was her drink too, rich and comforting.

When we arrived on Christmas Eve, we put up the tree and strung popcorn chains with cranberries on the pine branches. Judy's boyfriend stopped by to help, though she told Mother and Daddy he was her *friend,* not her *boyfriend.* I thought Robert Laurence was as goofy-looking as he'd seemed in his picture, but he kept smiling at my sister, and she kept grinning back, so I guess he was okay.

Daddy had bought Granny a TV for Christmas. She hadn't had one before. "Don't need one, either—you shouldn't have spent the money" is what she said. But after dinner she was the one who said, "Well, as long as that contraption's here, you might as well set it up."

So while Mother and Judy and I hung the stockings, David and Daddy unwrapped and positioned the new set. We all sat down with a cup of hot chocolate and a bowl of roasted chestnuts to watch the ten o'clock news.

The weatherman was just starting his report. "Now, tonight

we've got something extra special on radar," he said, a twinkle in his eye. "It seems to be a man on a sled being pulled by reindeer." He paused for a moment, examining his screen. "Yes, sir," said the weatherman, grinning, "I do believe Santa Claus is on his way!"

Granny laughed so hard, I was afraid her false teeth would fall out.

After the news, Judy and I went up to her room. There were two twin beds and a small desk where Judy did her homework. Even though we were in the same room, I could feel the distance between us. "Which bed should I take?" I asked.

"You can have the one by the window," said Judy.

I sat down on the worn quilt. There was a large chestnut tree just outside the window.

"Did Granny get the chestnuts from the tree?" I asked. Judy didn't respond. When I turned to look at her, I realized she was already asleep.

I could never sleep on Christmas Eve, so I sat up and gazed at the moon and stars through the branches. Even though I knew I was too old, I kept hoping to see Santa. I didn't feel tired at all, but I guess at some point I must have put my head on the pillow, because a moment later, Judy was shaking me awake. "Merry Christmas, Marlee."

I smiled back. "Merry Christmas, Judy." I put on my robe and followed her down the stairs.

Daddy stood at the bottom, leaning against the railing and sipping a cup of coffee. "There you girls are."

He winked at me and said, "I think Santa might have left you something."

There were oranges and walnuts in my stockings. Judy and I each got new socks and a new sweater (cashmere—mine was pink, and hers was green), and I got a copy of the new Buddy Holly album, *That'll Be the Day*. I was just going to ask to use Granny's record player when Daddy cleared his throat and said, "I believe there's one more present no one has opened yet."

I glanced around the room. I didn't see any unopened boxes. "Where?"

"You have to find it," said Daddy.

"Who's it for?" asked Judy.

"All of you," said Daddy.

Judy and David started searching then, looking in corners and boxes and under scraps of paper. I sat still for a moment and watched Daddy. He kept glancing at the tree.

I went over and looked between the glass balls and the popcorn chains for an ornament we hadn't hung there the day before. It only took me a minute to find it—a small wooden airplane, hand-carved, with a note taped to the tail.

"Marlee's found it!" exclaimed Daddy.

Everyone crowded around me. "What does it say?" asked David.

I unfolded the note and cleared my throat: "This entitles the Nisbett Family to one airplane ride from Pine Bluff to Little Rock."

"An airplane ride?" Mother asked.

"Oh, Daddy," Judy exclaimed, racing over to give him a big hug. "How exciting!"

"Wow!" said David.

"An airplane ride?" I repeated Mother's words.

Daddy picked up the small wooden plane and made it soar through the air, like a little boy playing with a toy. "Flight is one of the modern miracles. Why, I tell you, there's nothing like soaring high over the trees like a bird."

Flying meant we'd be high in the air, looking down. Kind of like standing on the top of the high dive. And that was not an experience I wanted to have again.

"An airplane ride is expensive," said Mother. "We usually buy the children savings bonds."

"Thought we needed something a little more exciting this year," said Daddy.

"Are you going to come with us?" Judy asked Daddy.

"Nah, I've already been up in an airplane twice. Besides, somebody's got to drive the car back to Little Rock."

"How about Granny?" asked David. "You want to come along?"

Granny shook her head. "I remember the first time I rode in an automobile. Seemed unnatural then to move across the ground so quickly. But flying? No, thank you. I'm not a bird, and I'm keeping my two feet firmly on the ground." Then she smiled sheepishly. "Besides, I want to stay home and watch my new TV."

Everyone laughed then, everyone except me. I was longing for a savings bond.

32

THE AIRPLANE RIDE

While we were at Granny's, Judy talked about Robert Laurence so much, David threatened to start charging her a nickel every time she said his name. To be fair, she also asked about my math lessons with Mr. Harding and painted my nails and listened to the Buddy Holly album with me until we both knew all the words by heart. But there was still a distance between us, silences in our conversations where there used to be none. No matter what I did, I couldn't find the right moment to tell her about Liz.

All too soon, it was December 31 and we were driving to the airport. My stomach was one big knot. I knew I was going to hate flying. I didn't like new things. I didn't like heights. Planes were new, and they went high in the air. Plus, they sometimes crashed. All those things were bad.

I wished I could stay with Granny, watching the nice, safe TV. But Daddy was so excited and had spent so much money on the tickets, I couldn't disappoint him. Besides, Liz would kill me if I had a chance to go up in an airplane and didn't take it. At least I had the feather she'd given me in my pocket. A black feather had helped Dumbo fly. Maybe it could help me too.

The Pine Bluff airport was a new building of cement block.

There was a small waiting area with seats and tables and two big doors with numbers over them. A man with a cart was selling Cokes and candy bars. We had about an hour before our flight, so Daddy went over to him and came back carrying a bag of treats.

I opened a PayDay, and the smell of peanuts and caramel, which I usually loved, made me feel sick. Great. The first time in my life I ever got a candy bar all to myself, and I couldn't even take a bite. The others chatted and ate, and the minutes crept by, both too long and way too short.

Daddy drained the last of his Coke and glanced at his watch. "Only ten more minutes. I'm going to check you all in at the gate."

Mother and Judy got up to look at the plane out the window, but David stayed at the table with me. "You gonna eat that?" he said, pointing at my candy bar.

I shook my head.

He picked it up and took a bite. "What's going on with you and Judy?" David asked, his mouth full of peanuts.

"I don't know what you're talking about," I said.

"Come on, Marlee. Usually you and Judy are all up in your room girl-talking so fast, I can't understand half of what you say."

I hadn't realized anyone else had noticed.

"You're acting funny now too," he said.

"No, I'm not."

"You scared about the plane ride?"

"People aren't supposed to fly. Granny said so."

"Granny also said TV was a silly invention. Back before she got one of her own."

I made a face.

"Besides," said David, "I thought you wanted to build rockets."

"Build them, not *fly* in them."

David laughed, and I stuck my tongue out at him. He made me feel a little better. I didn't think Daddy would purposely try to kill us all, but I couldn't shake the feeling that this was a very bad idea.

Daddy came back then, bouncing in his shoes. "It's time. They're going to start boarding."

We threw our trash away, and I made sure the black feather was safely in my pocket. Daddy rounded up Mother and Judy and made us all stand in a line before one of the doors. He handed each of us a small piece of paper which read *Trans-Texas Airways: Pine Bluff, AR, to Little Rock, AR.* Then Daddy went down the line and kissed us all. Like we were going on a long trip. Like we were going off to war. Like he was never going to see us again.

"Have fun!" he called as he waved and walked off. A woman with a cute, short haircut and a navy blue suit took our tickets and ushered us out the door. We stood on the runway until another woman in a matching suit led us across the cement to the plane. There was a set of metal stairs going up to the plane.

"I can't do it," I mumbled, standing in front of the stairs. They looked just like the high dive. The engines were warming up, and it was so loud, no one could hear me.

"I'm not going!" I yelled.

Mother was ahead of me. "What?" she called, turning back briefly, but she wasn't really listening. I automatically followed her. I willed myself to stop and after a moment, I did, right on the second step.

David leaned over and shouted into my ear. "Keep moving, sis."

I shook my head, but he pushed me from behind. I would have fallen, but my stupid feet caught me, and I started going up the stairs. The wind picked up and blew my hair in my face. I felt dizzy. My hands were hot, and my feet were cold, and everything sounded funny, like people talking underwater at the pool. It was like when I did the class presentation. I'd been sure I was going to faint then too.

But I hadn't.

I'd actually done a pretty good job.

I stuck my hand in my pocket and touched the tip of the feather. Before I knew it, I was ducking inside the plane. It was just a metal tube, with two seats on each side of a narrow aisle. Mother sat with David, and Judy and I sat next to each other. The stewardess showed us how to buckle our seat belts. When I looked out the window, I could see a man directing the plane onto the runway.

The plane began to move, and I closed my eyes. I squeezed them tight, until I saw silver stars on the insides of my lids. I wasn't going to open them again until this was all over and we were safely on the ground. Or until we were dead, smushed all over the concrete. I thought the second possibility was much more likely.

But then, the plane gave a funny lurch, like nothing I had ever felt before, and without thinking, I opened my eyes and glanced out the window.

We were only a few feet off the ground, but the plane got higher quickly, rocking back and forth as it climbed. It was a gentle motion, not scary, like being in a cradle for grown-ups.

We flew over the airport parking lot, and I caught a glimpse of Daddy standing by the car and waving like a madman.

A moment later, he was gone. The trees were smaller now, and the roads looked like strips of paper. We were sailing over an old quarry and a river and lots and lots of forest.

I turned to Judy. "Isn't this amazing?"

Judy was staring directly ahead, her face pale and her lips green.

"Are you okay?" I asked.

"Don't talk to me!" Judy snapped.

I glanced over at David and Mother. Mother had one hand on her forehead and was leaning against the seat in front of her. David tried to smile.

"You all right?" I asked.

"Just a little sick," said David.

I felt great. We were flying over a highway now, racing the cars that looked like toys on the road below. Everything went white, and it took me a moment to realize we had flown into a cloud. The cloud looked so solid, I'd have sworn I could jump on it like a feather bed, and yet the plane cut through it as easily as a hot knife in butter. After a moment, I could see the green ground below again, playing peekaboo with me through holes in the clouds.

The woman in the navy uniform came by. "Would you like anything to drink?"

Judy shook her head.

She turned to me. "Coke or coffee?"

"Coke, please," I said firmly, just like a grown-up. Then I realized. I had spoken to a stranger. And I hadn't even counted prime numbers first.

161

The stewardess handed me a small glass bottle, exactly like the one I had been unable to drink at the airport a few minutes before. I was suddenly starving, and wished I had saved my candy bar instead of offering it to my brother. As if she had read my mind, she handed me a package of peanuts. "First time in a plane?" she asked.

I nodded. "For all of us." The words were bubbling out now, fizzing like a shook-up soda. "It was a Christmas gift from Daddy."

The stewardess smiled at me. "How nice of him!"

I glanced over at Judy. She still had her eyes closed.

"Don't worry about your sister," said the stewardess. "Some people get motion sickness. I'll get you a bag in case she needs to be ill."

I nodded again.

"How about you, sweetie? Are you feeling okay?"

"Great," I said, popping a handful of peanuts into my mouth.

"An iron stomach." She laughed. "Maybe someday you'll grow up to be a stewardess like me." Then she turned away to take care of Mother and David.

A stewardess like her. In a fancy blue uniform and flying in a plane like this every day. It sounded like a dream. I stared out the window and watched the clouds and the crops, planted in neat square rows, and I tried to remember every detail so I could tell Liz all about it.

Too soon, the stewardess came back, making sure we had our seat belts fastened because it was time to land. My eyes grew dry as I stared out the window, refusing to blink, refusing to miss a single second of watching the trees and roads and cars and houses slowly grow larger and larger.

There was a bump when we landed, and I heard Mother cry out, but truthfully, it wasn't any worse than going over a pothole in the car. On the ground, I could feel how fast we were going. The brakes screeched and we slowly came to a stop.

"Thank God!" said Judy. She had the bag the stewardess had given her clutched in one hand.

"Amen," said Mother.

I thanked God that neither one of them had actually thrown up.

We got out of our seats and followed the rest of the people to the front of the plane. The door to the cockpit was open, and there were two men in uniform inside, with hundreds of buttons and wires behind them. They stood, greeting each of the passengers as they exited.

"Hello, there," the older man said to me. "Did you enjoy the flight?"

I grinned, too overwhelmed to say anything.

"You don't even need to ask, Bill," said the younger man. "Look at the way her eyes are shining."

As soon as we got home, I called Liz. I told her all about the plane ride. Must have talked for ten minutes straight. "Turns out I have an iron stomach," I finished. "And I didn't even know."

"Wow," said Liz. "Wish I could have been there."

"Me too." I smiled. "You know what?"

"What?"

"I was really scared of flying, and it turned out okay. No, not okay. Great." For the first time, I was thinking out loud. And it was fun. "I think it might be time to try some other things I'm afraid of."

"Like what?" asked Liz.

I wasn't sure. I opened my mouth and just trusted that something would come out. "Talking," I said. "I think I'm going to try talking. Not just to you and Judy and the people on my list, but to everyone."

"Good for you, Marlee," said Liz, and she sounded proud.

"And if I change, maybe other things will change too. Maybe Sally will be nicer. Maybe Mother and I will find more in common. Maybe the schools will reopen!"

"Maybe," said Liz, laughing, and then it was time to hang up.

I wasn't really serious. I knew my talking wouldn't change all that. But as I drifted off to sleep, I thought about what Daddy had said when we were talking in the car. He'd said that things could be different in Little Rock, if only the right people could find their voice.

I wanted to be one of those people.

33

NEW YEAR'S RESOLUTIONS

The first day of school after winter break, I woke up early. Pretty Boy chirped at me from his cage. "Yes," I said, pulling on my new pink sweater. "It is a beautiful day."

Mr. Harding asked for the answer to number fourteen, and no one spoke up, so I raised my hand. It was the first time I'd volunteered an answer, and he grinned just like David as he called on me. I got it right, of course—6,049 divided by 23 is 263. The other kids stared, and their eyes on me made my skin crawl, but then Mr. Harding called on someone else and the itchy feeling was gone.

At lunchtime I asked Mr. Harding if we could work on algebra every other day, so I could still see the other kids too. He nodded. "You know, Marlee, engineers work in groups. I think that's a great idea."

So for the first time in a long time, I walked back to the cafeteria. I stood in front of the closed doors and concentrated, imagining myself a princess, making a grand entrance at a ball. I counted 13, 17, 19, 23, pushed open the doors and went inside.

No one even looked up. JT was at a far table, talking with his friends. Little Jimmy sat alone, and Nora and Sally were at our old table. I silently counted my steps as I walked over to them. "Hi," I said. It came out a lot louder and shriller than I intended, but when Sally looked up, she smiled.

"Marlee," she said. "You're back!"

Nora pulled out a chair for me. "You all done with the math stuff?"

"Not all done," I said, sitting down. "But the rest can wait until tomorrow." This was easier than I thought.

"Doing math for fun." Sally laughed. "Marlee, you're such a square."

Or not so easy after all. I couldn't believe Sally was starting again with the insults, and I hadn't even been there five minutes. I touched the feather in my pocket. This time, I wasn't going to let it go. "I do think math is fun," I said. "But don't call me a square."

Sally rolled her eyes. "I was just teasing. Don't be so sensitive."

"It's mean," I said. "And I don't like it."

Sally looked at Nora, as if to say, *Can you believe her?*

Nora shrugged. "She's right. Sometimes you are kind of mean."

Sally opened and closed her mouth several times. I could almost see the words floating through her head as she struggled to find something to say. Finally, she just shrugged. "Sorry," she said.

Nora gave a nervous giggle. Sally had never apologized before.

I shrugged too. "I am probably a little square," I said, and we all laughed.

Nora started talking about winter break. It felt good to sit back and eat my cheese sandwich and listen to her complain about little sisters and socks for presents and all sorts of normal things. Then I remembered I didn't have to just sit back and listen. I could say something too. I could tell them about the airplane ride.

I was trying to find the right moment to speak up, when JT walked over to our table. "Hi, Marlee," he said, real friendly. "I need a favor."

I gave him a look. It was supposed to mean *go away and leave me alone,* but apparently he thought it meant *please go on,* because he kept talking.

"Mr. Harding said I was missing a couple of assignments." He put a piece of paper down on top of my sandwich. "They're listed there. You can give them to me tomorrow in homeroom."

I was beginning to think JT was like the nasty phone calls—scary, but all hot air. And there was only one way to find out if I was right.

"No," I said.

"What?"

"I'm not doing your homework anymore."

I braced myself for his anger. The shock. The threats. The drama of the shy little quiet girl saying no to the big strong football player. But JT didn't look surprised. He didn't even look irritated. He seemed kind of amused. In fact, he was grinning at me. "I always knew you were a pretty girl, Marlee, but you're even cuter when you're angry."

"I'm not angry." Of course I was angry. I'd been doing his homework all year!

He shrugged. "It's no problem. I'll just find someone else to do the work for me."

"You can't do that," I said. "It's cheating!"

JT laughed.

Of course, it had been cheating when I'd done it too, but I preferred not to dwell on that fact.

"I like your pink sweater!" JT called out as he walked off.

I wasn't sure if I was proud of myself for finally standing up to him, or embarrassed it had taken me so long to do so.

The next Tuesday at the rock crusher I was planning on telling Liz all about standing up to Sally and JT. But as soon as I got there, Liz started talking. "You know Curtis, right? Betty Jean's son."

"Yes."

Liz blushed, which made me even more curious to know what was going on. "He's in youth group with me at church and in ninth grade at Dunbar, but he'd never spoken to me. Then today he saw me writing in my journal, and he came over to see what I was doing. We started talking, and we realized we both know you."

"That's great." Actually, I was worried. What if she dumped me for him like Judy had done with Robert Laurence? I wanted her to stop exploding when she was teased, not get a boyfriend! But I couldn't say that, so I just asked, "You didn't tell him we were still friends, did you?"

"No," said Liz. "But I think he guessed."

"Yeah," I said. "I think Little Jimmy guessed too. He says *hi*."

"Hi." Liz looked pleased. "You tell him *hi* right back."

"How long can we keep this up?" I asked.

"I don't know," said Liz. "But I hope for a really long time."

I hoped so too.

34

MAIL, MEASLES AND MORE

My thirteenth birthday was January 27, 1959. Daddy gave me a pink purse, Granny sent me ten dollars, David gave me a new satchel for school, Judy sent a card *(Happy Birthday, Little Sis! Hope you have a great day. Send me a piece of cake!)* and Mother gave me a silver letter opener. "I noticed you're getting more mail," she said. I guess she meant the WEC flyers and the letters from Judy, though those were usually postcards. Still, it was a nice gesture.

"Look," Mother pointed out, "I had your name engraved."

Sure enough, *Marlene Nisbett* was written on the blade. I didn't have a middle name. David had one. Judy had one. By the time I came along, I guess my parents were both too busy to pick one out.

"Did I ever tell you I named you after Marlene Dietrich?" Mother asked.

No, she hadn't.

"She was my favorite movie star. So glamorous. Even as a baby, I knew you were someone special."

Suddenly, having no middle initial didn't seem quite so bad. I ran my finger over the engraved letters and slipped the letter opener into my new purse along with the black feather from Liz.

While my talking experiment was going well with Sally and the other kids at school, I still couldn't figure out how to speak to Mother. The problem was, we hadn't had a conversation in so long, it seemed like we didn't have anything to say. So we didn't talk, and by not talking, we made it even worse.

It was like a repeating decimal. You can divide 10 by 3 for as long as you want, but all you're going to get is 3.33333 with ever more 3s after it. There had to be some way to finish the problem. Daddy and I talked after dinner while we did the dishes, and once I caught Mother watching us, envious, as if she were trying to figure out the easy flow of conversation she and I could never catch.

The next day, I didn't feel quite right. I dragged myself through school, determined to show off my new stuff (Nora liked the letter opener, Sally liked the money), but when I got home, Betty Jean took one look at me and ordered me up to bed. I didn't complain. Not even when she brought me a bowl of chicken soup and ordered me to open my mouth.

Betty Jean pulled my lower lip gently and looked at my gums. "Yup, white dots. Girl, you got the measles."

She was right. The next morning, I had a fever, cough and fine red spots all over my body. All I wanted to do was sleep.

Everyone else had had the measles, of course. Mother and Daddy and Betty Jean a long time ago, and Judy and David a year or two before I was born. But I had a bad case—my eyes turned red, and I had to lie in the dark in my room hour after hour.

Miss Winthrop stopped by one afternoon, a few of her blond curls escaping from the scarf she'd tied over her head. "Thought you could use some company," she said. "Nothing

170

worse than sitting in the dark alone. I brought some WEC flyers for us to fold to keep our hands busy."

I felt well enough to sit up and help her for a while. Betty Jean brought up the radio from the kitchen, and it felt like a little party, until we heard the news. February 3, 1959. There was a small plane crash in Clear Lake, Iowa. Buddy Holly, Ritchie Valens, and J. P. Richardson, a.k.a. the Big Bopper, were all aboard. There were no survivors.

Miss Winthrop gave a little gasp, and I thought she was going to cry. We didn't fold anymore, just listened to the radio play "La Bamba" and "Chantilly Lace" and "Peggy Sue" over and over again.

When Miss Winthrop left, my fever got higher and higher. In the evening, Mother called Dr. Agar, our family doctor. He brought his black bag and pulled out his stethoscope. It was cool on my back. He gave me a lollipop, like I was a baby. I was too tired to lick it, so I put it on my dresser as he turned to talk to my mother.

"There's isn't much I can do for her," he said. "Measles has to run its course. Just try to keep her comfortable."

That night I dreamed of flying and plane crashes and Judy stealing my lollipop. In the morning, I woke up more tired than when I went to sleep. But I was thirsty, and no one came when I rang the little bell Betty Jean had put next to my bed, so I pulled on my robe and crept down the hall.

Daddy had already gone to work, but Mother was sitting at the table, the paper open in front of her.

"Mother?"

She jumped and sat up quick, like she was a burglar and I'd caught her stealing.

"Marlee, you should be in bed."

"I'm thirsty."

"I'll pour you a glass of tea."

I sat down at the table, tired by my walk down the hall. Mother went to the fridge. There was a big article in the newspaper about the plane crash and Buddy Holly. Underneath it was another smaller article: *Closed Schools in Virginia Reopen; School Crisis in Little Rock Drags On.*

Mother handed me a glass of tea and followed my gaze.

"Ever since I was a little girl, I've been proud to live in Little Rock. Proud to be from the South. But this . . . it's been going on too long."

I held my breath.

"Frankly, I don't care who she goes to school with anymore. I just want Judy to come home."

Me too. "We should do something about it," I said finally.

"What can we do?"

I went back to my room and brought out the box of flyers Miss Winthrop and I had been folding. I handed one to Mother. It said:

Saying what you think is as important as thinking it!
Speak out for public schools!

I sat down and started folding, and after a moment, so did Mother. We didn't say a word, but I couldn't help thinking maybe this was it. Maybe this was the way Mother and I would finally connect. Working on a project together had turned Liz and me into friends. Maybe it would work with Mother too.

35

MOTHER GETS INVOLVED

I was home sick for most of February. Liz called once or twice a week, pretending to be "Lisa, from math class." On Valentine's Day, Little Jimmy showed up on our front porch, with his skinny legs and his old bike. I was in my old pink bathrobe when I opened the door, which was kind of embarrassing, but Little Jimmy smiled at me like I was wearing a ball gown.

"Hello," he said.

"Hi."

"I brought you your school assignments." He handed me a page, torn out of his notebook, that listed all my work.

"Thanks," I said. And for the first time I noticed that his large eyes were a pretty golden-brown color like a caramel candy.

He turned to go, and I suddenly called out, "Liz says hi too."

Little Jimmy smiled.

"You won't tell anyone?" I asked.

"Of course not!" said Little Jimmy. "Feel better, Marlee."

That night, I searched through all the papers and books he had brought, looking for a card or paper heart, but I didn't find one. I was a little disappointed.

It was early March by the time I was well enough to go

back to school. When the day finally came, I was excited. "Ready to go, Daddy?" I asked.

"Mother's going to take you today."

"Why?"

"I'm going to be subbing at your school," said Mother.

"What?"

"The school board came up with the idea of using the high school teachers as substitutes at the schools for the younger students," explained Mother. "They get qualified substitutes, and the school system saves money, since they're paying us regardless."

"You two can take the car," said Daddy. "I'll ride the bus."

Now, I love my mother. I was glad she had helped me fold the flyers. But the only thing I could imagine that was worse than being in junior high was having Mother come with me to junior high.

"Some of the other teachers are against it," Mother continued as we drove to school. "I guess they think it's beneath them to teach the younger grades. Or maybe they're afraid of maintaining order. But I'm thrilled to finally have something to do."

I nodded and prayed that no one would see us together. Soon as we arrived at school, I waved to her. "Bye!" I said. "See you at home."

She headed off to the office to get her assignment.

I went on to Miss Taylor's class and found my seat. Sally leaned over to me. "Welcome back."

"Thanks," I said.

"Was that your mother I saw outside the school this morning?" Sally asked.

"No," I lied, and got up to sharpen my pencil.

JT caught up with me at the sharpener. "Marlee!" he exclaimed. "You're back."

I sighed. "Hi, JT."

"Am I ever glad to see you," he said. "I tried cheating off Sally, but she's not so good at math, and Mr. Harding said if I don't get help soon, he's going to have to hold me back."

"JT," I said, "I told you I'm done helping you."

"Okay, okay. Can't blame a guy for asking. One of these days you'll change your mind."

Not in a million years.

The bell rang, and we both took our seats.

Miss Taylor still wasn't there. I can't believe I didn't realize what was going to happen, but I didn't, not until the door opened and she came in.

My mother smiled at me. She actually waved, like she was on stage or something. I tried to sink down into my seat and disappear.

"Hello, class. My name is Mrs. Nisbett." She wrote her name on the board in big block letters. "Miss Taylor is out sick with the flu, so today I'm going to be your teacher."

JT raised his hand. "Aren't you Marlee's mother?"

"Why, yes." Mother looked pleased. "Yes, I am."

What I wouldn't have given for another case of the measles.

In the cafeteria, the talk was all about Sally's upcoming birthday party. She was going to have it at Troy's Roller Rink and had invited everyone. When I'd had my fill of discussing cake flavors and party dresses, I got up and walked over to where Little Jimmy was writing in his notebook. "Hi," I said.

"Hi," he said, and blushed.

"Thanks for bringing my homework by my house."

Little Jimmy shrugged. "No problem."

"Want to come sit with Sally and Nora and me?" I asked.

He glanced at Sally and Nora, then back at me. "Why?"

"Well," I started, "it's a big table, and Sally always sits at that end, and I'm in the middle, but there's no one at the other end. And you're here by yourself, and I just thought, why use two tables when one would work?"

"Oh."

"And I wanted to say thank you for bringing by my homework," I finished.

"You mentioned that," he said.

"So will you?" I asked.

"Sure." He smiled and picked up his notebook.

I took his bagged lunch and moved it to the far end of our table.

"Marlee, what are you doing?" asked Sally.

"Inviting Little Jimmy to join us for lunch," I said.

"Why?" asked Sally.

"If it's a problem . . . ," said Little Jimmy.

"No," I said. "Sit down."

He did.

Sally rolled her eyes and continued her discussion of party decorations with Nora.

Little Jimmy kept his eyes on his notebook. He still had his pen in his hand, as if he couldn't decide if he should talk to me or continue writing. I remembered what Liz had said to me. "Don't worry," I whispered. "You don't have to actually talk to me. Just sitting here is enough."

Little Jimmy smiled and put his pen down. His eyes

crinkled, and I knew what he was doing. He was saying the words in his head. I wondered what was going to come out.

Just then, Mother came over to our table.

"Marlee, do you know Mrs. Dalton's boy, that nice James-Thomas?" asked Mother.

Of course I knew JT. But Mother pointed him out like I'd never seen him before. He turned, as if he could feel her gaze, and waved. She grinned in return.

"Yes," I said finally.

"Well," said Mother, "he told me he was having trouble in math, and you're so good at it, I thought you could tutor him. He said that would be swell and to meet him today after school in the library. I've got some paperwork to do anyway, so I'll wait for you, and then we can drive home together."

What? I'd finally told him *no*, once and for all, and my mother had gone and told him *yes*. I was so mad, I couldn't think straight. The words bottled up in my throat like people running from a fire, all trying to rush the door at once.

I glared at her, hoping she would notice something was wrong. But she just looked pleased with herself.

"Well, I have to go get ready for my next class. See you after lunch, Marlee!"

Little Jimmy watched her go. Then he turned back to me, with his big brown eyes. "Are you okay, Marlee?"

I shook my head.

The final bell rang, and it was time to go to the library. I trudged there, my feet as heavy as my heart. JT was sitting on a table waiting for me. "Hi, Marlee!"

I opened my own math book and did the assignment.

Furiously. Pressing the pencil down so hard, it broke. Twice. Each time I had to get up to sharpen it, I told myself I could just walk out of there. I could flee. I wasn't chained to the desk or anything. I could just go to Mother and tell her everything, tell her I had liked JT, but now I didn't, and I didn't want to do his work anymore, but I needed help telling him no, and she wasn't helping. JT kept whistling the entire time, flipping through the pages of a comic book.

When I was done, I picked up the paper and threw it at him. But paper doesn't throw very well, unless you fold it into a paper airplane, which I hadn't done, so it just kind of slid into his lap.

"Thanks, Marlee," said JT as he placed the homework in his comic book and closed it. "See you around." And he started to stroll out of the library.

I hated him. I was going to tell him so. I was going to throw words like daggers at him, I was just figuring out which ones to say. *If you ask me to do your homework again, I'll tell Mr. Harding. I'll get my big brother to come beat you up and—*

My mother walked into the library. "You kids done already?" she asked.

"Yes, ma'am," said JT.

"Well then, come on. I'll drive you home."

I sat in the backseat as far away from JT as possible, pressing myself into the side door. Neither he nor Mother seemed to notice. Mother chattered the whole way home, and JT laughed at all the right spots. When we reached JT's house, Mrs. Dalton was waiting on the front porch with a tray of lemonade.

JT climbed out first, and Mother turned back to me. "Get out, Marlee, and let's go say hello."

I shook my head.

"Marlee!"

I got out of the car. Mrs. Dalton looked like a delicate bird wrapped in a silk scarf, huddled up in a wicker chair on her porch. She acted glad to see us, though she didn't say much. The lemonade was too sweet, and the cookies were dry and crumbly. Mother and JT chatted and laughed, while I got quieter and quieter.

"Are you going to Sally's party next month?" JT asked.

I nodded.

"What's this?" asked Mother.

"Sally McDaniels is having a birthday party at the roller rink," explained JT. "I wanted to ask if Marlee would go with me."

What? Like a date?

"Oh, that would be lovely," said Mother.

No, it wouldn't. It would be terrible.

But even Mrs. Dalton nodded. "I'd be happy to drive them there and pick them up."

"Then it's decided," said Mother.

No one even asked me what I thought. And I didn't say a thing.

36

FACING FEARS

Tuesday afternoon in the rock crusher, I felt pretty down when I met Liz. "I've been doing so well!" I moaned. "Speaking up, saying what I mean. And then my mother had to come to school and ruin it all!"

Liz and I were leaning against the big stone in the meadow and looking at the sky. "I don't understand why you're so upset. I thought you kind of liked JT."

I'd never told her what JT had called her when he'd found out she was colored. I didn't see a reason to now. "That was ages ago," I said. "JT is a jerk."

"Maybe you like someone else?" asked Liz. "Little Jimmy?"

I laughed. "He's four feet tall and as skinny as a bean pole."

She shrugged. "People grow. I always thought he was kind of nice."

He was kind of nice. On the float, asking about Liz, I'd thought he liked her too. And he'd brought me my homework on Valentine's Day. Maybe Liz was right. Maybe I really should give him a second look.

"Come on," said Liz. "It's a beautiful day. Tommy has an extra-long practice. Two hours. There must be something I can do to cheer you up."

It was a beautiful day. It was only March, but it was warm

and the field was full of wild crocuses, jonquils and Indian paintbrush. When I was little, Judy and I would spend every afternoon like this in the rock crusher, picking flowers and wading in the creek.

"Let's catch crawdads," I said.

"Ugh," said Liz. "Isn't there something else you want to do?"

I turned and looked at her in surprise. Liz was usually game for anything. "What's wrong with crawdads?"

Liz blushed. "I don't like creepy-crawly things. Spiders. Roaches. Crawdads."

I had to keep myself from grinning. It made me feel good to know that there was *something* she was afraid of. "Isn't it important to face your fears?" I asked.

"Do I have to get in the water to catch them?"

"Oh, yeah," I said. "That's the best part."

"Then, no."

"You weren't afraid of turtles."

"They are reptiles. With a nice hard shell. And no scary pinchers."

"Come on, Liz."

She looked at me a long time. "What are you afraid of?"

"Talking."

Liz laughed. "Besides that."

I thought for a moment. "Heights."

"Fine," said Liz. "I'll catch those crawdad thingies with you, but then you have to climb a tree with me."

"Facing our fears, huh?"

"You know it."

And because I realized I wasn't thinking about JT or Mother or the roller-skating party anymore, I agreed.

Which is how we found ourselves with our shoes and socks off, holding our skirts up as we waded in the creek. The water was cold, but the sun was warm on our backs. "My toes are freezing," complained Liz.

I ignored her. "What you have to do is flip over a rock or old log or something. Anything where a crawdad might like to hide."

I flipped over a rock. There was a huge crawdad, six inches long, just sitting there. I scooped it up with an old tin can we had found in the woods and brought it over to show Liz.

She took one look at it and shivered. I grinned and dumped it back into the stream.

"Your turn now," I said. Liz turned over a rock or two but found nothing.

"You need bigger rocks," I said, and pointed to a small boulder a few feet away.

It was heavy, so I helped Liz flip it over. "I see one!" she exclaimed, and was so excited, she dropped her skirt in the water.

I handed her the can. "Scoop it up."

"It might pinch me."

"Put the can in the water, a few inches behind the crawdad, but far enough away that you don't scare it."

Liz, moving slowly, placed the can into a crevice between two stones directly behind the crawdad. I handed her a stick. "Now wiggle the stick in front of the little guy. Pretend you're a fish or a snapping turtle or something."

Liz looked doubtful, but splashed the stick in the water right in front of the crawdad. Just like I knew it would, it moved a few steps backward.

"Again," I said. "Keep him moving back into the can."

Liz didn't breathe as she wiggled the stick. The crawdad moved into the can. Only one little pincher was peeking out.

"What now?" whispered Liz.

"Now you pick it up."

Liz bent over and put her hands in the water. She reached for the can, and slowly drew it out of the water. She was so quiet, we could hear the crawdad scrabbling inside. "I got it!" she breathed.

"Not so bad, was it?"

Liz couldn't stop grinning. "Come on," she said. "Let's catch some more."

An hour later, it was my turn. We stood in front of a huge oak tree on the edge of the meadow. I looked up. "You expect me to climb this?" I asked.

"Hey," said Liz. "I caught those creepy little things."

"You liked it," I said.

"Well, then, maybe you will too."

I sighed. "What do I do first?"

"Reach up and grab that branch," said Liz.

I did so.

"Now pull yourself up."

I gave her a look.

"Just that branch," Liz said. "You don't have to go any higher."

So I pulled, and she pushed, and then I was up in the tree, my arms wrapped around the trunk. You'd think that after going up in an airplane, climbing a tree would be easy. But it wasn't. You can't fall out of a plane. There's a seat belt. And the wind blows, but it's outside, not trying to loosen your grip on the branches. I felt dizzy and closed my eyes and started to count . . . 2, 3, 5, 7 . . .

Then I felt Liz's hand on my shoulder. "Open your eyes," she said.

I did. I was only about five feet off the ground, but already I was surrounded by leaves and oak flowers. It was a different world. There were even a few old bunches of acorns from last fall, clinging to the branches.

"Are you all right?"

I nodded. And it was true. My heart was beating fast and I was scared, but I knew that feeling now. I'd had it before. When I did the presentation at school and when I got on the airplane, and both times I'd been okay.

"All you have to do," said Liz slowly, "is watch my hands and feet. Put your hands where I put my hands. Place your feet where my feet go, and you'll be fine."

I nodded.

Liz started to climb. I stared at her white lace socks and saddle shoes, and I watched where her right hand went (she had a bit of dirt under her thumb) and where her left hand went (there was a bit of old red nail polish on her ring finger), and I repeated times tables in my head until I was able to follow her. Pretty soon, we were high enough that I could feel the tree swaying back and forth in the wind.

"It's okay," said Liz. "It's not going to blow over or anything."

But I wasn't worried. "It's like flying," I said. "The airplane rocks like that when you take off."

"Isn't the view amazing?" Liz sighed.

I was still staring at her feet. Taking a deep breath, I gripped the tree tighter and wrenched my gaze away from her saddle shoes.

The view was beautiful. In one direction, I could see the large rock we liked to sit on, and in the other, the rolling Arkansas hills. The late-afternoon sun turned all the new light green leaves to gold, like King Midas had been walking through the forest.

"It worked," I said. "You cheered me up."

Liz didn't say a word. She didn't have to. We stayed in the tree a long time, watching the leaves and the squirrels and listening to the birds. Together.

37

THE ROLLER-SKATING PARTY

The week before the party, Mother and I went to Cohn's Department Store to buy me a new dress. I knew Mother was trying to be nice, but I would have preferred to have worn a hand-me-down from Judy and spent the money on a new package of graph paper, a box of pencils and a new protractor. The whole time we were at the store, I kept thinking, *I don't want to go with JT.* But what kept coming out instead was "Do you like this color?" or "Is this one too expensive?" I ended up getting a yellow dress with a full skirt that flew out like a buttercup when I twirled around. Mother said I looked beautiful. But I was disappointed I hadn't managed to say one real sentence to her, not one that told her how I was really feeling.

The night of the party, Daddy took my picture and wiped pretend tears from his eyes. "My little girl is growing up." He sniffed, and I smiled as I waited by the window for JT to pull up.

It was raining, but finally an old gray Chrysler Windsor pulled up to the curb and JT walked up to our door. He had a suit on, a bit too big, but he looked nice, if only I didn't think about how he was a cheat and a racist. Daddy snapped one more picture, and we walked out to the car. I had my pink purse in one hand and Sally's present in the other.

JT opened the door, and we slid into the backseat. The car started moving, and I looked into the front seat, expecting to see Mr. or Mrs. Dalton. Instead, Red sat behind the driver's wheel.

My heart started beating in time with the windshield wipers, only twice as fast.

"You still friends with that colored girl?" asked Red at a stoplight.

I didn't answer. My stomach hurt as if my mother had dosed me with castor oil.

"Leave her alone," said JT.

"JT's in looooooove," teased Red.

"No, I'm not," snapped JT. Then he looked at me, aghast. "I didn't mean . . ."

He needn't have worried. I certainly wasn't in love with him.

Finally, about ten hours later (for some reason my watch only said eight minutes), we turned onto Asher Avenue, and there we were. A neon sign blinked at us from the parking lot: TROY'S ROLLER RINK.

"When's this stupid thing over?" asked Red.

"Nine," said JT.

"Well, don't keep me waiting," Red snapped. "I got better things to do than drive you two around."

The car rolled to a stop, and we jumped out. Mrs. McDaniels was waiting for us at the door. "Welcome, Marlee, welcome, JT. Everyone's inside."

When she said everyone, she wasn't kidding. In order to get the maximum number of presents, Sally had invited every single person in our class. There was a gift table by the door, so I put my present down and looked around.

I'd been to Troy's with my sister once or twice before, but

never for a party. The rink was a large, open room with a hard wooden floor. There was a snack bar, where Mr. McDaniels was setting up a cake, and an organ in one corner, where old Mrs. Chapman, the piano teacher from down the street, was playing a polka. The strangest thing about Troy's was a huge quote painted on the wall. It read *The more you skate, the more you learn. The more you learn, the more you skate.* I could never quite figure out what that meant.

I sat down to put on my skates (I had to rent a pair since I didn't have my own), and when I was done, Sally and Nora skated over to me. Sally's dress was so pink and frothy, she looked like a piece of cotton candy. She had new white leather roller skates, and I couldn't help feeling a little envious. Nora was in lime green, the color all wrong for her complexion.

"Glad you made it, Marlee," said Sally. "We're going to do the limbo later!" And with a flip of her hair, she was off.

JT rolled up to me then, in black leather skates, carrying a cup of punch. "For you," he said with a little bow.

I nodded, took the punch and put it on the side of the rink.

"Oh, come on, Marlee," JT pleaded. "Don't be cross. Let's skate."

He took my hand and pulled me onto the floor, linking his arm through mine. I kept my arm stiff, standing as far from him as possible as we started to skate in circles around the room.

"Why don't you like me?" asked JT.

"Why do you care?" I asked.

"Maybe I want your good opinion."

"Maybe you want help with your math."

JT smiled. I could see a little bit of the golden child who got away with everything.

"I mean it, Marlee. What'd I do?"

I thought for a moment. What was the harm? I might as well tell him the truth. "You called Liz a name," I said. "When we all found out she was colored."

"You're upset because I called your friend a ni—"

"Don't call her that!"

"Gosh, Marlee, you're a square tonight. Defending your *colored* friends."

"Why shouldn't I defend my friends?"

"Negroes are not your friends," said JT. "They are trying to destroy our schools and—"

"Who told you that?"

"Red. And my father. They said—"

"Liz never did a thing to you. You liked her. Probably would have been trying to get her to do your English homework for you if she were still here."

JT laughed. "Yeah. That sounds like me."

We skated for a moment without talking, the polka music oompahing along.

Finally, JT shrugged. "Maybe you're right. I didn't much care last year when those nine students first started at Central. But then my father said it wasn't right. Red skipped school to make signs and protest. And Liz did lie to us! I don't like dishonesty."

I snorted. "Don't seem to have a problem with it when it comes to math homework."

"Yeah, well . . . I got no problem with Negroes, long as they stay in their place."

"Which is?"

"Driving your car and shining your shoes and cleaning your house."

"Liz is about ten times smarter than you. Why should she clean your house?"

"Marlee, you can't say stuff like that. People will call you a communist."

"I don't care."

"Well, I do. And my brother wouldn't say those things if they weren't true."

"Really?" I snapped. "Red's a great scholar, is he?"

"Shut up."

We skated in silence again. The organist switched over to a waltz, and the lights dimmed, but JT gripped my arm, and we kept skating. Little Jimmy was watching us from the side of the rink. I waved at him, but he just scowled and looked away. I suddenly remembered Judy had said waltzes were for couples. Did Little Jimmy think . . .

"Are you still friends with her?" JT asked.

I said nothing.

"Red says you are, but I didn't think you'd—"

I nodded.

"But she's, she's . . . ," JT sputtered.

"A Negro?" I supplied.

"A colored girl and a white girl can't be friends," said JT.

"Says who?" I asked.

"Says everyone!" exclaimed JT. "That's why we go to different schools and churches, and . . . that's why the high schools are closed!"

"Then maybe," I said quietly, "everyone is wrong."

I finally dropped his arm and skated away from him, and it wasn't as hard as I'd thought it would be. JT drifted on, finally coming to a stop in the middle of the floor. Even with a frown on his face, he still looked handsome, and it irked me. Sally skated over to him and grabbed his arm, and he waltzed off with her.

I sat in a metal folding chair on the edge of the room until the song was over. My fingers were cold. I shouldn't have told JT about Liz. It had been reckless and foolish, and yet it had felt good to speak my mind.

I imagined a magic square to calm down, all the rows and columns and diagonals adding up to fifteen. Fifteen. How old I'd be in two years. A year older than Emmett Till was when he was killed. For the first time, the magic square didn't really work.

It was time for the limbo then. I threw myself into it, trying to stop thinking. Maybe because I'm small and short, I was good at it. Pretty soon, Sally and I were the only ones left. I'm pretty sure I could have won, but it was her party, so I tripped on purpose.

Sally got a bouquet of flowers as the winner, and I got a single rose as the runner-up, and Mrs. McDaniels made us take a victory lap around the rink so she could get some pictures.

"You know," said Sally as we were skating, clutching our flowers, "I didn't throw away my hairbrush."

"What?" I didn't know what she was talking about.

"The one I loaned to Liz. I know I said I did, but . . . it's a nice brush. I washed it in the sink, but then I thought, if I hadn't gotten lice yet . . ."

Had she overheard JT and me talking? Was she saying she was wrong?

"I just wanted you to know I hadn't thrown it away," said Sally.

"But you said—"

"What you say with your friends is one thing," she said. "How you really feel, that's another."

Not with Liz, I thought. With her, I say how I really feel.

For the first time, I felt a little sorry for Sally, that she didn't have a friend with whom she could do the same.

"Come on," said Nora, skating up to us. "Let's go have cake."

The organ lady played "Happy Birthday," and we all sang, and Sally blew out the candles. While I was eating the sweet cake, I noticed the quote on the walls again: *The more you skate, the more you learn. The more you learn, the more you skate.*

It made sense this time. It was about practice. The more I talked, the better I got at it. The better I got at it, the more I wanted to do it. I'd been waiting for it to feel natural for me to talk to my mother, waiting for just the right moment. But maybe that was the wrong approach. Maybe I had to talk to her first, and then, after I did, maybe it would start to feel natural.

In any case, I knew one thing. I didn't want to ride home with Red. I had a dime in my purse and found the pay phone in the corner. Watching the numbers go around and around as I dialed made me dizzy. I wished I had a napkin or something to jot down what I was going to say, but there weren't any nearby, and I didn't have a pen anyway. I'd just have to figure it out on my own.

"Hello?"

Drat, it was Mother. I'd been hoping Daddy would answer the phone.

"Hi," I said. "It's me."

"Marlee?"

"Can you come pick me up?"

"Why?" said Mother. "I thought the Daltons were bringing you home. It's not even eight thirty."

"I don't feel well."

"Womanly troubles?" asked Mother.

That was her way of asking if I had cramps.

"Something like that," I said. "I don't want to say anything to JT and—"

"Oh, of course not," agreed Mother. "I'll be right there."

I told JT I wasn't feeling well, and he didn't say a word. I wanted to tell Sally I was leaving early, but she was busy opening presents. I put my street shoes back on and went to wait by the door.

Little Jimmy walked up to me. "Why'd you come with JT?" he asked.

I shook my head. "It's too complicated to explain."

"Oh," he said, shifting from one skate to the other, like he wasn't really comfortable on them. "Well, I wanted to give you this." He handed me a piece of folded paper.

I unfolded the paper. It was a page from his journal, dated February 28, 1959. *I'm planning to ask Marlee to go with me to Sally's skating party when she comes back to school. I hope she says yes.*

"But then I heard you were going with JT," Little Jimmy said when I looked up at him. "So I never asked."

"Oh, Jimmy," I said. "I wish you had."

"Yeah," he said. "Me too."

A horn honked then, and it was Mother.

"Bye," I said. "See you at school."

"See you."

I slid into the front seat, and Mother drove off before I could even figure out exactly what had happened.

"Hi, sweetie," Mother said. "Are you feeling any better?"

I almost said *yes* or shrugged or made up some other lie. But then I remembered, *The more you skate, the more you learn,* and I thought about Liz and doing what you were afraid of, and I realized I'd never have a better chance.

"No," I said.

"I'll get you a hot water bottle when we get home."

I could let it go, or I could speak up. "That's not going to help."

"What?"

I took a deep breath and counted 17, 19, 23, 29. "JT's been making me do his homework for him all year, and when I finally told him *no* because it was cheating, you made me do it again. And then Red drove us there tonight, and he hates colored people and eggs houses and is really creepy." Once I started, I couldn't seem to stop. "And Little Jimmy was planning on asking me to go to the party with him, and I actually think I like him, but you set me up with JT first. And Sally still brushes her hair." Okay, so that last bit didn't make sense without an explanation, but Mother didn't seem to notice.

The blood drained from Mother's face, like I'd seen it do only once before, the time she'd got the phone call telling her that Granddaddy had died.

"Marlee," Mother said, her voice breaking, "I thought you liked JT?"

"I did," I said. "About four months ago." I hadn't said this much to her in years.

"I'm sorry," she said. "I didn't mean to interfere."

I waited for her to lecture me about cheating on homework, or say I shouldn't be scared of Red, or at least ask what I meant about Sally's hair. But Mother didn't. She didn't say another word.

38

SECRETS ON THE BUS

Judy came home for Easter. Things were still odd between us. We'd only exchanged a few postcards since Christmas. I did an extra-thorough job cleaning up my room the night before she arrived, just in case she wanted to be roommates again. But Daddy put her bag down in David's room, and she didn't tell him to move it.

So I was kind of surprised when she suggested we take the bus across town to see David at college one evening. Mother and Daddy agreed and gave Judy some money for dinner, and before I knew it, we were on our way.

The bus wasn't crowded. We sat next to each other, not touching. In the old days, Judy would put her arm around me, and I'd lean my head on her shoulder. I kept expecting her to start talking, to give me advice like she always did. But she didn't. I wanted to tell her something—anything—so we'd have another secret to share.

"Judy?" I said.

"Hmmm?" It was raining outside and the bus was warm.

"You know that friend I had? Liz."

"The one who was colored?" asked Judy.

"Yeah."

"What about her?"

I glanced around the bus to make sure there was no one I knew. There wasn't. "I'm still friends with her."

"What?" Judy sat up.

"Sometimes we talk on the phone. And on Tuesdays we meet in the rock crusher."

"Marlee!"

"Don't tell Mother and Daddy."

"Of course not. But why—"

"You're the one who was always telling me to find someone I had stuff in common with, someone I liked. Well, I did. It's not my fault she's not exactly who I expected."

Judy gave me a long look. Before she could say anything else, the bus reached our stop and we stumbled out into the rain.

David was waiting for us. "Hey, sis one and sis two," he said. "Long time no see." I ran over and gave him a hug.

We went to a cafeteria near his dorm. I ordered fried chicken and chocolate pudding and pecan pie, and no one said a word about me not selecting a single vegetable. It didn't take long before David was talking all about the high schools being closed. "Most of the displaced white students have found some-where to go to school. Like ninety percent or so."

"Not Red," I said.

"That's his choice," said David. "His parents could totally afford to send him to private school. But fifty percent of the colored students haven't been to school at all."

"Where'd you learn all this?" asked Judy.

"Meetings."

"What kind of meetings?"

"There are a couple of colored students here now. I talked to one and—"

"I work for the WEC," I said. "That's the Women's Emergency Committee to Open Our Schools."

"I know," said David. "Daddy told me. That's how I got the idea. One of my friends knows a professor at Philander Smith. That's a Negro college in town. We all got together for a meeting at the house of one of the professors. He served us wine and everything. Anyway, everyone's in a tizzy over Act 10."

"What's that?" asked Judy.

"It's a new law requiring all state employees to turn in a list of all the organizations they belong to. It has to be notarized and everything."

"So?"

"So!" said David. "The governor and his friends are going to use those lists to fire anyone they suspect of being an integrationist."

"But I thought people were allowed to associate with anybody they wanted, long as the group wasn't doing anything illegal," I said.

"Exactly!" said David. "A couple of the professors are refusing to submit a list."

"I'll have to ask Miss Winthrop about it," I said. "See what the WEC is planning to do about—"

"Can we talk about something else?" said Judy. "I'm only home for a little while."

So we did. We joked and poked at each other and talked about nothing in particular. It was wonderful. When it was time to go, David pulled me aside and said, "Keep up the good work."

"Will do," I said.

Judy was quiet on the bus ride home.

"I'm sorry we made you feel left out," I said.

197

"What?"

"I mean, when David and I were talking about the schools being closed. I know you're suffering the most. Being sent away from home and living with Granny and . . ." I tried to think of something positive. "But at least you have Robert. I bet you spend a lot of time with him."

Judy picked at a thread on her skirt. "He broke up with me."

"I'm sorry," I said. "When?"

"Last week. He asked me to give back his jacket and everything."

"Oh, Judy, that's awful." She started to sniffle, and I patted her back like she was a lost puppy.

"He wanted to give it to Lou Ann." Silent tears started rolling down her checks like the rain on the windows of the bus.

"Is this a good time to tell you I always thought he was kind of goofy looking?"

Judy snorted.

"And he smiled like a raccoon," I added.

Judy hiccuped as she tried not to laugh. "See, Marlee?" she managed finally. "You always know what to say to make me feel better."

"You're the older one. I thought that was your job," I said.

"Shut up," she said.

Sometimes it's good to have a sister.

39

ROBES IN THE CLOSET

Every Sunday afternoon in April I spent at Mrs. Terry's house. The first week when I arrived, there was a young woman in the dining room balancing a toddler on her lap as she tried to type a letter. The child was fussing.

"I'll take her," I said.

"Thank you." The woman stood up and handed her daughter to me. "I'm Mrs. Knowlton. Her name's Jackie."

"Hi, Jackie," I said. "I'm Marlee."

The child screamed.

"I'll take her back," sighed Mrs. Knowlton.

"No, let me try something." I scooped up Jackie under her arms and spun her around in a circle, just like my father used to do with me.

Jackie was so surprised, she stopped crying. I stopped spinning.

"More! More!" she cried.

I started spinning again. Jackie laughed.

"Hey, Miss Winthrop," called Mrs. Knowlton.

Miss Winthrop poked her head in the room.

"Got any more volunteers like her?" she said, pointing at me. "'Cause if you do, we'll have these schools opened by next week."

Jackie and I kept spinning, spinning, until we fell down, laughing in a heap. The room spun, but the compliment remained. Since I was the youngest, I'd always wanted a baby sister or brother. I cradled Jackie, and she put her head on my shoulder as I walked around the parlor. When she was finally asleep, I put her down on the couch and went back to the dining room.

"You got her to take a nap?" her mother asked.

I nodded. "I sang to her."

"What?"

"The times tables," I said.

Mrs. Knowlton laughed.

I watched Jackie every week after that, and once she was asleep, I'd sit down with the others at the huge, dark oak table in the dining room to help with paperwork. Mrs. Brewer was usually there, talking on the phone, and Mrs. Terry, of course, and Miss Winthrop and Jackie's mother, and Mrs. Dalton, silently putting flyers into envelopes.

I looked at the flyer. It had a picture of a child with a suitcase in one hand and said *Will this be your child next fall? Over 1,000 children had to leave Little Rock to go to school this year. There is no substitute for Public Schools.*

"My brother was telling me about the Act 10 thing," I said as I started folding. "Is the WEC going to do anything about it?"

"I believe," said Mrs. Brewer, "that Mr. Shelton—he's a colored teacher at Horace Mann—is working on filing a suit with the NAACP."

"Yes," said Miss Winthrop. "And Vice Principal Powell from Central is going to join him."

"Until the suit is filed and the courts rule on it," said Mrs. Brewer, "public employees will have to sign or not sign as they see fit."

Mrs. Terry walked into the room then and placed a large pile of mail addressed to the WEC in front of me. "Marlee, would you mind opening these?"

"Sure," I said.

"Thank you. Just put them into a pile and let me know if there's anything you think needs my immediate attention."

I nodded and pulled my silver letter opener out of my purse. Miss Winthrop hummed softly as we all worked. The first few letters I opened were just routine correspondence, bills, membership applications, stuff like that. But the next three . . .

"Some of these aren't very nice," I said.

"What do you mean?" Mrs. Terry asked.

"*If you go out today, you will be hit by a car and killed,*" I read.

Mrs. Terry plucked that letter from my hand.

"There's also *Say good-bye to your loved ones* and *I thought you were a good Christian woman. I'm ashamed of you.*"

Mrs. Terry took both of those too. "I'm sorry, Marlee. The threats go in a separate file. I'm afraid this is not an appropriate task for you. Perhaps you could go back to stuffing envelopes?"

Miss Winthrop took over the mail-opening duties, and we all went back to work. But no one hummed anymore. I wanted them to think I was mature and grown-up, but I couldn't help asking, "All those letters. Aren't you scared?"

"Of course we're scared," said Mrs. Terry. "But you can't let that stop you."

"It's like the phone calls," said Mrs. Brewer. "The first one is awful, but by the hundredth, well, you hope those people are all just talk."

"What is it your husband does again when he gets the calls?" asked Miss Winthrop.

"Oh, sometimes he reads them poetry. Or he starts talking

to them in French. Or singing an aria from an opera. Mr. Brewer has quite a good voice."

We kept working in silence for a while. "Another one for your file," said Miss Winthrop.

I glanced at the letter before anyone could stop me. *You and all the others who think like you should be tied to a car and dragged down Ninth Street, as did happen once before.*

"What's it talking about?" I asked.

Mrs. Terry sighed. "The lynching. The last one in Little Rock was in 1927."

"What happened?" I asked.

"No," Mrs. Knowlton said. "She's too young to know."

"She's helping us," said Miss Winthrop. "I say that makes her old enough."

Mrs. Terry sighed. "A colored man, John Carter was his name, was taken by a mob of people. No one did anything. Not the police or anyone watching. Nobody even tried to save him. They hung him and shot him and dragged his body down the street and then burned him. It happened at the edge of the Negro district, on Ninth and Broadway. This house is only eight blocks away. From my front porch, I could see the glow of the fire and hear people screaming."

We were all silent then. I heard the ripping of the paper as Miss Winthrop opened the envelopes. The squeeze of the sponge as Jackie's mother wet a stamp. Someone cleared her throat, and I looked over to see that it was Mrs. Dalton. She hadn't said a word the whole time.

"I'm here, helping," she whispered, "because once I found white robes in my husband's closet. I was too ashamed to ask him what they were. I guess I knew. And I was too scared to throw them out. But when the schools were closed, I realized I had to do something."

"If your husband is part of the Klan," Miss Winthrop said, "aren't you worried he'll find out you're helping us?"

"Yes, I was." Mrs. Dalton shook her head. "But according to him, this is just a ladies group. Harmless. We won't accomplish anything."

The baby woke up then, and I was glad to get up and give her a bottle. I even started whispering the times tables again. I might have claimed it was to soothe her, but really, it was so I didn't have to think about lynchings and death threats and robes in the closet.

40

DYNAMITE

One evening in early May, I finished my homework and came into the kitchen to find my parents sitting at the table with a man I didn't recognize. He wore a suit and hat, and it wasn't until I saw his stamp that I realized he was a notary. And I remembered that Mother and Daddy, as teachers, were both state employees.

"Act 10?" I asked, once the man had left.

Mother nodded. Daddy's face was pinched and pale.

"Did you list them all?" I asked.

"Yes," said Daddy.

"Even the Arkansas Council of Human Relations?"

"Of course. I'm a member."

Daddy got up and left the room.

Mother and I looked at each other. "Will he lose his job?" I asked.

"I hope not," said Mother. Then she went to the sink and started washing the dishes from dinner.

The next day was Tuesday, and I was meeting Liz at the rock crusher. She wasn't there when I arrived. I waited awhile, then put my satchel on the big rock and started to climb the oak tree. It wasn't as scary this time. If I concentrated and held on real tight, I could almost do it without counting. Almost. I was halfway up when I heard a voice call out, "Hey, Marlee!"

I was so surprised, I nearly fell out of the tree. I looked up.

There was Liz, looking down at me. "Sorry," she said. "I didn't mean to startle you."

"I didn't know you were there."

"You climbed up without watching me this time."

"Yeah, I guess I did."

Liz grinned at me.

"You're in a good mood," I said, pulling myself up to the branch she was sitting on.

"Yeah," said Liz. "Curtis asked me to a baseball game this weekend. We had a great time. Shirley was there too and she just about fell off the bleachers when she saw I was there with a ninth-grader!"

"Wow," I said. But the truth was, I was worried. If things were going so much better for Liz, how much longer would she need me?

"Bring anything to eat?" Liz asked.

"I've got some apples," I said. "But I left my satchel on the rocks."

"Never mind," Liz said.

"No, I'll go get them." I started to climb down. It was a long way. I was just jumping down from the lowest branch when I heard something, like someone biting into an apple.

"Hello, little mute girl."

Red and JT were sitting on the stone table. My satchel was open, and they were eating my apples. I was glad I was on the ground, because I suddenly felt so weak, I didn't think I'd have been able to hold on to the branches.

"We followed you," said JT.

I wasn't sure if they knew Liz was here or not. She was a long way up. I wasn't sure she could hear us, but I had to warn her not to come down.

"Why, JT and Red," I said, as loud as I could without yelling. "What a surprise to see you here!"

"Where's your friend?" Red asked.

"I came here by myself."

"Why were you up in the tree?" JT asked.

"I was looking at the view," I said.

Red went over to the tree and looked up. My heart started beating furiously. But the branches were thick with spring growth. "Sure there's not anyone else up there?"

"I think I would have seen them if there were."

I held my breath and willed Liz to be silent. I recited the times tables myself, until finally Red looked away from the tree and turned his piercing blue eyes on me.

"I heard you stopped doing my brother's homework," said Red.

JT was eating my apple intently without looking up.

Suddenly, I wasn't just scared. I was angry too. "You going to beat me up, Red?" I asked. "You going to beat up a girl?"

Red didn't answer. "Anything in the bag?" he asked JT finally.

JT rummaged inside. "Two dollars." He handed the money to his brother.

Something fell out of the tree.

We all turned and looked. An acorn. Then another one. And the sound of something—or someone—coming down the branches.

No. No, Liz. Stay in the tree. I have it under control. I don't care if they steal what's left of my birthday money.

"What was that?" Red asked.

I shrugged, my heart beating so hard, I was sure they could see it through my sweater.

JT and Red walked over to the tree and looked up.

"You see anything?" asked Red.

"Nothing," said JT.

"I'm going to climb up and make sure."

At that moment, two more acorns fell. Red grabbed a branch, about to swing himself up, when a squirrel jumped down, spooked, and jumped on Red's head. "Ahh!" Red screamed. "Get it off of me!" He fell to the ground.

JT was laughing too hard to do anything.

"It's just a squirrel," I said. I went over and picked up my satchel. "I'm leaving. You two can stay and play with the rodents if you want."

I turned and started walking, praying they would follow me. After a moment, they did.

"I know you're a race mixer," said Red. "We'll catch you at it one of these days."

I didn't say a word.

I guess it made him mad that I didn't respond, because he grabbed the satchel from my shoulder and tossed it into the forest.

It took reciting all twenty-five prime numbers under one hundred, but I didn't get angry. I didn't say a word. I just left the path and went to get my bag. It had fallen into a little ditch, full of weeds and tree roots and ferns. On the way back to the path, I tripped on a rock and fell down. "Ow!"

JT came over to me. "You all right, Marlee?"

"Why do you care?" I asked.

But he held out his hand to help me up, and I took it.

That's when we realized it wasn't a rock I had tripped over. It was a box. An old box. Labeled DYNAMITE.

"Wow," said JT. "Red, come look at this!"

Red crashed through the underbrush, his boots much better suited for tramping through the weeds than my saddle shoes.

"Dynamite!" he breathed. "Holy moly, JT, your girl's good luck after all." Red reached to take the lid off the box.

"Don't touch it!" I screamed. "Do you want to kill all of us?"

"Don't you know nothing? Dynamite's stable. It won't go off unless there's a charge of some sort. Besides, you tripped over it. If anyone was likely to kill us, it was you."

I stood there and watched as he pulled the lid off. There was a whole layer of dynamite inside, nine or ten sticks. He whistled. "Must have been here since this place was a working quarry. Tonight, we'll have some fun for sure."

"What are you saying?"

"I'm saying," said Red, "we'll find your little friend and show her whole family what we think of niggers who try to pass."

"Red!" said JT.

"Daddy's right," said Red. "You are a little coward."

JT said nothing.

"Give me your bag," said Red.

I didn't move.

"I said, give me your bag."

I just stared at him.

Red came over and grabbed it off my shoulder.

"What are you doing?" I yelled.

"We," said Red, "are taking this dynamite home." He started

placing the sticks of dynamite in my satchel. "JT!" he barked. "You gonna help me or not?"

JT glanced at me, then at his brother. He started placing the dynamite in the bag.

I turned and walked off. Slowly at first. I figured, if I ran, it'd be tempting them to follow, like dogs after a fox. Also, my knee hurt, and my tights were ripped. I'd have to tell Mother I'd lost my school satchel, and we'd have to buy a new one. I didn't dare go back to find out if Liz was still in the tree. Hopefully, she'd snuck down and had already made it out another way.

I stumbled home, unsure what to do. I'd have to tell my father about the dynamite. I'd have to warn Liz. We'd thought we were safe at the rock crusher because it was so isolated, but clearly we were wrong.

When I got home, Betty Jean was waiting for me in the kitchen. She looked me over, from the twigs in my hair, to my ripped skirt, to my bloody knee. Finally she waved a piece of paper in the air. "I have a message for you," she said, then handed me the paper. "From your friend Lisa."

I took the paper and read it: *I'm home and I'm fine. Call me.*

"Thank you, Betty Jean." That was one thing off my chest. Liz was okay. I'd give her a quick call and jump in the shower and . . .

Then I noticed Betty Jean was still looking at me, her arms crossed, a frown on her face, and I started to think I wasn't going to get that shower. "I don't think I've ever met your friend *Lisa,* have I?"

"No," I said quietly. "I don't think so."

"Funny thing is," said Betty Jean, "her voice sounded awful

familiar. I couldn't figure out who it reminded me of at first. But then it came to me. Elizabeth Fullerton. She's in youth group with Curtis. Nice girl. Pretty. Sometimes goes by the name of Liz."

Oh, no. She knew.

There was a glass of iced tea and a piece of pecan pie on the kitchen table.

"Now, sit down, Marlee, and start talking."

41

CONSEQUENCES

I had to tell the whole story three times. Once to Betty Jean. She made me call Mother and Daddy when I was done, and after they rushed home, I had to tell them everything again. Then Daddy called the police.

Sergeant Pike was an older man with silver hair and beard, and he shook my father's hand like they knew each other. He had kind eyes like a grandfather's and listened to my whole story without an expression on his face.

"Well, young lady," he said when I was done, "you have gotten yourself into a great deal of trouble." He sighed. "I'll pay the Daltons a visit. But if they don't want to let me search their house, there's not a lot I can do."

He turned to Betty Jean. "Has the colored girl's family been informed?"

Betty Jean nodded. She'd made a bunch of calls while we were waiting for Sergeant Pike to arrive.

"Good. I'll ask my officers to increase patrols in that neighborhood. Can you give me the address?"

Betty Jean nodded again. "My husband is going to go over and sit up with them tonight."

It was the policeman's turn to nod. "That's probably a good idea."

"But Red doesn't know where Liz lives," I said. "Or what she looks like. He's just blowing off a lot of hot air. Isn't he?"

No one in the room answered. And I realized it wouldn't be that hard if he really wanted to find out. Even though I was at home, with my parents and a police officer, I suddenly felt scared. I couldn't go to the rock crusher anymore. I couldn't meet Liz anywhere.

The policeman finally left, but dinner was worse than the telling had been. I could barely choke down a piece of pot roast. I had to know what they were going to do to me. Anything would be better than not knowing my punishment.

"I've called Granny," Daddy said finally. "We'll drive you to Pine Bluff tonight."

"What?" I asked.

"You're going to stay with Judy and your grandmother."

"No!"

"Marlee, I warned you to stay away from Liz. You should have listened. For her sake, if not your own."

"It's not my fault about the dynamite!"

"No," said Daddy. "It's your fault Red is targeting Liz. If you'd left her alone like I asked, he would have forgotten all about her by now."

The worse part was, maybe he was right.

"Have you not been paying attention to anything going on in Little Rock?" Daddy continued. "The FBI came to David's graduation because there were so many threats made against Ernest Green. The FBI!"

"I know it's serious," I said. "But—"

There was a knock at the door.

"I'll get it," said Mother.

Daddy and I stood frozen. Why hadn't Mother said

anything? Did she want me to go? A minute later, Mother returned with Miss Winthrop in tow. Her face was flushed and red, as if she had been running. "I've been calling all afternoon!" she exclaimed. "The line was always busy."

"Miss Winthrop," Daddy started, "we've had a stressful day and I think—"

"Oh, so you've heard the news?" Miss Winthrop asked.

"What news?" asked Daddy.

"Mrs. Brewer asked me to tell you personally because . . ." She paused. A long dramatic pause. "You've been fired."

"What?"

"The school board has fired a whole bunch of teachers! Forty-four people in all. Including you."

No one said a word.

"Actually, it was half the school board, and you weren't really fired, but your contract wasn't renewed for next year."

"Sit down," said Mother, "and start from the beginning."

Miss Winthrop drank half a pitcher of tea and ate a sandwich as she filled us in. The school board had been having a normal meeting. They were supposed to rehire all the teachers for the upcoming year. But when it became clear that the board president was going to go through the list one by one and try to fire anyone he thought was supportive of integration, Lamb, Tucker and Matson walked out of the meeting.

"Why'd they do that?" I asked.

"They'd been told by their lawyer that without them there, there would be no quorum and all the teachers would be automatically rehired. But then, after lunch, those still there, McKinley, Rowland and Laster, declared themselves a quorum and started firing thirty-four teachers, seven principals and three secretaries. Including Mr. Shelton from Horace Mann and Vice

Principal Powell from Central and Principal Wood from Forest Park Elementary and—"

"And me," said Daddy quietly.

"And you," Miss Winthrop agreed.

"Is that legal?" asked Mother.

"I don't think so," said Miss Winthrop. "But they did it, and I don't know who is going to stop them. Before I left, I stood up and asked, 'Why are they being let go?' I knew the answer, of course. Every single person on it is a supporter of integration. But I wanted to make them say it. McKinley just cut me off and said there was no time for discussion."

Miss Winthrop wiped her mouth. "Thanks for the meal. I hadn't eaten all day. The Forest Park PTA is meeting tonight at seven to discuss the firings. I hope you'll all be there. Now if you'll excuse me . . ."

Mother walked her to the door.

I sat by Daddy at the table. He looked completely stricken. I'd never seen him so defeated.

"I'm sorry, Daddy."

He shook his head. "What are we going to do?"

"We," said Mother firmly, walking back into the kitchen, "are going to that meeting. I was president of the Forest Park PTA, and I have a few things I want to say."

I didn't usually see Mother like this, confident and in charge. It was nice. "What about Pine Bluff?" I asked.

"Pine Bluff," said Mother, "is going to have to wait."

42

MOTHER'S SPEECH

The Forest Park auditorium was filled to overflowing when we got there—and it held over four hundred people. Mother put her name on the list of speakers, while Daddy and I went to find seats. There was a police car out front and an officer in the lobby.

There were a lot of people who wanted to speak. I tried to listen, but I had a hard time, because next to me Mother was getting more and more nervous. Most people start to fidget when they're anxious, but Mother gets stiller and stiller, until pretty soon, it's like sitting next to a statue. I had to do something.

"Mother?" I said.

"What?"

"Do you remember *Dumbo*?" I knew she did. When I was little, she'd taken me to the film at least three times herself.

"Yes."

I pulled the black feather out of my purse. "This is a magic feather," I said. "When you get up there and feel nervous, rub your fingers across the feather, and you'll know what to say."

Mother gave me a look.

"I know. It sounds silly, but—"

There was clapping and then a man on the stage said, "Former PTA president Maurine Nisbett will speak next."

Mother held out her hand. "Give me the feather."

Mother made her way up to the podium and adjusted the microphone. Daddy leaned forward. He seemed as nervous as Mother. I held my breath. But when Mother began to speak, her voice was calm.

"When the schools were closed last September, I wanted to believe our elected officials were doing what was best for our community. Maybe, like me, you sent a child away to go to school, thinking it would be temporary, a few weeks at most. I didn't want to get involved.

"Months later, maybe, like me, you've become more and more frustrated as this crisis has dragged on and on. Maybe you've begun to question our officials' disregard for court rulings, their prying into our personal activities.

"Now, with the firings of seven principals, three secretaries and thirty-four teachers, including my own husband, I realize it is no longer enough for me to think these things. I need to say them."

Mother looked at me, and I suddenly remembered the WEC flyer we had folded together: *Saying what you think is as important as thinking it! Speak out for public schools!*

"Maybe, like me, you're afraid. I know I was when my husband first started to take a stand on these issues. I was worried, not that he was wrong, but about what others might think. I was afraid the neighbors might call me names. Me, a grown woman, concerned about appearances.

"Or maybe you're a businessman, and saying to yourself, 'But if I speak out on this issue, there will be real consequences for me. Not just words, people will boycott my store. I might lose business.' I'm not going to pretend that isn't a risk, because it is. But it's time. Time to take a stand. The risks—to our students, to our schools, to our town's reputation—are too great if we stand aside and say nothing.

"It was my younger daughter, who is rather quiet herself, who convinced me of the need to speak out. She left this in my purse." Mother pulled out a piece of pink stationery and held it up. "This is from 1 Peter 3:14. *But even if you do suffer for righteousness' sake, you will be blessed. Have no fear of them, nor be troubled.*

"For months now, I've carried around this quotation. But no matter which way I look at it, I can come to only one conclusion. If my own daughter realizes that we must speak out, how can I do any less?

"Now, I don't know what Principal Wood's views are on integration. I don't much care. When my daughter wouldn't talk in school, Mrs. Wood was the one who reassured me that Marlee would be okay. She saw that Marlee was brave and perceptive and smart, and she made me see it too. Mrs. Wood is the best educator I've ever known, and the idea that she should be fired for anything she believes or does on her own time is absolutely ridiculous."

Mother stopped talking then. One man started clapping and then another and another, until the whole room was applauding. I glanced over at my father, and he was grinning too. And Mother, behind the podium, was holding up a tiny black feather.

43

AFTER THE SPEECH

Brave and perceptive and smart. My mother thought I was brave and perceptive and smart. That's all I could think of. It was a funny feeling. I didn't remember hearing her say that before, but it was really nice. We were almost home by the time I realized that no one had said anything about Pine Bluff since Miss Winthrop had shown up at our door. Suddenly, the nice feelings evaporated, and I couldn't stop wondering if I was going to have to pack my bags when I got home.

"Daddy?" I asked.

"Yes, Marlee?"

"Are you still going to send me away?"

He didn't answer.

"Because I'd really like to stay. I know I've been disobedient and you can punish me, but—"

"But Red . . ."

"There have been threats before. Those notes you got in our newspaper, remember? And the phone calls. You didn't send me away then."

Daddy was silent.

"Marlee has a point," said Mother. "You didn't even quit that group when I asked you to. You said it was important to take a stand."

"And I've been thinking," I went on. "Those Negro students who went to Central last year with Judy and David. The Little Rock Nine. They were in danger. But they didn't run away. They were brave. They kept going to school, even though it was scary. Even though their parents must have been worried about them. They kept going, because they believed in something. Believed they had a responsibility to make things better. Believed they could make things better, even though they were still just kids. I think I'd like to be like them."

I held my breath.

"If you stay . . . ," Daddy said.

Then I knew I'd won.

"I said, if you stay, I don't want you seeing that girl anymore."

"But—"

"I mean it, Marlee."

In the past, I would have accepted what he said. At least I wouldn't have said anything. But things were different now. I was taking a stand. "I won't meet her in public anymore," I promised, "but she is a really good friend. I'd still like to talk to her on the phone."

Daddy didn't say anything.

"Her parents would have to agree," said Mother finally. "I'll give them a call in the morning."

"All right," agreed Daddy.

"Sounds fair to me." I didn't say a word the rest of the way home, too scared he'd change his mind.

That night, I was just about to turn out the light when I realized there was something I needed to do. Daddy was still in the kitchen, talking on the phone. I went to Mother and Daddy's bedroom and knocked on the door.

"Come in," said Mother.

She was sitting in bed, cold cream on her face, in an old flannel nightgown, reading a book. I'd had a fancy speech rehearsed in my head, but when I saw her there, all normal and ordinary, it suddenly seemed like too much and all I said was "Thank you."

"I figured," said Mother, "if you could work up the courage to tell me the truth about JT, you were brave enough to stay home."

Mother held out her arms then, and if I ran into them and both our eyes filled with tears, I'm not admitting it, because it sounds too darn corny, and it wasn't corny at all. It was nice. For a moment, I got to be four again, and my mother was the one who could make everything okay.

44

STOP THIS
OUTRAGEOUS PURGE

The next morning, as I gulped down my oatmeal, Mother kept her promise and called Liz's house. Her mother answered. "Mrs. Fullerton," said Mother. "This is Mrs. Nisbett, Marlee's mother."

Liz's mother talked for a long time. The oatmeal sat like a lump in my stomach as I waited to see what she would say.

"I know, I know," Mother said finally. "We've forbidden Marlee from meeting Liz in person too. But to deny them all contact seems to be inviting rebellion, don't you think?"

Mrs. Fullerton talked for a moment longer, then finally Mother handed me the phone. "You have five minutes."

"Hi," said Liz when I put the phone to my ear.

"Hi," I said. "Are you okay?"

"Yeah. Daddy and Pastor George sat up all night on the porch. But nothing happened. They got a schedule all worked out for the rest of the month."

"Sounds scary," I said.

"Yeah," said Liz. "How are you doing?"

"Daddy was going to send me to Pine Bluff to live with Judy, but Mother and I convinced him not to. I can't see you anymore, though."

"Yeah, me either. Mama made me swear. And if I disobey, I have to go live with Aunt Ida and her fifteen cats in Atlanta."

Fifteen. A three-by-three magic square adds up to fifteen no matter which way you look—up, down or diagonal. And no matter which way I looked at our situation, I could come to only one conclusion. "Are we going to be able to stay friends?" I asked. "I mean, if we never get to see each other."

"We can talk on the phone," Liz said. "We didn't see each other much anyway."

And I remembered that while a traditional magic square always adds up to fifteen, if you use a number twice, or leave one out, you can make a square that adds up to something else. You can even make a multiplication square or a square with letters. It might not look like a regular friendship, but maybe we could find some way to be friends.

"It won't be forever," said Liz. "Maybe someday things will change and we'll be able to meet at the zoo again."

"Sure," I said. "Someday I'll see you by the lions."

Things had been awkward at school since Sally's party. I'd thought Little Jimmy had been on the verge of asking me to the movies (not that I could go, since I was grounded), but he hadn't said a word about it. I'd thought Sally was going to open up, start really talking to me, but she didn't either.

After the crazy night the day before, I was ready for a nice quiet lunch, full of numbers, variables, quadratic equations and not much else. But Mr. Harding was out sick, and on my way to the cafeteria, JT cornered me in the hall.

"Why'd you call the police?" he demanded, holding up an arm, blocking my way.

I ducked under his arm and continued walking.

"Marlee!" If he'd sounded angry, I'd have just kept going. But he sounded kind of scared. "Red thinks I did it."

"Why?"

"I didn't want to take the . . . stuff. We got in a big argument about it after you left."

"Not my problem," I said. "Besides, I didn't call the police. That was my father. And I'm glad he did. Now it's over."

I started to walk off again, but JT gripped my arm. "But that's just the problem," said JT. "It isn't over. My father let the police search the whole house. But they didn't find anything. Red had stashed it in the shed, but I guess he moved it, because when the police looked there, it was gone."

My fingers and toes suddenly went cold. Daddy had been on the phone with Sergeant Pike the night before, and he didn't say anything when he hung up. I'd assumed that meant everything was okay. "Red still has the dynamite?"

JT nodded. "At Sally's party . . . the things you said . . . I did like Liz, before I knew. And while I don't want to go to school with nig . . . Negroes, I don't want anyone to get hurt."

I didn't want that either.

"I shouldn't have followed you into the woods," JT said. "But it was Red's idea."

"JT," I said gently, "you're thirteen. Your brother is not an excuse. It's time you started thinking for yourself."

I strolled off then. I think I looked all confident, like I was sure it would work out, like I didn't care. But that wasn't true. It was my fault. If I had stayed away from Liz . . . I didn't go to lunch. I might have looked like I thought everything was okay, but I really went to the bathroom and cried.

• • •

When I got home from school that afternoon, both of my parents were sitting in the living room with Dr. Agar and Miss Winthrop. Mother was still reporting to her empty classroom when she wasn't subbing, and Daddy had been let go for next year, but he still had to finish out this one. I glanced at my watch. "What's going on?" I asked. It was only three thirty P.M.

"We came home early," Daddy said. "Dr. Agar is organizing a group called STOP."

"Stop This Outrageous Purge," Mother explained.

"We're going to circulate a petition asking for a special election to recall the board members who voted for the teacher purge," Dr. Agar explained.

I must have given him a look like I didn't understand (which I didn't), because Daddy said, "We're going to try to get the three school board members who fired the teachers removed."

"Why?" I asked.

"If we can get three more moderate school board members elected, they can join forces with the three who walked out. Then instead of everything being deadlocked, we can move forward on reopening the schools."

"I thought the governor closed the schools," I said.

"The governor got the legislature to pass laws closing the schools. But a new school board," Mother said, "might make a difference. They're the ones who set the start dates for the schools and . . ."

I couldn't remember the last time I'd seen my parents like this. Working together on a project. Enthusiastic like Judy about Pine Bluff before Robert Laurence dumped her. It was kind of nice. In any case, this sounded like the best chance we'd had in ages.

"So what can I do?" I asked.

"STOP will be working with the WEC," Miss Winthrop explained.

"We need to gather six thousand three hundred names," Dr. Agar said. "That's fifteen percent of the registered voters. If we get all the names, we'll get our special election."

"Six thousand three hundred names," I said. "That's kind of a lot. How are we going to . . . ?"

"We're organizing a petition drive at War Memorial Stadium this Sunday. People will be able to just drive up, sign the petition and go on their way."

"The thing is, I'm sure the segregationists are doing the same thing," said Miss Winthrop, "trying to remove the school board members we want to keep."

This was so confusing. I was trying to remember everything I'd learned in history about elections and voting. If we could do this, Judy could come home. Someday Liz and I might go to the same school.

Betty Jean came in then, serving cake and coffee. Seeing her gave me an idea. I followed her back into the kitchen. "Betty Jean," I asked, "are you registered to vote?"

"Course I am," she said.

I grabbed her wrist and dragged her back into the living room, where I made Dr. Agar explain everything again. Betty Jean listened quietly as he talked, till finally she said, "I think I might know a couple of people who might be willing to sign a petition like that. If you don't mind accepting help from some colored folks, that is."

"Right now," said Dr. Agar, "we're going to need every name we can get."

I called Liz again that evening. She'd already heard about the petition drive and how Betty Jean and Pastor George were organizing the colored folks. "Our youth group is helping too. On Sunday we're going door-to-door."

"Great," I said. "Now I have something else to tell you." I quickly repeated what JT had told me.

"Call the police again," said Liz.

"And tell them what? *Red has dynamite.* I already told them that."

Liz said nothing.

"Who's on the schedule for tonight?" I asked.

"Pastor George," she said.

"Are you scared?" I asked.

"Yes," whispered Liz. "I am."

45

MAYBE BRAVE

The next morning when I woke up, I had an idea. I was pretty sure Mother wouldn't like it, but at least I could ask. "Mother?" I said over breakfast.

"Hmm." She didn't look up from the paper.

"Any chance you'd let me stay home from school today so I can help STOP get a head start on those petitions?" The words came out in a rush.

Mother thought for a long time. "I guess so."

"Really?"

She nodded. "In fact, I think I might call in sick myself and give you a hand."

I was too shocked to say a word.

"Unless you'd rather go with Miss Winthrop," Mother said, suddenly very interested in her toast.

"No," I said. "I'd rather go with you."

Mother smiled.

"Does this mean you think it's okay if Judy goes to school with Negroes now?" I asked.

"You know," said Mother, "I think it does."

Two hours later we'd been up and down our street and had a handful of new names on our petition. Old Mrs. Chapman was the first one to sign. Turned out, before she was married, she was a music teacher.

Mrs. Madison (the mother of Jill, the little girl I'd taken trick-or-treating) was a different story. Mother barely got out what we were doing before Mrs. Madison started to scold us. "Maurine Nisbett, what is a smart woman like you doing with a group like that?"

Mother was flustered. "Well, Debra, I don't think—"

"I'm ashamed of you, Maurine, supporting those communist race mixers!"

Mother took a deep breath. "If you would just listen to what I—"

Mrs. Madison slammed the door in our faces.

"Well, I never!" said Mother, which was about as close as she ever got to swearing.

A few houses later, I saw Sally and her mother walking around as well. I waved and ran to meet Sally in the street. "You're working for STOP too?" I asked.

Sally stuck her nose up in the air, so high a bat could fly right in it. "Of course not," she sniffed. "We're with CROSS."

"What's that?"

"The Committee to Retain Our Segregated Schools. We're working to keep the schools segregated."

"Oh," I said. "I guess I thought after what you said at the skating rink, you'd—"

Sally grabbed my arm and pulled me away from where our mothers were trying to pretend they hadn't just realized they were on opposite sides. "Truthfully," Sally said, "I don't much care which side of this issue I'm on, as long as I get to skip school and get new clothes. Mother bought me this." She pointed to her new sweater set. "Just in case a TV reporter comes by and we get to be on television. I want to look my best."

Pure Sally. "Oh," I said. "Well, good luck. With getting on TV, I mean."

As I walked off, Sally called, "Hey, Marlee!"

I looked back at her.

"Good luck to you too," said Sally.

"Thanks."

We smiled and went our separate ways. For the first time in ages, I felt okay about Sally. She was only against integration because her mother was. Eventually, she'd come around.

"Are you still friends with Sally McDaniels?" Mother asked. "After JT, I just thought I'd better ask, because . . ."

"Yeah," I replied. "I think I am."

At lunchtime, we took a break and went to Krystal to grab a burger. On the way into the restaurant, I noticed someone had placed a bunch of advertisements by the front door. I bent down to pick one up.

It was a card inviting us to join the KKK.

"What is it?" asked Mother.

I handed the card to her.

She bit her lip. "Daddy found some of these at a newsstand last week." She glanced around. "Quick. Let's pick them all up."

After we had gathered and thrown away all the cards, we went inside to order. I'd lost my appetite, but Mother insisted I get a burger, fries and a chocolate shake. She ordered a cheeseburger, onion rings and a cherry Coke. We shared a little tub of ketchup.

"This is nice," she said as we took turns dipping into the

ketchup. "We should do this again soon. Spend time together, I mean. Maybe go to the zoo?"

I nodded. "I'd like that."

"It's not too babyish for you?" Mother asked.

"No, I love the zoo."

"You always did," she said. "Especially the lions."

"Really?" I asked.

"Do you remember when we moved to our house?" asked Mother.

I shook my head.

"You had just turned four. It was our first night in the house, and the lions started roaring. Judy, David and I were terrified. But you went right over to look out the window. You weren't scared of getting eaten; you wanted to see them."

"I was only four," I said. "I didn't know any better."

Mother shook her head. "No, you were brave. Like I said at the PTA meeting."

"You were just giving a speech."

"No," said Mother. "I meant it."

I finished the last of my chocolate shake. Brave? That was crazy. But if you had told me Mother would ever let me skip school, I would have said that was crazy too. Brave? Maybe I was.

The next day at school, JT had a black eye. He kept his head down all day, but I saw it, we all did. After math, this time I cornered him in the hallway.

"What happened to you?" I asked.

"Red."

"Your brother hit you?"

JT shrugged. "Not the first time."

"Why don't your parents do anything?"

"I didn't tell them! They think I ran into a tree."

I was pretty sure they didn't believe that. "Why?"

"I told you, Red thought I'd betrayed him. I hadn't, but"—
he gestured for me to come closer—"the dynamite is locked in
the trunk of his car. I saw it this morning, and he saw that I saw
it." He pointed to his eye. "He said if I say anything to Mother
or Father, he'll kill me." JT bit his lip. "But he didn't say anything about telling you."

"Thank you, JT."

He nodded.

Sally and Nora walked up then, and we jumped apart.
"What's wrong with you two?" Sally asked. I shook my head
and ran off.

As soon as Daddy got home, I told him what JT had said.
Daddy frowned, but called his friend at the police station. His
face was grim when he hung up. "They already searched Red's
car. There was nothing there."

"He moved it," I said.

"Maybe," said Daddy. "Or maybe JT was mistaken. Or lying
to upset you. In any case, try not to worry. The grown-ups will
take charge of things."

I nodded, but what I was really thinking was, *So far they
aren't doing a very good job.*

46

SAINTS, SINNERS AND SAVABLES

At the petition drive on Sunday, May 10, my job was to greet the cars as they drove up and bring the petition for them to sign right up to the car window. Mother or Daddy would come by with the notary to check their driver's license. No one even needed to get out of the car. Lots of people I knew came by. Mrs. Brewer, of course, and Reverend Mitchell from church. Even Mr. Harding and Miss Taylor from school.

Late in the afternoon, Betty Jean and Pastor George stopped by to drop off all the signatures they had collected. I was thrilled to see that Liz and Curtis were with them. "We've been gathering names since nine this morning!" exclaimed Liz. "Only one person we asked refused to sign. Marlee, I think this just might work!"

"You should have seen her," said Curtis. "If someone was hesitant or nervous about signing, Liz just started talking, and by the time she was done, not only had the first person signed, but he'd gotten three of his friends to sign too."

"Liz can be very persuasive," I said.

"You can say that again," said Curtis. Liz blushed, and he beamed at her the way I'd always wished a boy would look at me.

By Monday, STOP had enough names, but CROSS got their petitions in too, so all six board members were being recalled. The special school board election was set for Monday, May 25. That afternoon, Dr. Agar and Mrs. Brewer came to our house to talk to my parents about the next step for STOP.

"We have a copy of the poll tax book listing all the registered voters in Little Rock," said Mrs. Brewer. "We need to put their names, addresses and phone numbers onto note cards. Next, we'll divide the city into sections, assign each section a ward captain, and give each captain a shoe box full of cards with the names of all the voters in their area. Block workers will then personally contact as many voters as possible before the election."

"Do you think that will help?" asked Mother.

"It has in other cities when there was a tight election," said Mrs. Brewer. "But we won't win without the Negro vote."

"Pastor George and I will handle that," said Betty Jean. There were already tea and cookies on the coffee table. But this time, instead of going back into the kitchen, she was standing in the doorway, listening to the conversation.

"Good," said Dr. Agar, "then there's only one problem."

"What?" asked Daddy.

"There are thirty thousand registered voters in Little Rock," admitted Mrs. Brewer.

"Thirty thousand?" repeated Daddy. "But the election is only two weeks away. By the time we get all the cards organized . . ."

Mother shook her head. "It's impossible."

But I was doing some calculations. "No, it's not."

They all turned to look at me.

"Thirty thousand names sounds like a lot," I agreed. "But if you divide it up between thirty people, that's only a thousand names each. If you figure it takes a minute per card, that's a thousand minutes, or about seventeen hours. That's not forever. It's one long weekend."

They all stared at me. What can I say? I've always liked long division.

"Marlee is very good at math." Mother sounded proud.

"If you have more people," I said, "it'd take even less time."

Dr. Agar looked at Mrs. Brewer. She nodded. "We'll see what we can do."

For the next forty-eight hours, all the WEC members we could round up worked frantically, putting the names, addresses and phone numbers of all thirty thousand registered voters in Little Rock onto note cards. Miss Winthrop and Mrs. Dalton both came over, and they stayed working late into the night. Mrs. Brewer went to the county clerk's office and got copies of the recall petitions. Everyone who signed the STOP petition was listed as someone we could count on for their support. Everyone who signed the CROSS petition was labeled as someone it probably wasn't worth our time contacting. We were going to focus on those who weren't on either list.

While I copied names at home, Liz copied names at church. "We've got the saints, the sinners and the savables," she'd commented to Pastor George. The joke was repeated, and Mrs. Brewer liked it so much, we started putting a halo in the upper right-hand corner of each card for the saints, an X for the sinners, and a question mark for the savables. When we were done, there were one hundred shoe boxes stacked in our living room, full of three hundred cards each.

The plan was simple: on election day, we had to get all the

saints to the polls. We didn't want to do anything to remind the sinners that there was an election going on, though Mrs. Brewer nixed Miss Winthrop's idea of letting the air out of their car tires. We would spend our time on the savables, contacting them and trying to win them over to our cause.

Mother kept one of the boxes for herself. Every minute she wasn't at school she spent on the phone, or having tea, or just dropping in on neighbors we hadn't talked to in years. At night, she'd tell Daddy and me about whom she'd contacted, and whom she'd won over.

Betty Jean got her own shoe box of people in her neighborhood, and Daddy told her to make free use of our phone, so she got real good at dialing and cooking, sweet-talking and folding laundry. Her box was mainly full of saints and savables—the real problem was convincing people it was worth taking the time to vote.

Liz organized some students from Philander Smith College to provide rides to the polls on election day. "People want to vote, but we have to make sure they can get there." I helped with a rally STOP held on May 19 at Robinson Auditorium to get people energized about the election. Pastor George held a separate rally for Negroes at Dunbar Community Center the same evening.

I thought it was odd that even though we were working together on a common goal, we still had separate rallies. But no one else said a word about it.

47

THE KEYS

Mother and I were supposed to go to the zoo the following Saturday to celebrate finishing all 30,000 cards. But when Saturday came, Mother had a migraine and had to stay in bed. "I'm so sorry," she said. "We've all been working too hard. You go on and have fun."

I didn't think it would be too much fun by myself, but I went. On the bus, I thought about how Liz and I had often met at the zoo on Saturday afternoons last fall. Maybe she would be there today.

I tried not to get too excited, but I ended up running all the way down the hill to the lion's cage.

She wasn't there.

I was disappointed. Instead, two young men were standing there, their belongings spread out all over our bench. They were throwing stones at the lions. One of them, a big burly guy with a leather jacket, had bad aim, but the other, a blond guy, had a strong arm. He hit the poor cats again and again, and there was nowhere they could run to get away. I opened my mouth to yell at him to stop when he turned around to pick up another rock and I saw his face.

It was Red.

I ducked down behind a bush, trying not to shake. What

was *he* doing there? The zoo was *my* place, the place where I felt safe and comfortable, and he was ruining it! For the first time, I had an inkling of what it might be like to be Liz, to feel compelled to say something, and I actually had to recite the nines times tables to keep my mouth shut.

So I was already thinking about Liz, which is maybe why it didn't quite register when I saw her walking toward me. Right past Red and his friend.

I stood up when I saw her, but that was stupid because Red might see me, so I ducked back down again. Of course Liz *had* seen me, and through the bushes I watched as she opened her mouth to call out my name. I jumped up again, throwing my hand over my mouth to tell her to be quiet, and pointed over to the monkey cage.

My heart was pounding as she made her way over to me. "Marlee, what was that all about?" Liz asked. At least she had the good sense to whisper.

"That was Red," I said. "You walked right by Red."

Liz went pale. "Where?"

"By the lion cage."

Liz glanced back, though she couldn't see him from where we were standing. "I didn't recognize him. Not without his football uniform."

"I don't think he knows what you look like. But if he sees you with me . . ."

I didn't have to finish the sentence.

"What do we do?" asked Liz.

"JT said he has the dynamite in the trunk of his car."

"So?" said Liz.

I was doing it again. Thinking aloud. It seemed kind of dangerous to me. "Maybe we should check."

"How?" asked Liz.

"On the bench. Where we met and you gave me the magic square book. I saw a football jacket and some beers, and I think there was a ring of keys."

"That's crazy," said Liz.

It was crazy. "But the police aren't going to do anything," I said. "Daddy already called them."

"Well," said Liz after a long moment, "I guess it's up to us."

I nodded.

"By the way," she said, "it's nice to see you."

"Yeah," I said. "You too."

We spent the next hour hiding in the bushes, waiting to see if there would be an opportunity to snatch the keys. Red and his friend were drinking beer, which wasn't really allowed at the zoo (and they were too young anyway), but there was no one there to stop them.

Finally, just when I was beginning to think this would never work, they both went off to the bathroom, leaving their belongings on the bench. Including the large ring of keys.

I looked at Liz. This was our chance. Liz was here, Red was here, and his keys were on the bench. It couldn't be coincidence. This was fate. We'd never get an opportunity like this again.

"Then I'll watch the bathroom," said Liz. "You get the key." Before I could say another word, she ran off toward the bathroom.

I glanced over at the lions. One of them lifted her head and looked at me, as if saying, "Please save me from those rocks." Thinking about the rocks made me angry, and being angry made me forget about being scared, so I walked over to the bench and picked up the keys.

It was a simple silver ring, but there must have been a hundred keys on it. Okay, so it was probably more like fifteen, but still. Why did a guy like Red need so many keys? It felt like my fingers suddenly swelled to three times their size, like cooked sausages splitting their skin, as I tried to flip through them all. There were two with the word *Chrysler* on the top. I didn't know which one was for the trunk, so I decided to take both.

The first key came off easily, but the second one kept slipping. Liz came running back around the corner. "They're coming!"

I put the ring back on the bench, and we ran to the safety of the monkeys and the bushes. Red and his friend came back, picked up their stuff and went deeper into the zoo.

Liz sighed. "Thank goodness. They didn't notice anything was missing."

"But there were two keys," I said. "I only had time to get one." I'd been clutching it in my fist so tightly, it left a little indentation on my palm when I opened my hand to show it to her.

Liz nodded. "Some cars have one key for the door and ignition and another key for the trunk and glove compartment." She picked up the key and looked it over before placing it back into my hand. "Let's hope you got the right one."

We ran up the hill to the zoo parking lot, my clenched fist with the key by my side. My heart was beating as loud as an airplane engine. No one paid us any attention at all. There were only a few cars in the parking lot. One of them was the old gray Chrysler Windsor. I glanced inside. There were fishing rods and a tackle box on the backseat of the car.

"Is this it?" Liz asked.

I nodded.

"It was your idea," she said. "You try the key."

I knew I had to do it. I took deep breaths, trying to remember that I was brave, but I couldn't move. I was literally frozen to the spot. I couldn't believe it. I was going to ruin our one and only chance to steal the dynamite back because I was too big of a coward to open a trunk.

Then the lions did something I'd never heard them do during the day before. They roared. It was just a little roar, but it worked. I counted 2, 3, 5, and then I tried the key in the lock.

It got stuck. The lock was rusty, but the key probably wasn't the right one anyway. I sighed and tried once more. The key turned, and I heard a click.

The trunk popped open.

Inside was the dynamite.

My old satchel was in the trunk too, but the sticks had fallen out of it and were now strewn all about the trunk.

"Well, I'll be a monkey's uncle," Liz said. "JT was right."

I glanced around the parking lot. There was no one there. If someone did see us, we were just two girls, standing in front of an open trunk.

"Let's go," Liz said. "We'll call the police."

"No," I said. "We have to take it."

"What are you talking about?"

"I already called the police," I reminded her. "They aren't going to do anything."

"If you tell them you saw it with your own eyes—"

"Red'll move it! Even if we leave the key in the lock, he'll know someone was—"

Liz sighed. "Of course you're right."

We looked at the dynamite in the trunk. The cylinders stared up at us.

"I don't want to touch it," Liz said.

"Neither do I," I said.

"On the other hand," said Liz. "If it's been rolling around in his trunk for a week now and hasn't gone off yet, surely it's okay to . . ." She reached in and picked up a stick, and placed it carefully back into my satchel. "Just like picking up a crawdad," she said, but neither one of us smiled.

I picked up the next stick. No one blew up. It felt cool, kind of like a crawdad. I placed mine carefully in the bag and then it was Liz's turn again. We worked in absolute silence. I was sweating by the time I got to the last stick.

Liz reached in and picked up the bag.

"What do we do now?" I asked.

"Take it to the police station."

"And tell them?"

"We found it in the woods," Liz said, and shrugged. "It's almost the truth."

We started to walk away when I realized we'd forgotten to close the trunk. I ran back. I'm not sure what made me look in the trunk before I closed it. But I did. And there were two more sticks that had rolled out of the bag, way in the back.

I glanced toward the zoo entrance. No one was in sight. I just couldn't face the thought of leaving any loose ends, so I climbed into the trunk to reach the last two sticks of dynamite. But I accidentally kicked the lid as I scrambled in, and it fell shut.

"Liz," I screamed, "let me out!"

That's when I realized I was still clutching the key in my hand.

More voices. One I was afraid I recognized. I peeked out of an old rusted spot in the trunk.

Red and his friend.

They walked straight to his car. I could feel it lurch as they climbed inside. Red started the engine and drove off.

With me in the trunk.

48

GOD BLESS MOTHER

It was dark in the trunk, with only bits of light coming in. I was terrified, on-top-of-the-high-dive, getting-on-an-airplane, passing-as-a-white-girl-when-you're-really-colored terrified. If there was ever a time to prove Mother right, this was it. I tried to picture my four-year-old self, too stupid to be afraid. I tried to pretend it was dark because I was home in bed. I imagined so hard, I could almost hear the lions roar.

I felt a little better. The church bells chimed quarter after three. Red turned left, then right, then went straight for a long time. The air was terrible, full of exhaust. I wanted to cough, but I was afraid they would hear me. Red turned right onto a bumpy road. Just when I was sure he was going to drive forever, the car stopped.

"It's three forty-five," I heard one guy call out. "You're an hour late."

"Sorry," said Red. "This old clunker doesn't go over twenty-five."

"Bring anything to eat?" he asked.

I peeked through the rusty hole. Burly leather jacket guy slapped his friend on the back. "We're going fishing. I'll catch you something."

They finally walked off. When I couldn't hear them anymore, I made myself count to a hundred, then I tried to open the trunk. Only one problem. I could feel the lock, but there was no catch on the inside. Why would there be? Who would be stupid enough to jump into a trunk? I kicked at the trunk, even made a dent in the metal, but it still didn't open.

Think, Marlee, think. There had to be some tool, something I could use to pry it open. I felt around. My fingers closed on a cold, round cylinder. Yikes! The dynamite. I'd forgotten it was still there.

I dropped it like a hotcake and backed away, as far as the trunk would allow, which was only about an inch or two. I tried to imagine a magic square or the area of a circle or solving for y, but it didn't work this time. All I could think of was how when Red came back and opened the trunk to put the fish he'd caught inside, he was going to kill me.

Then I had a worse thought. What if he didn't open the trunk? How could he? I still had the key. Would he even notice it was missing? He thought the dynamite was still in there, safely locked away. What if I was locked in there for days? What if I had to go to the bathroom? How long could I survive in there? I hadn't even had a chance to say good-bye to Liz. Or David or Judy. Or Daddy. Or Mother.

Mother! Oh, God bless Mother. If I had my purse, the letter opener would be inside. I felt around in the darkness. My purse was still slung over my shoulder. I pulled out the opener and, fumbling in the dark, placed it next to the trunk latch. Maybe I could use the letter opener like a prybar to force the trunk open. I took a deep breath and slammed my hand down on the letter opener.

The blade broke off the handle. I felt around in the darkness, but the blade must have slipped down somewhere because I couldn't find it.

I kicked at the lock. Nothing. Panicked, I picked up the letter opener handle and pounded at the lock, again and again, until finally, the trunk popped open. Sunlight shone in, blinding me. I gulped in deep breaths of fresh air. I was free.

Then I froze, because I wasn't free. I was stuck in the woods with three scary boys, who would likely kill me when they realized I'd stolen their dynamite. So I did the only thing I could do. I grabbed my purse, counted 2, 3, 5, then jumped out of the trunk and ran.

I made it about twenty feet before I fell down. For a second, I'd thought I'd been shot, then I remembered they were fishing, not hunting. I listened. There was silence. The boys must still be down by the river. There was no one around.

Slowly, I got to my feet and began to walk home. I stayed close enough to the road that I wouldn't get lost, but far enough into the forest so that Red wouldn't see me if he drove by.

It was slow going. There wasn't really a path, and I felt achy all over. Brave? Stupid was more like it. How did I think we could prevent something bad from happening? Every time I tried, I made things worse. My thoughts got darker and darker, as did the sky. Pretty soon, it started to rain.

Finally, I came to a farmhouse. I didn't even care about getting in trouble anymore. I just wanted to go home. I went up on the front porch and knocked at the door. No one answered. There was no car in the driveway. I tried the front door. It was unlocked.

"Hello?" I called out. "Hello, is anybody home?"

Now, usually I'd hesitate at least a minute or two before I went into someone's house without permission. But I'd already stolen some dynamite and jumped into a car trunk today— what was a little breaking and entering? So I opened the door and went inside.

49

GOD BLESS DAVID

It was a pretty farmhouse, with old furniture, but neat and tidy. I walked into the kitchen. There was a phone on the wall.

I picked up the receiver and dialed Liz. She answered on the first ring.

"It's me," I said. My voice shook so much, I wasn't sure she'd recognize me.

"Marlee?"

"Yeah."

"Oh, thank God! Are you okay?"

"I think so." I was dripping water all over a clean white rug.

"I just about died when Red drove off."

"He decided to go fishing," I said.

"Fishing? Where are you?"

"I don't know." I looked around as if I expected to see a street sign in the kitchen. "What happened to the dynamite?"

"I left it by the back door of the police station with a note saying I'd found it in the woods. I don't think anyone saw me."

"Thank goodness," I sighed.

"Where are you?" Liz repeated. She sounded like she was about to cry.

"I don't know!" I was the one who was lost. There was a

pile of mail on the otherwise neat table. I picked up a piece. "I'm at forty-three Salamander Road."

"Where's that?" asked Liz.

"Do you have a map?"

She did.

"Start at the zoo. We went left, then right, then straight for a long time." Thank goodness I'd paid attention. "And finally another right."

"I see it," said Liz, "but it's a long road. How will I know where . . ."

I had an idea. I picked up a piece of mail and rummaged in my purse for a pen. It was three fifteen P.M. when Red drove off. I knew that because I'd heard the church bells. And it was three forty-five when we arrived. So that was thirty minutes. Red had said the car only went twenty-five miles per hour, and he was late, so he'd probably been driving that fast the whole way. I made a few notes on the piece of paper. Thirty minutes was half of one hour, and half of 25 miles was 12.5.

God bless math. "I'm about twelve miles down the road," I said.

"How—"

"Just find someone to come and get me."

"Who?" Liz moaned.

My brain felt thick and slow. If I called Mother or Daddy, I'd be going to Pine Bluff for sure, no matter how many pretty speeches Mother made about taking a stand. Maybe David would come. He didn't have a car, but perhaps he could borrow one.

"Call my brother," I said, and gave her the number. "Tell him it's an emergency and to please come now."

I heard the front door open and steps in the living room. A

moment later a figure appeared in the doorway of the kitchen. "Who are you?"

Startled, I hung up the phone.

It was an old lady, with a faded dress and worn hands.

I burst into tears. I swear it wasn't calculated, but apparently it was just the right thing to do. I must have looked pretty pitiful, because instead of getting mad, she turned concerned. "It's all right, sweetie," she said. "Just tell me what's wrong."

"I got lost in the woods," I mumbled. That much was true. "I was fishing with my daddy, and I wandered off and . . ." A fresh batch of tears. I wasn't quite sure if I was acting or not anymore. "I knocked, but no one answered and . . ."

"There, there," she said. "Calm down." She patted my back like I was a puppy. I slowly stopped crying.

"I have a granddaughter your age," she said. "Let me go see if I can find you something dry to wear."

I was still sniffling but felt better. Maybe she'd even offer to drive me home. I could call Liz back and . . . I turned over the piece of paper I'd used to get the address. It was a CROSS flyer.

I stood up and ran. Out the front door and down the street. Ran and ran and ran. I figured out pretty quickly that was a stupid thing to do. It was still raining. And it wasn't like being a CROSS supporter made her a wicked witch who ate children or anything.

It wasn't exactly cold, but my skirt was soaked through, and my feet were wet. I hate wet shoes. They squish and squash, and twelve miles was a long way to walk in squishy shoes. David probably wouldn't be able to come. No, Liz would have to call my parents, and I'd be in Pine Bluff before I could even say good-bye. Well, at least we had gotten rid of the dynamite.

Except for the two sticks I'd left in the trunk. In my rush to get away from the car, I'd forgotten completely about them. All this had been for nothing. Red still had some dynamite, and I'd lost the nicest birthday present I'd ever received from my mother. Probably the last present I'd ever get once she found out what I'd done.

I went on like that, feeling sorry for myself, till I saw a car coming down the road. I thought about jumping in the woods to hide, but frankly, I was just too tired. As it came closer, the car slowed down. I could see a young man behind the wheel, grinning at me.

"Hey, Marlee," David said as he rolled up beside me. "Fancy meeting you here."

"Thanks for coming," I said.

"Course I'd come," said David. "You're my sister."

I got in the car, and we started home. "Try not to get mud on the seat," said David. "I had to borrow the car from my professor."

I peeled off my wet shoes and socks, and a wave of relief swept over me, like wet feet had been the worst of my problems.

"So," said David.

"So," I repeated.

"How about a deal," he said. "I won't tell Mother and Daddy, if you tell me the whole story."

"Okay," I said, and started talking. David was a good listener. He didn't interrupt once, but I could tell he was upset, because by the time I got to the end, his trademark grin was nowhere in sight.

"Jeez Louise, Marlee!" he said when I was done. "What were you thinking?"

"You promised not to tell," I reminded him.

"I did," sighed David. "But you've got to promise me never to do anything like that ever again."

"Gladly," I said.

He shook his head. "It's always the quiet ones who are the craziest." But he was grinning again, and I knew he was teasing. I leaned up against him like I used to do when I was four and he was ten and he was reading me a book. And even though I was worried about what was going to happen next, I felt happier than I had for a long time.

50

WORRIES

I was lucky. Really, really lucky. When David dropped me off at home, Mother was still sleeping. Daddy had left a note for me, saying he'd gone down to STOP headquarters. I called Liz to let her know I was home, ate a sandwich and went to bed. I was so tired, I didn't even have any dreams. It was wonderful.

The next Monday at school, JT cornered me again. "How'd you do it?"

"Do what?" I asked.

"Red was furious. When he came back from fishing, his trunk was open and the dynamite was gone. He thinks you did it."

"Why me?"

"Because you didn't want him to take it in the first place!"

I put my hands on my hips. "JT, how could I have done it? I don't have a key to his trunk." I was a better liar than I thought.

JT shrugged. "I can't figure out how you followed him to the middle of nowhere."

"That's because I didn't follow him." That was sort of true. I'd gone with him instead.

"Why," asked JT, "if you went to all the trouble to steal the rest—why didn't you take the last two sticks?"

"I didn't mean to leave—"

JT grinned at me. Okay, so he wasn't stupid. And, clearly, I was.

"So it was you," he said.

"JT, you can't tell—"

"Of course not. You'd look really awful with a black eye. But Red is pretty angry and looking for someone to blame. And he and my dad have been talking a lot about Birmingham."

"Why are they talking about Alabama?"

"Colored folks are starting to move into the white neighborhoods there, and well, there've been a lot of bombings. In one part of town there have been so many explosions, they call it Dynamite Hill."

"That's awful!"

"That's what I thought. But Red and Daddy were laughing about it, like it was some big joke. 'Ought to do that here,' said Daddy. 'That'll solve our school problems real fast.' Mother said they were only kidding, but . . ."

JT glanced around. No one was paying any attention to us.

"Remember last year, when there were those bomb threats at Central?"

"Yeah." Judy had told me about them on more than one occasion.

"Well, Red called in at least one of them. I know. I was home sick, but Red didn't know that, and I heard him make the call."

I said nothing.

"I never told anyone."

"Do you think he'd bomb my house?" I asked.

JT considered that, and the longer he considered it, the more nervous I got. "I don't think he'd bomb a white girl," he said finally. "But Liz is colored."

"He doesn't know what she looks like."

"Not yet," said JT. "But look at this." He pulled out our yearbook, which we'd gotten in homeroom that morning. I hadn't even looked through it yet. He flipped to a page in the back.

It was a picture of the cheerleaders at a football game. In one corner, sitting on the bleachers, Liz and I were clearly visible.

"Red hasn't seen this yet, has he?"

JT shook his head. "I'll hide my yearbook, but a lot of people have copies."

"Thanks for the warning," I said.

He shrugged. "It was kind of fun to see Red so mad." He swaggered off like a cowboy, but this time, I was pretty darn sure it was an act, like David's happy grin. And I hoped that JT wouldn't turn up at school the next day with another black eye.

I warned Liz about the photo, but there wasn't much she could do. Someone was already keeping watch at her house every night. There was now less than a week before the election on May 25, and I was a nervous wreck. I spent hours staring out our front window, watching for Red's old gray Chrysler Windsor.

Every morning as I sat in the car with Daddy on the short ride to school, I tried to decide if I should tell him about the trunk. I wanted to get it off my chest, wanted him to reassure me that two sticks were nothing, no real harm could be done.

But every time I opened my mouth to tell him, I stopped. What would it change? The police had done all they could. I would be sent to Pine Bluff. And it seemed like *not* being able to keep a lookout for Red would be even worse.

But I got quiet again. Like a turtle, I pulled back into my shell, conserving my courage and my words until I really needed them. At least that's what I told myself. I hoped it wasn't just an excuse for being quiet and afraid.

51

STOPPING BY BETTY JEAN'S

It was Sunday, May 24, 1959, the day before the election. Mother and I had spent all afternoon mimeographing a sample ballot. My arms were sore from turning the crank, and I had purple ink all over my hands, but we needed the copies. See, the election was a little confusing. We wanted people to vote AGAINST the recall of Lamb, Matson and Tucker (because they were the moderate board members STOP wanted to keep) and FOR the recall of McKinley, Rowland and Laster (because they were the ones we wanted to get rid of). If we could get rid of the segregationists, new school board members would be appointed. Since the school board determined the opening date for the schools, if we could get the governor's men off of it, the schools could reopen. STOP was going to hand out the ballots at the polls to make sure no one voted for the wrong person by accident.

We were making some extra copies for Betty Jean and Pastor George and were going to drop them off before dinner. The thought of going to Betty Jean's cheered me up a bit. I'd never been to her house before, but I was pretty sure Liz would be there. She was as excited about the election as I was. I cranked out the last few copies, washed my hands to try to get rid of the mimeograph ink (it didn't work), and Mother and I jumped into the car.

Betty Jean's house was small and white, with neat flower beds in the front. It was only two blocks down from where we'd seen Red egging that house last Halloween. Mother parked on the curb, and we went inside.

Pastor George smiled real wide when he saw us. "Mrs. Nisbett," he said, "always a pleasure."

Mother smiled.

"And Marlee," he said. "Any more secret messages?"

I blushed. "No. Only some sample ballots."

"Thank you," he said as he took them from me. "Wouldn't want anyone accidentally voting for the wrong person."

Betty Jean poked her head out of the door. "Marlee, Liz and Curtis are in the living room, if you'd like to say hello."

I ran off before Mother could say we had to go home and make dinner. Curtis was putting the finishing touches on a bunch of signs. Liz sat next to him. As I watched, he leaned over and put a drop of paint on her nose. She giggled. It sounded unlike Liz.

She liked him. He liked her. I was just the third wheel in the room. I was going to lose her, just like I'd lost Judy to that awful Robert Laurence. I almost turned and went back outside, but then Mother appeared behind me and said, "Let me finally meet this famous Liz."

When she said that, Liz looked up, and a grin broke over her face. "Marlee!" She ran to give me a hug. I felt bad for ever doubting her.

"This is my mother," I said quietly. "Mother, this is my friend Liz."

Liz and Mother shook hands and looked each other over. Liz was almost as tall as Mother and looked her straight in the eye. Mother smiled and clasped Liz's hands in both of hers and said with real warmth in her voice, "It's a pleasure to meet you."

"You've got quite the daughter," Liz said.

Mother laughed. "Don't I know."

Then Curtis stood up and walked toward us, and Liz said, "This is my friend Curtis." And she blushed.

Curtis glanced at me, and we both said, "We've met." We all laughed, and he shook Mother's hand. I remembered how Judy had come back, even if I'd lost her for a bit, and Liz seemed so happy, how could I be sad? I turned to look out the front window so no one could see the jumble of emotions on my face.

That's when I saw the old gray Chrysler Windsor drive by.

I blinked and the car was gone. Had I imagined it? Mother was sitting on the couch, and Betty Jean had brought in sweet tea and oatmeal muffins. Liz was talking, and Mother and Curtis and Betty Jean were laughing at something she'd said, and everything seemed so normal. Just when I was sure I'd imagined it, the car drove by again, very slowly, then turned the corner.

I had to say something. I had to do something. But it was a common car, and it would be awfully embarrassing if I was wrong. On the other hand, what if Red had followed us here? Hurting Betty Jean would be the perfect way to get back at me. Maybe he knew Liz was here too. If it really was Red . . .

The car drove past the house for the third time, and I could see a dent in the trunk.

I jumped off the couch, causing Mother to spill tea all over her dress. "Marlee!"

"Get out," I yelled, pulling her off the couch. "Now."

"What is it?" asked Betty Jean.

"Go," I said.

I guess they heard something in my voice, because Liz grabbed Curtis's arm, and Betty Jean pushed them both into the kitchen, where Pastor George was talking on the phone.

"Outside," I said.

I thought he was going to argue, but he took one look at my face and hung up the phone. A few seconds later, we were all huddled on the back stoop.

We waited, frozen, for a long moment. Nothing happened.

"Marlee," said Pastor George finally, and he only sounded the tiniest bit irritated, "could you please tell me what's going on?"

"I saw Red's car drive by."

Mother got a little paler, but she didn't move. Liz clutched Curtis's hand.

"I see," said Pastor George. "Red is the boy with the dynamite, yes?"

I nodded. "He has a gray Chrysler Windsor."

"I'll go look," he said.

As soon as he was gone, the whole thing seemed ridiculous. Red wasn't really going to bomb anyone. Boys love to talk, Daddy always said. Nothing was going to happen, certainly not to my friends. Lots of people owned dark gray Chrysler Windsors. It was probably a neighbor, waiting to pick someone up, and driving around the block while he waited. I'd panicked, panicked like a fool. Had I even seen a dark gray Chrysler Windsor? A lot of cars look similar.

Pastor George came back. "I don't see anyone there."

"Marlee's been a bit on edge lately," said Mother finally.

My face burned red, and I willed myself not to cry.

"Well," said Liz, letting go of Curtis's hand and winding her arm through mine. "Better safe than sorry."

Betty Jean opened the back door and held it open, gesturing for her husband to go inside. But then we suddenly heard a car pull up in front of the house.

We all froze.

There was a crash and the sound of breaking glass.

A screech of wheels, driving off.

And then, an explosion.

52

AFTERWARDS

I'd been right. Something had happened after all. Something bad. I'd never known I could be so upset about being right. Mother reached for my hand. Her fingers were trembling. Everyone was silent.

After a minute or two, the smell of smoke wafted out the open back door. Betty Jean glanced over at Pastor George. "Stay here," he ordered, and he went back into the house again.

Curtis moved to follow him, but Betty Jean grabbed his arm. "You heard your father."

The next-door neighbor poked her head out a window. "You all right?"

"I think so. I—" Betty Jean choked up and couldn't finish.

Liz shook her head. "Marlee, if you hadn't said something . . ."

I glanced over at Liz. She was biting her lip, but I could still see it quivering. Curtis put his arm around her.

Pastor George came back then. "Someone threw a brick through our front window. It landed on the couch. From the damage to the living room, there must have been a couple of sticks of dynamite too."

And like a picture in slow motion, I could imagine it. Red leaning out of the window of his car. Pitching a rock at us, like he'd done with the eggs. The window shattering like the ice on a pond in spring and covering us all with little bits of glass. All of us standing frozen, shocked, glittering as the sun shone in the ruined window, not noticing the dynamite until it was too late.

"We should call the police," said Mother.

Betty Jean nodded, but she didn't move. I realized she was crying, great big tears that flowed down her cheeks without making a sound.

Pastor George sat down on a stump in the backyard and covered his face with his hands. I imagined, as a pastor, he'd had experience giving bad news to people, but it must have been different when it was your own wife and son. I knew I should be scared too. We could have been killed. But all I could think was, *The dynamite is gone. Red doesn't have any more.* And no one was hurt.

The next-door neighbor came out then. She was old and tiny, shorter than me, with white hair and a lined face. "I already notified the authorities," she said. "You just tell me who else you need me to call."

Liz's family arrived first. Her mother wore a yellow dress, which looked beautiful against her dark skin, though half of the dress was wrinkled and the other half was not, as if she'd been ironing when she got the call. Her father was light-skinned and movie-star handsome, like Montgomery Clift and Harry Belafonte rolled into one. I thought Liz might introduce me, but her father put his arm around her shoulders, and her mother led her away, and only Tommy looked back at me and glared.

Daddy ran up then and threw his arms around Mother and me.

"It was Red," I said.

He nodded, and Mother started to cry.

The old neighbor offered me a cup of coffee, and I took it. My hands were cold, even though it was a warm evening, and it felt good to hold the cup. I tried to take a sip but only managed to spill half the coffee on the ground.

A few minutes later, the police arrived. There were two of them, an older man who went off with Pastor George to look at the damage in the house, and a young man with a mustache, who seemed most interested in talking to Mother and me.

I told the policeman everything, about Liz and me running into each other at zoo, and taking Red's keys, looking in his trunk and—

"Oh, Marlee!" Mother exclaimed.

"It gets worse," I admitted.

I told them about getting stuck in the trunk. My daddy sucked in his breath as I told them about the letter opener and forgetting the last two sticks and David coming to pick me up. And even though I knew I was going to get in trouble—I deserved to get in trouble—it still felt good to tell.

Finally, I took a deep breath. "Since I spent so much time in that car, I knew it when I saw it. And you know the rest."

Silence again. The policeman gave me an odd look.

"Say something," I pleaded. "I know I'm in trouble, but—"

Mother began to laugh then, a nervous, hysterical laugh.

The police officer glared at my mother. "You don't actually believe this nonsense, do you?"

"What?" said Daddy.

"It's ridiculous. Stealing keys, climbing into a trunk. Who can believe a story like that?"

"It's true," I said. "You can ask Liz."

263

"If you're lying, I'm sure the colored girl will too."

"My daughter does not lie," said Daddy.

"You're saying it was Red Dalton, the football star, right?" the police officer asked.

I nodded.

The policeman shook his head. "No way he'd pull a stupid stunt like this."

"But—"

"What I'd like to know," he said, "is why you are at this colored family's house."

"What does that have to do with—" Daddy started.

Mother put a hand on his arm. "We were just dropping off some flyers. There's an election tomorrow."

"Was it some sort of integrationist meeting?"

Mother shook her head.

"And what if it was?" snapped Daddy. "Aren't you supposed to protect all of us?"

"All citizens of Little Rock," he agreed. "But if it was some commie meeting—"

"My wife and thirteen-year-old daughter are not communists," said Daddy. "Where is Sergeant Pike?"

"Out of town," said the older officer, coming out of the house. "You were lucky. If anyone had been sitting by the window . . ."

No one wanted to finish that sentence. Numbers flowed through my head, prime numbers, times tables, pi to as many digits as I knew. But it didn't help. The police didn't believe me. They weren't going to do anything. They were acting like Betty Jean should be grateful to only have a broken window and a burnt-up couch.

53

THE ELECTION

It was late when we finally got home—way past dinnertime—but none of us were hungry. Mother and Daddy said good night and headed off to their bedroom.

"Aren't you going to punish me?" I asked.

Daddy crossed his arms. "Doesn't seem to do much good."

"I'm sorry I . . ."

Mother held up her hand. "No, Marlee. I'm too tired for this. We'll talk about it tomorrow."

"Tomorrow's the election."

"Then Tuesday," said Mother. And they closed their door.

I slept badly that night, dreaming of bricks crashing through our front window, dynamite exploding, and Mother and Betty Jean and Liz walking through our house with makeup on their faces and diamond tiaras. I wondered when my dream had turned into Cinderella's ball, but then I realized it was broken glass in their hair, and it wasn't rouge on their cheeks, it was blood.

I called Liz first thing the next morning. "Who is this?" Liz's mother asked.

"Marlee Nisbett," I admitted.

"Marlee," she said softly. "All I ever wanted was for Elizabeth to have the best education possible. But associating with you nearly got my daughter killed. She won't be talking to you again."

"But I—"

Mrs. Fullerton hung up the phone.

It was hard to concentrate in school. JT wasn't there, and despite myself, I was kind of worried about him. Mr. Harding seemed distracted too. He was teaching the class percentages, but he kept getting the problems wrong. Three-fourths was 75 percent, not 34 percent. I corrected him the first time, but he looked so embarrassed, I didn't dare correct him again. Besides, no one else in the class was paying attention.

I kept waiting for someone to mention what had happened at Betty Jean's, but no one did. Sally had a new haircut and dress and talked nonstop about how she was going to get her picture in the paper at the CROSS victory party. Because, of course, she was sure her side would win.

When I arrived home, there was a postcard from Judy in the mail.

Good luck! Win the election and bring me home.
                        Love, Judy
PS. I need new laces for my saddle shoes. Black please, extra long.

Shoelaces. Such a normal concern.

"You voted?" Betty Jean asked as I walked into the kitchen.

"Betty Jean," I said, "I'm only thirteen."

"I'm asking everyone," she said without looking at me. She sniffed the air, then turned to the oven. As soon as she opened it, a puff of smoke drifted out. "Oh, Lord," she sighed, "this is the second batch I've burned this afternoon."

"Betty Jean?" I asked.

"What?"

I wasn't sure what to say first. Betty Jean had kept my secret about going to the Gem, and I'd repaid her by almost getting her killed. "Are we going to talk about what happened yesterday?"

"No." Betty Jean was scraping what appeared to be burnt cookies into the garbage.

"I'm sorry," I said. "I know you told me to stay away from Liz, but—"

"Marlee," interrupted Betty Jean.

"What?"

"I need this job. We're still paying back the money from when Curtis was arrested, and now we need a new living room too. You know the best way to lose your job?"

I didn't answer.

"Yelling at the daughter of your employer. I don't want to do that, so I'd appreciate it if you'd kindly be quiet and leave me alone."

But that wouldn't help anyone—not me, not Liz and certainly not Betty Jean. I tried to imagine what Liz would do.

"You know," I said finally, "I think my parents would appreciate it if you'd yell at me. They haven't gotten around to it themselves, and I know I deserve it, so it'd save them the trouble."

Betty Jean snorted and kept her eyes on her cookies, but I could tell she was trying hard not to smile. "You're a strange girl, Marlee."

"I'm so sorry, Betty Jean."

"I know," she said. "I know."

Mother, Daddy and I listened to the results come in on KLRA radio station throughout dinner, and afterwards. I did my homework, Daddy graded papers, Mother did the dishes and none of us said a word. The STOP candidates were ahead all evening, but when KLRA went off the air at twelve thirty A.M., it was still too close to call.

I was sure I wouldn't be able to sleep, but I put my head on my pillow, just to rest, and the next thing I knew, I heard the front door open as Daddy went out to get the paper. I washed my face and got dressed, anxious to know what had happened, at the same time dreading it.

As soon as I walked into the kitchen, Daddy held up the paper:

STOP Wins Recall Victory: Purgers Thrown Off Board

Mother grinned at me.

Daddy said, "We did it!"

I burst into tears.

"Marlee, we won," said Mother.

But I couldn't stop crying.

I'd thought winning the election would solve everything. But now that the big day was here, I realized it wasn't the end after all. It wasn't even close! New board members needed to be appointed by the Pulaski County Board of Education. There were legal challenges to integration in the courts. Even if the high schools did open, Liz and I still wouldn't be at the same school.

"What is it?" asked Daddy.

"Tears of joy," I lied, and my parents seemed to believe me.

I called Liz again before I went to school, but this time no one answered.

All morning, I couldn't wait for lunch to come so Mr. Harding and I could do some math and forget about everything except algebra. But when I pulled out my book and tried to do the first problem, I couldn't copy it down correctly because my eyes kept filling with tears.

"What's wrong, Marlee?" Mr. Harding asked gently.

"Have you ever looked forward to something for a long time, and then when you finally got what you wanted, it wasn't what you expected?"

Mr. Harding nodded.

"I'm happy we won," I said. "So how come I don't feel better?"

He looked thoughtful and said nothing for a long moment, then pulled out a pencil and started to write on the blank piece of paper I had before me. "I think what's happened, Marlee, is that you've realized the world isn't an addition problem."

He wrote $3 + 4 = 7$ down on the paper. "We tell kids that sometimes. We pretend the world is straightforward, simple, easy. You do this, you get that. You're a good person and try your best, and nothing bad will happen.

"But the truth is, the world is much more like an algebraic equation. With variables and changes, complicated and messy. Sometimes there's more than one answer, and sometimes there is none. Sometimes we don't even know how to solve the problem."

He wrote $x^2 + 4x - 21 = 0$.

"But usually, if we take things step by step, we can figure things out. You just have to remember to factor the equation, break it down into smaller parts."

I stared at $x^2 + 4x - 21 = 0$. Pictured it factored into $(x - 3)(x + 7) = 0$. Imagined the solutions, $x = 3$ and $x = -7$, and felt a little better.

"You're right, Marlee. Winning this election isn't the solution. But it's a start."

"Mr. Harding," I said.

"Yes?"

"At the beginning of the year, I was helping JT cheat on his homework."

"I know."

I looked at him, surprised.

"I grade your homework every day. I recognize your handwriting."

"Why didn't you say anything?" I asked.

Mr. Harding shrugged. "I thought it would be better if you told me yourself."

I nodded. "Are you going to punish me?"

"Yes," he said. "I'm going to make you do extra math during your lunchtime."

I smiled.

"Now, come on." He pushed the algebra book toward me. "Let's start solving the world's problems. One step at a time."

I was in the kitchen doing my homework when Liz called me that afternoon. "I can only talk for a second," she said.

She sounded awful. "Why? What's wrong?"

"I'm not going to be allowed to see you anymore. Ever. Not even by accident. If we happen to end up in the same place, I have to turn around and leave. And if I don't . . ." Liz couldn't finish.

"Are you crying?" I asked.

"No," said Liz.

But she was.

"Marlee, we were almost killed!" said Liz. "And not just us, but Curtis and Betty Jean and the Pastor and your mother too. There's nowhere left for us."

"What are you talking about?"

"We need to find other friends. People we can actually do things with."

"What?"

"Marlee, I don't want you to be lonely. I want you to have friends you can talk and laugh with and—"

"There's no one I like at school!" I wailed.

"Then you're not looking hard enough," said Liz. "I'm not always a cup of warm milk with a dash of cinnamon. And Little Jimmy is more than just apple juice!"

"But—"

"I'm sorry, Marlee. This is just how it has to be. As long as there are people like Red in town, we just can't . . . I'm sorry."

"Are you telling me good-bye?" I asked.

"Yes," said Liz. "I am. Good-bye, Marlee." And she hung up.

I sat there for a full minute, staring at the receiver. This was exactly what I'd been afraid of. I went to my room and sat on my bed and thought. Looked at the problem from all angles, added things up from all sides. I could come to only one conclusion. Liz was right. Summing people up as a cola or a coffee wasn't really fair. Most people were a whole refrigerator full of different drinks. Trying to force them into one cup or one glass meant I never really got to know them.

But Liz was wrong too. As long as there were people like Red in town, it was more important than ever for us to be friends, to show all the others who were too afraid that it was possible. I needed her to point out when I was wrong and teach me new things, and I was pretty sure that she needed me too. There had to be a way.

Mr. Harding said when you were stuck, you should factor the equation. Liz was too afraid to be friends with me anymore. There had to be a part of that problem I could solve. Some way to give her back the courage she'd given me. Some way to . . .

Red. He was only one part of the equation, but he was a large part. If I could deal with him, maybe it would help, at least a little.

I thought and thought and thought, and by the time my parents came home that evening, I had a plan.

54

SPEAKING UP

I explained my plan to Mother and Daddy over dinner. I didn't think they would like it much, but at least they listened. "She's right about one thing," said Daddy when I was done. "Something does need to be done about Red."

"Mrs. Dalton isn't a bad woman," Mother agreed. "Perhaps it wouldn't hurt to talk to her."

"Maybe we should call the police again," suggested Daddy.

Mother shook her head. "I had Miss Winthrop check our files. Of the police officers who live in our district, twenty-three signed CROSS's petition. Only six signed STOP's. But if we all went to talk to the Daltons together . . ."

Daddy nodded. "It's worth a try."

So twenty minutes later, my parents and I were knocking on JT's front door. A colored man wearing a butler's uniform answered the door. "We were hoping to pay a call on Mr. and Mrs. Dalton," said Mother. "Are they at home?"

The man nodded and ushered us inside. I still had the black feather. It was bent and crumpled, and now that Liz wasn't talking to me, I wasn't sure it had any magic anymore. But it made me feel better as the man led us down the hall and out onto the back porch.

Mr. Dalton was holding a drink and reading the paper. JT and Red were on the lawn, tossing a football back and forth. Mrs. Dalton sat in the corner, sipping an iced tea and reading a book. JT dropped the football when he saw us.

"Mr. Nisbett," Mr. Dalton said, "what did we do to gain the pleasure of this visit?" His voice made it clear it was anything but a pleasure.

"Mr. Dalton," said Daddy, "I'm not sure you were aware of recent events involving your son, Raymond Edward Dalton."

I'd always wondered where Red got his nickname, since he didn't have red hair. It was silly when parents gave their kids names that had initials that spelled words, like Daisy Ursula Montgomery or Peter Ivan Galveston or . . .

No. I wouldn't drift off. I was going to listen. Listen to every word, until it was time to do my part. And then I would talk.

"The police were already here this morning," said Mr. Dalton. "Again."

We all turned to look at Red, but he stood still, as calm as can be. It was JT who looked afraid. I wondered, for the first time, what it would be like to have an older brother like Red. Someone you loved, because they were your own flesh and blood, but someone who was nasty too. Sometimes even horrible to you.

And I remembered how, when JT was in the third grade, he fell out of his tree house and broke his leg. At least that's what they said. But I remember being surprised, because it was a nice tree house, with walls all around the top. If you were clumsy, maybe you could fall out, but JT wasn't clumsy. If your brother was mad at you, though, it'd be really easy to push you out.

JT had been in the hospital a long time. Mother even took

Sally and me to see him. I was nervous, because even then, JT was something of a golden boy, the alpha lion of the pack. Sally chattered a blue streak. I put a vase of daffodils from our garden in the window.

Everyone said the doctor did a fabulous job and that his leg healed perfectly, but that wasn't true. After a long day of school, sometimes, maybe if it was about to rain, JT had a slight limp. Once last year, coming off the football field, I saw him rubbing his hip when he thought no one was watching. Everyone assumed he wanted to be just like his brother, but what if he didn't? What if he'd rather be someone else?

"The police came to talk to my son," repeated Mr. Dalton, pulling me out of my own thoughts again. "And they accused him of throwing a bomb through a poor Negro's front window. Now, I assured them my son would never waste his time on such a prank, and seeing as how there was no evidence anyway, the good officer agreed and apologized for wasting our time.

"So what I'm wondering is, why are you all here to bring this up again?"

The father would be no help.

"Our daughter was trapped in the trunk of your son's car, while she was removing the dynamite Red had stored there." Mother's voice was calm and clear, but her hands were shaking.

"My son never stored dynamite in the truck of his car," said Mr. Dalton. "Though he did recently have the lock broken off. Had to get a new one installed. I don't suppose your daughter would know anything about that?"

I counted 2, 3, 5, and said, "Yes, I do."

For the first time, Mr. Dalton looked surprised.

"I broke it off with a letter opener," I continued. "I'll pay for the lock, but I'd like the opener back."

Mrs. Dalton looked up from her book. JT almost smiled. Red had absolutely no reaction at all.

"Thought you were mute," said Mr. Dalton.

"No, sir," I said. "But as I said, I left the opener in the trunk, and I'd like it back."

"Well, that's the most ridiculous thing I've ever heard. Get out of here. All of you! And if I ever hear one word about this again, I'll have you arrested for slander."

Mrs. Dalton stirred her tall iced tea. I thought of the time we'd spent together stuffing envelopes. I waited for her to say something, but she didn't.

The butler held the door open for my father. "Out!" Mr. Dalton barked again. I began to see why Red had turned out the way he had.

I looked over at JT. "Please," I whispered.

JT held my gaze for a long time, then went over to his mother and touched her arm. "Mama," he said, "Marlee is a square, but she's not a liar."

Red turned as red as his name.

Mrs. Dalton reached up and ran her fingertips across her scar.

"Go!" said Mr. Dalton.

Mother took my arm and started to lead me off.

"No," said Mrs. Dalton. She rose from her seat, clutching JT's hand.

"What?" snapped Mr. Dalton.

"I'd like to see if this girl is telling the truth."

"Why?" asked Mr. Dalton.

"It's a simple matter to check." Mrs. Dalton's voice was growing stronger. "Let's go look in the trunk of Red's car. If there is a letter opener in there, I'll believe her story. If not, you can call the police."

Red shrugged, and I suddenly had the awful feeling that he'd already found the letter opener and thrown it away. But maybe he had only found the handle. Maybe the blade was still there.

Mr. Dalton sighed. "Fine, let's go settle this once and for all. But afterwards, you have one minute to get off my property before I call the police."

So we marched back through the house and out to the car in the driveway. Mr. Dalton glanced at Red, and he unlocked the trunk without protest. We all crowded around to look inside.

There was nothing there.

Mrs. Dalton sighed in relief. Red grinned. Mr. Dalton just crossed his arms. "Satisfied?" he snapped.

I wasn't. I knew it had been Red. And before anyone could stop me, I jumped back into the trunk.

"Get your crazy daughter out of my . . ."

Daddy held the lid open so I wouldn't get trapped. I bent down and pulled back the lining of the trunk. There, in a crack in the side, something silver flashed. I reached in and pulled out a slip of metal. Daddy helped me out of the trunk, and I held it up.

Mr. Dalton clenched his teeth. "Red, what is the meaning of this?"

"It's just a piece of metal," said Red, with a shrug. "I don't know where it came from."

I turned the metal so they could all see my name, ungraved in the blade, shining yellow in the setting sun.

Red lunged at me, trying to grab it away, but his own father held him back. Red broke free and spat on the ground.

Mr. Dalton's face was bright red. "What the hell were you thinking?"

"I didn't know they were going to be there!" snapped Red. "I was only after the colored girl. I saw her go into that house and thought that was where she lived. You said yourself she deserved—"

"Shut up!" roared Mr. Dalton. "Get in the house before—"

"No," said Red. His bangs fell into his eyes, and he pouted. It made him look about five years old.

"I'm still bigger than you, boy," said Mr. Dalton. "And there's a switch in the back closet I'm not afraid to use."

Red's eyes blazed with hatred, but he turned and slunk into the house. Mr. Dalton followed him without even glancing at the rest of us.

Mother, Daddy, JT, Mrs. Dalton and I were left standing awkwardly on the sidewalk. Finally, Daddy cleared his throat. "I'm afraid we're going to have to call the police."

Mrs. Dalton nodded. "I know."

JT was staring at the ground. I walked over to him. "You okay, JT?" He looked as shocked as I'd felt after the bombing.

"No," he said. "I never really thought he'd do it."

I took his hand and held it for a moment.

"Come on, Marlee," said Mother. "It's time to go."

55

THE LAST DAYS OF SCHOOL

We were silent most of the way home. I didn't mind. After seeing JT's parents, his father so angry and vicious and his mother as passive as a wallflower, my family's little spats seemed like a child's game. Daddy was just turning onto our street when he said, "We need to talk about your punishment."

"I'd say she deserves to be grounded until the end of the school year," said Mother.

"That's fair," I admitted. Actually, that was more than fair. The end of the year was only two weeks away. I'd expected worse.

"Marlee," said Daddy, "taking the dynamite from Red was reckless and impulsive."

I nodded.

"But it was awfully brave too." He almost sounded proud of me.

"Marlee listens to lions," said Mother, and Daddy didn't even ask what she meant. I guess somehow he knew.

I tried calling Liz again the next morning, but her number had been disconnected. Even though I knew it wasn't fair of me, I suddenly hated Liz's mother.

. . .

On the last day of school, JT came up to me while I was cleaning out my locker. "Red's gone," he said.

I nodded. I wasn't sure what to say.

"There wasn't enough evidence to charge him with a crime," JT explained, "but my father made him join the army. He's only seventeen, so my dad had to sign an extra form, but he's gone."

"I'm sorry," I said.

"No," said JT. "I'm glad. Things are a lot better at home. Mother's not having so many headaches and—" He stopped. "But I miss him too. Isn't that stupid?"

I shook my head.

"Anyway," said JT, "I told Mr. Harding I'd been cheating in math and I should probably repeat his class next year. I didn't want to tell him you were the one helping me and get you in trouble, but—"

"It's okay, JT. He already knew."

JT shook his head. "With Red gone, I'm trying to make a fresh start. Do things the right way, you know? But admitting when you've done something wrong . . ." He shivered. "It makes my skin crawl. How do you stand it?"

I shrugged. "You sleep better at night."

"Well, that would be nice." JT gave me a funny look. "You don't want to go to the movies with me sometime, do you, Marlee?"

There it was. JT finally asking me on a real date. After all this time. "No, JT," I said as gently as I could. "I don't think so."

"Okay," he said. "No hard feelings."

"Good." And I meant it.

"Hey, do you think Sally'd say yes if I asked her?"

I smiled. "I think she'd love it."

Sure enough, by lunchtime Sally was over the moon. I never knew you could talk about a two-sentence conversation *(Want to go to the movies sometime? Sure!)* for twenty minutes. Nora and I glanced at each other. She rolled her eyes, and I tried not to giggle. I'd never really gotten to know Nora. I'd always thought of her as Sally's sidekick, never as being her own person too.

Little Jimmy sat down at our table, and I thought about what Liz had said to me on the phone. About us needing other friends. Ones we were allowed to see. "Hey, Jimmy," I said, "you going to the pool this summer?"

"Yes."

My stomach gave me a funny little lurch. Never thought I'd be asking *him* out. "Maybe I'll see you there?"

"That'd be great," he said. "We could jump off the high dive."

"Sure," I said automatically. Then I wanted to kick myself. I didn't want to jump off the high dive.

"Great," said Little Jimmy.

The bell rang and he started to walk off. I was stupid and dumb and never learned and . . . and one step at a time. If I didn't know what to do, I should factor the equation. "Jimmy!"

He stopped and turned.

"Actually"—I counted 2, 3, 5—"I don't like the high dive."

"Oh," he said. "How about I buy you a Coke from the snack bar instead?"

"That'd be nice."

He nodded and walked off. And it was funny, because Little

Jimmy hadn't grown a bit, but now when I looked at him, he seemed kind of cute. I wasn't thinking about getting married or having kids or anything like that at all. Just about sharing a Coke with a friend on a hot summer day.

Maybe Liz was right after all.

56

SUMMER

A lot of things happened that summer.

In June, new school board members were appointed, and they voted to rehire the purged teachers. Daddy received his teaching contract for the next year on June 18. He signed it and returned it to the post office the very same day.

David changed his major yet again. He was studying politics this time and went to live with a friend in Washington, DC, for the summer.

Mother gave Betty Jean a raise.

And Judy came home. I expected it to be awkward, like our visit at Christmas, or tense, like over spring break when I had to watch every word. But it wasn't. It was comfortable. Like reuniting with an old friend. After dinner, I went into her room to watch her unpack.

"And tomorrow," said Judy, "maybe we can go to the zoo and then the pool."

"Actually . . . ," I said.

"What?"

"I already have plans."

"Oh."

I couldn't read her face. Was she disappointed or surprised or something else? "I'm going to the movies with Nora. We're going to see *South Pacific* downtown and out for ice cream afterward."

"Oh. Nora, huh?"

"You can come too if you want."

"Nah, I really wanted to catch up with Margaret." To my surprise, Judy was smiling. "I was just trying to be nice to you. But it sounds like you don't need me to arrange your social life anymore."

"No," I said. "I guess I don't."

"You don't sound too happy about that," said Judy. "It's a good thing, Marlee."

"I know, it's just . . ." And then I told her about Liz, and our final phone call.

"Oh," Judy said when I was done. "Well, last time she disappeared you sent her a note, didn't you?"

"Yes," I said.

"Well," said Judy, "maybe you should try it again."

So I wrote Liz a note. It was really more of a letter this time. I told her about how Little Jimmy and I had had our Coke by the pool, how we'd eaten a burger at Krystal and gone skating at Troy's on a rainy afternoon. I told her that Nora, it turned out, liked cards, and was almost as good at hearts as I was. I told her how JT and Sally were going steady, and how it had seemed to make them nicer to everyone, at least most of the time.

Most of all, though, I told Liz about how I went to the zoo, every Tuesday afternoon, by myself, and thought about her and the past year. I told her how Red was gone, and that I still had the book of magic squares. Every time I added up a row, column or diagonal, I thought of her. I promised to be at the zoo every Tuesday afternoon that summer, just in case she ever wanted to join me by the lions.

I was just getting ready to seal the letter and run it over to Pastor George to give to Liz at youth group, just like I'd done before, when I thought of something else. I looked through my purse and found the tattered black feather. I tucked it inside and licked the envelope shut.

I waited week after week by the lions, but she never showed up.

The high schools were scheduled to open early that year, on August 12, 1959, before the pools even closed. The elementary schools and junior highs wouldn't open until the day after Labor Day, like always.

When August 12 finally came, Daddy and I got up with Mother and Judy, in a reverse of the day last fall when Daddy and I had gone to school and they hadn't. We all got into the car and drove Mother to Hall High School and dropped off Judy at Central.

On the way home, one of the streets was blocked off. Daddy parked the car and we got out to see what was going on.

There were more than two hundred people in the street, some in cars and some on foot. In the front walked a man holding a Confederate flag. Others held signs reading ARKANSAS IS FOR FAUBUS and RACE MIXING IS COMMUNISM.

"What's going on?" I asked.

"They're protesting," said Daddy in a monotone.

"We're marching to Central," a man called out. "Stopped them last year. We will again."

"No," Daddy muttered. "Not again."

A car was playing "Dixie" way too loud.

"This is how it started in 1957," whispered Daddy. "Protests that turned into mobs. And the police did nothing." Daddy and I turned and saw police and firemen up ahead. They'd set up a small barrier. Daddy shook his head. "They're going to let the protesters pass, just like they did two years ago."

But I thought I saw something different in their faces, a determination to make Little Rock a different place than it was before.

One of the officers held up a megaphone. "Stop. You are not allowed to get any closer to the high school."

The protesters just kept marching on.

I'm not sure who was more surprised, Daddy or the protesters, when the firemen turned the hoses on. In an instant, the segregationists were soaked.

Most of the protesters left immediately, wet and soggy as they made their way home. But a few became enraged and started throwing rocks, bottles, the very signs in their hands.

But before we could run back to the safety of our car, the police moved in and began arresting people. Daddy and I stood and watched, frozen. "It's not going to happen again." And when he grabbed my hand, I thought he was going to cry.

In a few minutes, over twenty people were arrested, and the street was empty again. They'd been stopped just a block from Central High School.

Daddy looked at me.

"Have no fear of them," I quoted Peter at him. *"Nor be troubled."*

He gave me a hug. "That's my brave girl."

At dinner, when we asked Judy how school had gone that day, she said, "Fine. There weren't even any protests this time."

Daddy and I glanced at each other, but we didn't say a word.

In the end, there were only three colored students at Hall—Effie Jones, Elsie Robinson and Estella Thompson—and only two at Central—Carlotta Walls and Jefferson Thomas. There were no colored students at the junior highs or elementary schools. "Only five students," said Mother, shaking her head.

We still had a long, long way to go.

57

THE HIGH DIVE, PART 2

The next Tuesday, like always, I spent wandering around the zoo. I visited the gorillas, Ruth the elephant, the zebras and flamingos, and finally, when I was tired of walking, I stopped by the lions.

There, on our bench, sat a tall girl with black hair and skin the same color as mine. She was clutching an old black feather in her hands.

"Hi," I breathed. Nothing else would come out.

"I'm sorry I couldn't come sooner," Liz said. "It took me this long to convince my mother to let me . . ."

I shook my head. "It doesn't matter." She was here now.

"I showed her my notebook. I wanted her to know about the turtles and the crawdads and the quiet lessons. After my mother read it, she said I could come see you. One last time."

I didn't know what to say.

"She's actually just over there, waiting by the monkeys," said Liz.

I glanced up and caught a glimpse of Mrs. Fullerton. She was watching us, and if she wasn't smiling, she wasn't frowning either. I thought of how scared she must have been this past year, and suddenly I no longer blamed her for keeping us apart. I waved, and after a moment, she nodded in return.

"So," said Liz. "The schools reopened."

"Yes."

"Integrated. Even if it is just a token number of Negroes, it's . . ."

"Integrated," I finished.

"Yeah," said Liz.

There was a long pause. Finally, I sat down on the bench next to her.

"How's Curtis?" I asked.

"Fine," Liz said, and blushed, which told me everything I wanted to know. "How's Little Jimmy?"

"I like him a lot," I said. "Though I think just as a friend. Anyway, you were right. I did need other friends. Even if they aren't friends as good as you."

"Are we still friends?" asked Liz.

"Of course," I said. "We'll always be friends."

"Even if we don't ever get to see each other?" said Liz.

"I've thought about it a lot," I said. "I think a friend is someone who helps you change for the better. And whether you see them once a day or once a year, if it's a true friend, it doesn't matter."

"You're pretty good at saying what you think now."

"I learned from the best."

Liz smiled. "Remember when we saw *The Wizard of Oz* at the Gem?"

"Of course I remember," I said. "It was the first movie we saw together."

"It was the only movie we ever saw together," Liz said.

"There'll be others."

"Someday," said Liz.

"Things will be different," I agreed.

"Somewhere," said Liz. "Over the rainbow." She stood up. "Until then, call me." And then she was gone.

On the seat where she'd been sitting was another three-by-three magic square. The first two and last two digits were the year, 1959. And the other five numbers, well, they were her new phone number.

As soon as I got to the pool that afternoon, I knew what I had to do. I didn't say a word to anyone, just put my towel down next to Judy and waved to Little Jimmy and walked over to the five-meter platform dive and started to climb. It was a beautiful clear day, and when I got to the top, the wind danced the ends of my hair so they tickled my neck.

I walked to the edge of the platform and looked down. It still made me dizzy. Everything was the same and yet not the same. I looked up. A plane flew overhead and my eyes cleared. I imagined Liz and Curtis and Betty Jean at the pool, swimming with Nora and Little Jimmy and Mother and me. Somewhere. Over the rainbow.

And so I jumped.

I wish I could say it was a perfect swan dive. Actually, it was more like a crazed belly-flop, and all the air was sucked out of me as I hit the water at a funny angle. I floundered under the water, my skin stinging all over, sure I was drowning. Then I opened my eyes.

The water was blue and full of chlorine, and my eyes stung, but I factored the equation and realized I was upside down and all I had to do was right myself and swim up. Sounds easier than it was, but I clawed my way to the surface. And when I took that first deep breath and saw the clear summer sky, and heard my sister and Little Jimmy and Nora and even Sally and JT cheering for me, I swear I heard the lions roar.

AUTHOR'S NOTE

In 1957, nine African American students integrated Central High School in Little Rock, Arkansas. The Little Rock Nine, as they came to be called, endured daily abuse and harassment so extreme that the 101st Airborne Division was called in to keep the peace. The story made headlines across the nation.

So when I sat down to write another book of historical fiction, setting it in 1957 Little Rock seemed like an obvious choice. My mother was born there, and I thought the events at Central would be an exciting backdrop for my protagonist. However, when I flew to Arkansas in 2008 to do interviews for *The Lions of Little Rock,* I found that while people there certainly remembered 1957 and the Little Rock Nine, what they really wanted to talk about was 1958, when all the public high schools in Little Rock, white and black, were closed in order to prevent integration. Their stories of that "lost year" were so compelling that after my visit, I decided moving my story to 1958 made sense for a number of reasons.

The first reason was that the events of 1957 are already quite well known. When I was in elementary school, my own education about the civil rights era was sketchy at best, but even I learned about the Little Rock Nine. Also, there are already a number of excellent books written about the 1957–58 school year, and I realized there was no way I could ever write anything as interesting as the Little Rock Nine's own firsthand accounts of what had gone on inside Central High. On the other hand, I had never heard of schools being closed to prevent integration, even though I later learned it had happened in my very own state of Virginia as well. This seemed like a story that needed to be told.

In addition, some of the people I interviewed (who lived in Little Rock but did not attend Central in 1957) said they really didn't discuss what was going on at the high school with their parents or anyone else, unless they saw pictures or it was otherwise unavoidable. Others admitted that, like many young adults today, they were rather self-centered and were more interested in what was going on in their own schools and with their friends. This changed in 1958. The conflict could not be so easily brushed aside when they saw their older brothers and sisters sitting at home or sent away to attend school. Perhaps it wasn't as dramatic as soldiers at a high school, but on an everyday basis, more people were affected.

Finally, 1957–58 was a terrible year. That the Little Rock Nine endured, and no one was killed, was probably the high point. Many citizens of Little Rock were embarrassed that the world saw only the hate and bigotry in their town. In contrast, by 1958–59, some people in Little Rock had started to speak out. The more I learned about the Women's Emergency Committee to Open Our Schools (WEC) and the Stop This Outrageous Purge (STOP) campaign, the more interested I became in this year when the city itself seemed to find a voice.

And finding a voice was something I was interested in. My mother and her family moved away from Little Rock in 1954, but if they had remained, my aunt would have been a member of the sophomore class at Central High School in 1957. This is what she had to say about it: "All my life I have wondered how I would have behaved if I had been a student at Central. I know without a doubt I would not have called names or been rude. But my real question to myself is, would I have been kind? I'm afraid I would have done nothing." Perhaps one can think of 1957–58 as the year many did nothing, when the voices of the segregationists drowned out the thoughts of everyone else. By 1959, however, many of those people with "kind thoughts" had finally started to speak up.

I don't want to give the impression that the struggle for integration in Little Rock was over in 1959—it wasn't. But it seems like the beginning of the end, in a way that 1958 clearly does not. My hope is that *The Lions of Little Rock* will allow a more complete view of what happened in Little Rock during those years.

Although this book is fiction, I have tried to be as historically accurate as possible, especially in my portrayal of the WEC and the STOP campaign. The books and videos listed below were invaluable in learning about the time, and are a great starting point for anyone wanting to learn more. I was fortunate enough to speak personally with Cynthia East, the daughter of Dr. Agar (one of the organizers of the STOP campaign), and I got to hear firsthand her memories of working on the election, receiving threatening phone calls, and being sent away from town.

Marlee and Liz are fictional characters. However, my uncle, who attended West Side Junior High, said that when he was a student there, he knew a boy who was "there one day and gone the next." The rumor was that the boy had been black, passing as white. While I have no evidence that this happened in 1958,

294

it seemed like perhaps it *could* have happened. With a bit of poetic license, it gave me the idea of how Marlee and Liz might have met and become friends.

The bombing, as described in the book, is fictional, though it was based on two separate real events. On September 7, 1959, the day before Labor Day, three bombs went off in Little Rock—one at the school board administrative building, one at the business offices of Mayor Werner Koop, and one in the station wagon of Fire Chief Gann Nalley (who had turned fire hoses on segregationist protesters just a few weeks before). More dynamite was found in the woods on the edge of town. Five white men, all linked to the Ku Klux Klan, were arrested and eventually convicted. The other event was the bombing of the house of Carlotta Walls (one of the Little Rock Nine) on February 9, 1960. As described in her book (see below), the investigation into this bombing was handled terribly, and included the questioning of her own father and the arrest of two family friends.

Finally, I hope this book expresses my admiration and respect for public schools. When I was in elementary school in the early 1980s, my mainly white neighborhood was paired with a mainly black neighborhood to create two integrated elementary schools, one for grades K–3 and the other for grades 4–6. When I asked my parents why I had to ride the bus to school instead of just going to the school nearest my house, they told me it was a great opportunity for me to go to school with people who were different from me, by race, social class, religion, et cetera. They said it was only fair that the busing be shared by both neighborhoods. Their enthusiasm for the pairing of our schools made a huge impression on me. Sometimes I think people today forget that public schools are not just about reading and writing, math and test scores, but also about bringing different types of people together. I'll never forget my parents' belief that school integration was important and beneficial to all of us, no matter what our color.

Kristin Levine
June 1, 2011
Alexandria, Virginia

Suggested Books for Learning More:

Warriors Don't Cry: A Searing Memoir of the Battle to Integrate Little Rock's Central High by Melba Pattillo Beals

A Mighty Long Way: My Journey to Justice at Little Rock Central High School by Carlotta Walls LaNier

The Power of One: Daisy Bates and the Little Rock Nine by Judith Bloom Fradin and Dennis Brindell Fradin

Finding the Lost Year: What Happened When Little Rock Closed Its Public Schools by Sondra Gordy

Breaking the Silence: Little Rock's Women's Emergency Committee to Open Our Schools, 1958–1963 by Sara Alderman Murphy

The Embattled Ladies of Little Rock, 1958–1963: The Struggle to Save Public Education at Central High by Vivion Lenon Brewer

Suggested Films:

The Lost Year: The Untold Story of the Year Following the Crisis at Central High School by Sandra Hubbard

The Giants Wore White Gloves: The Women's Emergency Committee to Open Our Schools by Sandra Hubbard

ACKNOWLEDGMENTS

There are so many people I want to thank for helping me make *The Lions of Little Rock* a reality. First of all is my amazing editor, Stacey Barney. With her infinite patience and insightful questions, she always helped me see how my book could be *more* than what it was. Thank you also to my agent, Kathy Green, for all her support and encouragement, and for making the business side of writing so easy.

My deepest appreciation goes out to everyone who talked with me about the late 1950s in Little Rock, both in person (LaVerne Bell-Tolliver, Katherine Downie, Cynthia East, Helen Harrison, Harry Otis Sims Jr., Judy Reed, and Marlene Walker) and via e-mail (Sondra Gordy, Sandy Hubbard, Martha Cornish, Irving Spitzberg, Chris Barrier, Susan Baker, Susan Altrui and Bobbie Forbush).

In addition, I want to express my gratitude to all the people who read different versions of this story, including Matt McNevin, Jessie Auten, Debbie Gaydos, Cynthia East, Pam Ehrenberg, Gwen Glazer, Kirsten Green, Brooke Kenny, Elizabeth McBride, Meredith Tseu and Farrar Williams.

With two small children, I couldn't have gotten this book done without babysitting help: thanks to Roseann Mauroni, Jessie Auten and Debbie Gaydos for volunteering to hang out with my kids. I'm also most grateful to the librarians at John Marshall Library for always making me feel like a star when I walked in, and Candy and Wil Briffa and their fantastic staff at Grounded Coffee for making their coffee shop such a pleasant place to work.

An extra special thank-you to my family—to my mother, Marlene Walker, for countless hours of babysitting; to my father, Tom Walker, and my sister, Erika Knott, who jumped in for extra babysitting whenever I had a deadline; and to my husband, Adam Levine, for keeping the household running when I was busy writing. Nothing says *I love you* like a clean house and dinner on the table. In addition, I'm most grateful to my mom and husband for being my emergency readers, who were always willing to read pages and give me comments, even if it was eleven o'clock at night.

And finally, thank you to my girls for their enormous patience when Mommy had to go work on her book yet again.